Their Nebr Marriage Deal

—— ♘ ——

STAND-ALONE NOVEL

A Western Historical Romance Book

by

Ava Winters

AVA WINTERS

Disclaimer & Copyright

This is a work of fiction. Names, characters, places and incidents either are products of the author's imagination or are used fictitiously. Any resemblance to actual events or locales or persons, living or dead, is entirely coincidental.

Table of Contents

Let's connect!

Impact my upcoming stories!

My passionate readers influenced the core soul of the book you are holding in your hands! The title, the cover, the essence of the book as a whole was affected by them!

Their support on my publishing journey is paramount! I devote this book to them!

If you are not a member yet, join now! As an added BONUS, you will receive my Novella "**The Cowboys' Wounded Lady**":

FREE EXCLUSIVE GIFT
(available only to my subscribers)

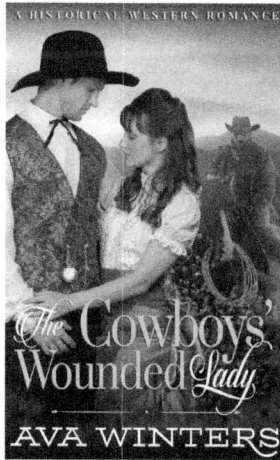

Go to the link:
https://avawinters.com/novella-amazon

Letter from Ava Winters

"Here is a lifelong bookworm, a devoted teacher and a mother of two boys. I also make mean sandwiches."

If someone wanted to describe me in one sentence, that would be it. There has never been a greater joy in my life than spending time with children and seeing them grow up - all my children, including the 23 little 9-year-olds that I currently teach. And I have not known such bliss than that of reading a good book.

As a Western Historical Romance writcr, my passion has always been reading and writing romance novels. The historical part came after my studies as a teacher - I was mesmerized by the stories I heard, so much that I wanted to visit every place I learned about. And so, I did, finding the love of my life along the way as I walked the paths of my characters.

Now, I'm a full-time elementary school teacher, a full-time mother of two wonderful boys and a full-time writer. Wondering how I manage all of them? I did too, at first, but then I realized it's because everything I do I love, and I have the chance to share it with all of you.

And I would love to see you again in this small adventure of mine!

Until next time,

Ava Winters

Prologue

Columbus, Nebraska

July 1883

Harry's boots scraped against the grit of the road, each step a leaden echo in the stillness of the night. The dim glow from the flickering street lamps barely pierced the darkness, casting long shadows that seemed to stretch out like fingers grasping at the tails of his coat.

It was too quiet.

When Calvin Hawkins had asked him to meet at his store at midnight, Harry had initially been annoyed.

"If you're having a problem with vandals, how are they getting in?"

But, every question Harry asked, Hawkins refused to answer. Something about it wasn't adding up, but the man refused to clarify anything he said, repeating the same thing until Harry agreed.

"Just be there, Sheriff," he'd said, looking over each shoulder as customers milled behind him, scooping up cups full of beans and measuring out lengths of fabric. "I can't keep having these vandals coming in, tearing my store apart. Mags and me have had a time of it, coming in every morning and cleaning it all up."

Harry didn't like it, but he agreed. It was one of the less appealing parts of the job, but it was his job all the same.

Now, he circled the shop, his unease building in the silence. There were no lights flickering in the windows, no sign anyone was here at all. No vandals, but no store owner either. He wanted to believe that the man had forgotten or fallen asleep in the warmth of his bed and missed their appointment—but a sense of foreboding clung to him as stubbornly as the dust on his boots. Columbus may not be much more than a dirt road cutting through a collection of farms, but he'd been sheriff long enough to know to trust his gut, and something here was amiss.

As Harry approached the dry goods store, the silence of the town grew more pronounced. Not even the regular creak of the wooden sign swaying above the entrance greeted him. He reached for the handle of the door, the metal cold and unwelcoming under his touch.

"Mr. Hawkins?" Harry's voice broke through the oppressive quiet, making him want to keep talking, just to keep the silence at bay. There was no reply, no shuffle of feet or clearing of throat from the corners of the shop. Only the sound of his own breath disturbed the air. His eyes, sharp as the edge of a blade, scanned the interior but found no trace of chaos, no sign of the vandalism that supposedly demanded his immediate attention.

A growing irritation pricked at him. He'd left the warmth of his bed, with Beth snuggled in beside him and their little girl—so pink and new—and all for what? The store was locked up tight, everything neat and orderly and in its place. All was as it should be, and yet his stomach was drawn tight, the hair on the back of his neck standing up. It didn't add up, and Harry Danvers wasn't a man who took kindly to puzzles with missing pieces.

He muttered a curse under his breath, his patience fraying at the edges. A ruse? It certainly appeared so, and the notion did little to quell the unrest that had settled in his chest. The urgency that had pulled him from his family now seemed to be nothing more than a fool's errand.

With a last sweeping glance over the shelves neatly lined with sacks of flour and sugar, tools hanging along the walls, unopened barrels of dried meat, and rolls of cloth, Harry turned on his heel. The store, with its eerie silence, held no answers—only questions that gnawed at the edges of his mind.

He backed away from the building, circling its perimeter one last time.

As he made it back to the front of the store, not another soul in sight, the inklings of certainty began to rise in his mind.

He quickened his stride, breaths sharp and shallow. Shadows loomed, stretching across his path. Each one seemed to whisper, "Hurry."

The sudden certainty settled into his gut like a stone.

Home. He needed to get home.

His mind spun scenarios, questions pounding in rhythm with his racing heart. His palms dampened on the leather of his holster, ready for any threat that might spring from the darkness as he leapt astride his horse and turned him toward home.

"Yah!" he shouted, smacking his flank, and the horse took off, pounding down the dark, empty road.

Finally, he saw it—the outline of his house. But something felt wrong; a thick tension hung in the air, replacing the comforting glow of lamplight that should have greeted him.

Darkness and silence. Suffocating silence.

And then chaos erupted.

Men on horseback burst from the shadows, their figures stark against the dim light of the half-carved moon. Hooves thundered, striking the hard ground as they fled into the night.

Desperation clawed at Harry's throat—a primal feeling of total panic and a fear until now unknown to him locked behind gritted teeth.

Instinct took over. Muscle memory guided his hands as he drew his revolver, though his mind screamed this was no time for caution or doubt. He urged his horse forward, propelled by fear and fury.

Shock registered briefly—Why here? Why them?—but was swiftly swallowed by the need to act. To protect. To reclaim what could still be saved. Harry's life had distilled to this single moment of pursuit, where nothing else existed but the fierce drive to chase down the unknown and shield his family from harm's cruel grasp.

He didn't know how this would end, but he knew it would not end without him fighting with every last breath.

He looked to the house, so ominously dark, and back to the men riding away. For a moment, he was paralyzed with indecision—go inside and check on his family, or follow the men?

Two of the horses caught his attention, the shadows of the riders atop both of them strangely large and wide, and he made his decision without, in that moment, fully understanding why. Harry trusted his gut, and his gut told him to follow the men, so he did.

The men were making for the wide open plains to the east. He knew this land. There was little to nothing out that way.

Harry spurred his horse into a gallop, the cold night air whipping against his face. His heart thundered in his chest, echoing the hooves that punched the earth beneath them. The moon cast a ghostly glow over the fields, transforming the familiar terrain into an ethereal chase ground. Shadows melded with light, creating a disorienting tapestry as he urged his horse faster, muscles tensing with each bound.

The thudding of his pulse became a metronome for the chase, each beat urging him on, fueling the fire that seared through his veins. He leaned low over the horse's mane, eyes fixed on the fleeing figures ahead—dark silhouettes framed by the soft silver glow of the moonlight. Over fences and through streams they raced, the landscape a blur, details smudged by speed and desperation.

Harry focused in on that shape, that odd shape that had caught his eye and made him decide to follow. He was gaining on those two horses now, benefited by being a smaller, lighter load on his horse while those two were burdened by more weight.

At first glance, it looked like a sack full of something. But as he narrowed the distance, his breath hitched; there was an unmistakable form to it, a gentle curve that didn't belong to any object but could only be....

"Julia," he gasped, horror slicing through the adrenaline.

It was not goods they had stolen, but something infinitely more precious—his newborn daughter, wrapped in her blanket, its tail flapping in the wind. Harry's mind reeled, thoughts fracturing under the weight of the realization, yet his resolve crystallized. He would not falter, not now, not when every second determined the fate of his child.

He flattened his back, leaning as low into the horse's neck as he could possibly go, urging him faster, faster; his hooves pounded the earth, breaths erupting in ragged snorts as they closed in on the horses. Harry's fingers clenched the reins, knuckles white with the strain of his grip, and then the shape of the other horse became clear—Beth, gripped to the side of one of the outlaws. Her long brown hair whipped in the wind behind her.

A guttural cry tore from Harry's throat, disbelief and dread tangling into a sharp knot within his chest. Questions pelted his thoughts like hailstones yet vanished as quickly against the shield of his resolve. He had to save them; there would be time to find answers later.

He drew his weapon, the cold metal a familiar weight against his palm.

"Come on," he whispered to himself, to his horse, to anyone who was listening.

With a glance skyward, he angled the barrel upward and squeezed the trigger. The gunshot split the night, a sharp crack that echoed like a thunderclap over the plains. Harry held his breath, the aftermath of the blast ringing in his ears, waiting for the reaction.

The outlaws jolted at the sound, their formation scattering like crows flushed from a field. The two horses holding his wife and daughter fell further behind, removed from the pack. Harry watched, unblinking, as the chaos unfolded, his hands shaking not from the recoil but from the high stakes of this deadly game. There was no time to second guess, no room for error. Only action, only the fierce drive to protect his family at all costs.

"Please," he uttered, a silent plea lost amidst the fury of galloping hooves and the stirring dust. It was a risk he'd taken, but in that perilous moment, it was all he had.

He shot again.

The outlaws veered off course, their previously tight ranks now a disjointed mess. Horses reared and bucked, spooked by the shattering of the night quiet, and their riders struggled to regain control. Desperation clawed at Harry's chest, his gaze darting between the silhouettes of his wife and daughter.

"Beth!" His voice was a hoarse whisper, drowned out by the sound of hoofbeats.

The outlaws were shouting now, their commands to one another curt and laced with panic. He saw an opportunity in their confusion, a flickering chance to act.

There was one answering call from the slowest horse ahead, and all of a sudden, everything slowed down, as if time crawled nearly to a stop.

One of the outlaws, a hulking shadow atop his mount, reached for Beth with a clumsy grip. Harry's breath hitched, time narrowing to a single, dreadful beat. They shoved her—his Beth—her body thrown sideways with a violence that seemed to slow the very air around her. She tumbled from the horse, her body moving too quickly, too quickly toward the hard earth.

"Beth!" Now his cry tore from him, raw and unbidden.

He spurred his horse forward, but his mind was already there, cradling her before she even touched the ground. The thud when she landed was a hollow sound, a nightmare made real, but before he could reach her, the other horse carrying Julia had slowed, the outlaw crying out as he did, but his words were nonsense in the panic filling Harry's head.

No, not Julia.

He couldn't breathe, but still he flew ahead, gaining more quickly now that the man had slowed.

"Stop!" he cried. "Don't!"

The outlaw looked back, his face awash in fear, and pulled his horse to a stop. He looked at the gun in Harry's hand and, holding the blanket, lowered it so that the baby, so small, so impossibly small, rolled down until she landed, naked and screaming, in the mud below. She fell with a thump and was silent.

"Julia!" he bellowed again.

He kicked hard, propelling his horse into a reckless dash that ate up the ground between them with hungry strides.

Time seemed to fracture, seconds splintering as he grew closer. Finally, he reached her, sliding off his horse until he landed beside her and pulled her into his arms. The contact jolted through him, a current of relief so sharp it was almost pain.

"Julia?" he said, his hands shaking as he stroked her face.

A wail pierced the quiet, small but fierce; Julia's cry was strong. She was alive, her fragile body trembling against his chest as he drew her close, examining her for signs of injury. Miraculously, she appeared unhurt.

Harry cradled his daughter, feeling her warmth seep into his chilled bones, her tiny heartbeat a defiant drum against his own racing pulse.

With every breath, Harry fought to steady himself, to push back the fear that clawed at the edges of his consciousness. There was no time for tears, not yet; there was only the weight of his daughter in his arms and the heavy knowledge of what must come next.

Harry's boots scuffed the ground as he moved toward Beth, the dust rising and then settling back down with a silence that mocked the chaos of moments ago. The cry of his daughter nestled in the crook of his arm was now a soft whimper, her mouth nuzzling his chest, seeking milk.

He knelt beside the still form of his wife, the motion awkward as he cradled Julia close. Full of uncertainty, he reached a hand toward her, her long brown hair splayed like dark tendrils against the moonlit earth. Her eyes, once wide and bright and full of life, were closed, her face still—too still.

"Please," Harry whispered, his voice strained and cracking. He reached out a trembling hand and brushed a stray ringlet from her forehead.

The world seemed to tilt as he realized what he was seeing, as he struggled to come to terms with this new reality.

Just a few hours ago, he had been in bed with her, the two of them holding each other, safe and close, the baby sleeping peacefully just feet away. And now—now—

"Baby," he said, the word a shard of glass in his throat, "I'm here. I'm here."

But the words fell flat, swallowed by the vast emptiness of the plains stretching unbroken around them.

In the silence that followed, the gentle rise and fall of Julia's breathing against him was the only sign that time had not stopped—that somewhere, life stubbornly persisted. But here, beside the lifeless form of his wife, Harry's world narrowed to a point of grief so acute it threatened to cleave him in two.

It was impossible to come to terms with her like this, not his loud, fierce wife, the woman so full of love and life it made everything around her bright, now still and silent. Her body was limp, and as he held her to his chest, he could imagine for just a moment that she was simply asleep as he dropped his face into her sweet-smelling hair.

Tears blurred his eyes as they began to fall.

She was gone.

He had failed her.

He held his wife and daughter together in his arms for one last time as he cried, alone in the dark. The weight of her absence settled over him, cold and unyielding, the darkness closing in with the stealth of a thief coming to claim his final prize.

Chapter One

Chambers, Nebraska

September 1886

May leafed through the pages, a small smile on her face as she noted the neat rows and columns of money in and out of the ranch, the amount left over after all their bills were paid up, and the circled total at the bottom.

"You get the same total as me?" Willa asked from her seat across from her.

The sight made May's heart twang. That was her seat, the soft, worn leather across the wide oak desk her grandaddy had built and used all his life, then passed down to his son. Pa had always said it would be hers one day, but she felt certain he had never imagined her in his seat so quickly. Once, it had been her across from him, checking the balances and totals. Whenever she would look up, announcing a total, his eyes would crinkle in pride. He was always especially proud when she caught one of his mistakes.

"May?" Willa prompted, and May forced herself back to the present, shaking away the specter of her pa's smiles.

"Let me see." She scanned the rows, pleased to see they matched up, and silently thanked God for her best friend. She couldn't imagine what she would have done these past few weeks without her. She shot a smile at Willa. "Perfect."

Willa sighed dramatically, slumping into the seat and swiping a hand across her brow. "What a relief. If I have to do one more sum, my brain will light on fire and burn to ash."

"How realistic." May rolled her eyes.

Salt and pepper, her parents had called the two of them. Best friends since birth, but with hardly a similarity to find between them, physical or otherwise. May was tall, her hair dark brown, always carefully curled and styled and shining, not a strand out of place. Willa was small and compact, her hair blonde and wild; she claimed it was untamable, but May was sure she just didn't have the patience to try to tame it.

Something in May's expression must have caught Willa's attention, and she narrowed her pale blue eyes. "What are you thinking?" Her eyes softened. "Are you all right?"

May had no time to wallow in nostalgia. She shook her head, handing the pages back and neatening the ones in front of her in a stack, knocking them briskly into shape and then sliding them into the top drawer. "Thank you for your help, but we should—"

The door to the office opened, slamming against the far wall and making the two jump.

"What the hell, May?" Edward strode through the door with all the ease and confidence of a man who was welcome and exactly where he was supposed to be.

May was a woman with strong opinions, and like anyone with strong opinions, there were a few things she hated. Being interrupted was easily the first. Lower on the list, but not by much, was her cousin.

"Excuse me?" She stood from her father's desk, hands flat against the smooth wood. "What are you doing here?"

"I just had to hear from a *farmer*, in *town*, that my aunt and uncle are dead!"

May and Willa exchanged quick glances.

"As much as I appreciate your condolences," May began dryly, "I am taking this time to gather myself and decide how best to move forward without them."

Edward was never one to falter in the face of a polite rebuke. "There's only one path forward for you and for this ranch." He pointed at himself, his thumbs jabbing into his overcoat. "Which is why I ought to have been sent for right away."

He dropped into the seat beside Willa, who straightened, pushing her unruly hair behind her ears and looking from cousin to cousin.

"I'm not sure what you mean." May lied. She knew exactly why he was here and couldn't stop herself from inwardly cursing the fool who had been trading her family's tragedy like petty gossip.

Edward smirked, the round cheeks of his face squishing his eyes distastefully. "May, you are a young woman left with no family. You are vulnerable." His words came out triumphantly, as if nothing had given him more pleasure than this situation. Likely, nothing had. "You need a man to take charge." On the arms of the chair, his hands—soft, weak hands, she knew—gripped and let go.

Her stomach started to churn.

Her mind flashed to the few childhood memories she shared with the man across from her. His family had visited the ranch often, until it became clear to her parents that something was wrong with the boy. She remembered him begging to watch the cattle and horses get branded, talking about the smell of burning flesh afterward like it was perfume. Her mother catching him spitting a mouthful of chewed tobacco into the casserole prepared for the hired workers was the final straw and the end to their visits.

May had never been so relieved.

But there were no parents here to protect her from his cruelty now, and her heartbeat quickened at the thought of having this man as her husband. She would rather be at the mercy of horse thieves and bandits, would rather spend the rest of her life a spinster and die alone, than suffer that fate.

Edward smiled and clapped his hands against his knees, standing once more. "So, it's settled. You'll marry me. I'll ride into town now and get a priest to carry it out. I'll get this ranch running like it should. I'm sure you've done your best, but what can a lady know about men's business?"

May flushed in anger. "Nothing is settled. The only place you're going is home."

He rounded the desk. He was a large man, not muscled, not strong, but tall and wide, his hands easily able to wrap around her arm, which he did now. He lowered his voice to a growl and leaned close. She could smell the stale tobacco on his breath but forced herself not to shrink away from him, holding his gaze with one of iron. "What are you going to do to stop me?"

"Let go of her!" Willa cried, coming around the desk. He shoved her back easily, knocking her against the back wall, not taking his eyes of May. "You can't do that!"

"Sure I can. I'm a man, and you're a woman with no people. I'll do exactly what I want to do." His smile was hard. "Who's going to stop me?"

May's brain was racing, desperate to find something, anything she could say to stop him.

Willa got there first.

"She's already married, so you had better take your hands off of her before her husband walks in and sees you mistreating her." Her voice was hard as steel.

May and Edward both froze and turned their gazes to her. Willa was still on the floor where she'd fallen, her skirts a tangle around her, but her eyes were blazing with fury and a righteous determination, not even a flicker of the lie to be seen in her face.

Edward whipped back to face May. "Is this true?" he demanded.

She swallowed hard.

Another thing May hated? Liars. But she had no other choice.

She straightened her shoulders and dropped her eyes to his hand. "It's true, and she's right. My husband can be quick to anger."

Edward shrank before her eyes, dropping his hand and taking two quick steps back from her. Her skin shone with his perspiration where his hand had clenched it, and she rubbed it against her apron, grimacing.

White-faced, he looked around the room, as if her husband would crawl out from beneath the desk. "Where is he, then?"

May looked at Willa. She had started this lie, after all.

"Hm?" Willa asked innocently, reaching out a hand for May to help her off the floor. May pulled her up.

"I asked where he is. This man of yours."

"He's away," May said.

"Buying horses," Willa added. "You had probably scoot before he returns. Wouldn't want him to get the wrong idea."

May could see the gears turning in Edward's head, could see him struggling to decide whether the risk was worth calling her on her bluff. His cowardice won out; she could have guessed.

His small eyes darted between them and then around the room. "I'll be back in a month," he said sharply. "We'll meet this husband of yours then. Married or not, I have a legal right to this ranch now that Uncle Joseph and Aunt Caroline are gone." He paused and then added as an afterthought, "Rest in peace." He briefly took his hat from his head and pressed it against his chest before replacing it and making for the door. "I will be back, and I will be wanting what's mine. And if this man thinks to keep me out, he had better be ready because I'm coming back with help."

Neither of the women took a breath until they heard his boots clomp through the front door, slamming it behind him, same as the way he'd come in.

They came together as soon as it was safe, clutching one another's forearms and looking each other over.

"Did he hurt you?"

"Are you all right?"

Their words overlapped, their worry palpable. After ensuring neither was harmed, they both sank into the side-by-side chairs, still holding hands.

There was no time for relief.

"What am I going to do?" May asked. "Willa, what in the world am I going to do?"

Willa's face was round, soft, her dimples famous in their little town. Her face was made for smiling, for humor, for sweet-natured mischief. May could only think of one other time her friend's face had looked this serious.

"We're going to have to get you a husband. You heard him. We both saw how serious he was. He's not going to let up, May. He comes back, and you're here alone?" She shook her head. "You'll be in danger. No. The only thing we can do now is get you married to a man who is not Edward."

May threw up her hands in exasperation. "How am I supposed to find a husband in two weeks?" she demanded. "There isn't a man my age in this town who isn't married already."

She knew this because it was a subject her mother had bemoaned regularly. She had worried so much for her daughter's future; May wished now that she could have told her to save all that worrying. The things her mother had feared, the lack of marriageable men in their area being just one of many, seemed minute compared to the worries May faced now without them.

"You'll have to put out an advertisement," Willa mused. "In the paper. Not one locally, though; imagine if Edward saw it."

May was shaking her head, but Willa was already standing, rounding the edges of the big desk and pulling a clean sheet of paper from the stack, dotting the tip of a pencil against her tongue.

"Willa—" she began, exasperated.

Willa was writing furiously.

"Willa! Setting aside the fact that I don't want to marry a man I don't know, how on earth am I supposed to get all of this done within a month's time?"

"That's exactly why we don't have a moment to waste," Willa said without looking up.

May threw her hands up in exasperation.

"Here," Willa said a moment later. "Read this."

May scanned the sheet. Then she lifted her eyes to meet her best friend's, feeling a smile beginning to grow on her face. For the first time, she felt a flash of hope.

"Okay," she said. "Let's take it now. You're right; I have no time to spare."

Chapter Two

Columbus, Nebraska

September 1886

Harry gripped his dusty hat in his hand as he trudged down the path leading to his mother-in-law's small, tidy home.

Evangeline had been a Godsend the past three years. He didn't know what he would have done without her. She was always ready and willing to step in and take care of Julia while he tracked stories of horse robberies, interviewed thieves, and went from town to town, talking to the sheriffs he knew and the ones he didn't, trying to find the men responsible for murdering his wife.

Evangeline would want to know if he'd learned anything that day, and he hated to tell her that the answer was not a single thing. His shadow stretched long across the planks, a silent partner to his fatigue. Dust from the plains clung to him like a second skin; it was under his nails, in the lines of his face, and woven into the fabric of his clothes. He couldn't remember the last time he'd taken a real bath, the last time he'd done more than dunk his clothes in the rain barrel, the last time he had sat and truly felt his muscles loosen and relax.

He couldn't imagine doing so until he brought those men to justice.

He pulled in a breath as he approached the front door, and for one brief moment, he allowed himself the luxury of closing his eyes, leaning heavily against the frame. This home had once only held happy memories. He could hear the echo of Beth's laughter in its bones every now and again, the only place that sound lived any longer.

25

But losing Beth had changed them all.

All except little Julia, who didn't know to miss what she didn't remember.

The thought of his girl spurred him forward, and he opened the front door, pushing inside.

"Jules?" he called, suddenly desperate to see her face, to smell her milk and sugar smell. "Papa's here."

"Harry Danvers, as quiet as a thunderstorm," chided a voice from the shadows. Evangeline emerged from the kitchen, a stern silhouette against the dim glow of the parlor lamp. "You'll wake the child."

"Apologies," he said, dropping his voice.

He immediately bristled at the old argument between the two of them greeting him as soon as he walked through the door. But he quelled that rising tide of irritation, knowing that here, under this roof, respect was his currency.

He removed his boots, set aside his hat, and answered her unspoken question. "Didn't learn anything new today," he said. "But I've got a new lead to hunt down tomorrow."

Her lips thinned.

"I'll get Julia and get out of your way," he said, moving past her to the narrow passage that led to the back bedroom she had made up for her granddaughter. He could almost hear Julia's gentle breathing if he listened hard enough, and he ached to hold her close, to reaffirm life's gentler promises amidst his own storm of vengeance.

"Leave her be, Harry." The words were soft but firm. "Julia's had a long day, too. She's finally resting. A growing girl needs her sleep."

"I appreciate the advice, but I'd like to take her home. She'll sleep better in her own bed." He struggled to keep his voice calm and steady. As frustrating as dealing with Evangeline had become, he couldn't risk alienating her.

"Will she?" Evangeline's voice was cool.

Harry's temper flared. "I know what's best for her. Don't forget she's my daughter," he snapped. "As much as I appreciate your help, she's still mine."

Evangeline lifted a hand. "Let's not argue. There's something I want to talk to you about. When we're done, you can decide whether or not you want to drag a sleeping child from her bed."

Bristling, he bit his tongue and followed her into the kitchen where two cups of coffee lay waiting, steaming into the cool darkness of the kitchen.

He hated coming into this house. At every corner, he saw Beth.

Beth, leaning against the shelves, on her tiptoes, reaching for the coffee can.

Beth, wiping her hands on her apron and laughing at something he'd said.

Beth, telling her mother they were going to have a baby.

His throat stung, and he shook his head to clear it, dropping heavily into the chair and taking a swig of the bitter coffee.

"Harry, look at you," she said, examining him with eyes that didn't miss a thing. "This...quest of yours. It's consuming you, and it's no life for a young girl."

The words stung, even though he knew she said them out of concern and not judgment. Still, the idea that he was not being the best father he could be made his heart twist.

27

"Julia needs stability, peace. She needs more than a father who rides in and out of her life, chasing shadows and retribution."

"Evangeline, I am trying to—"

"Are you?" she interjected sharply. "Or are you trying to fill the void left behind by..." she paused, swallowed, then forced it out, "Beth with the capture of these bandits? Because that won't bring her back, Harry. And it won't erase the need for a father in Julia's life."

Her words settled upon him, and he could feel the heavy truth in them.

"Julia comes first," he said, but the words rang false.

Did he mean that? He did, but his actions were putting first something else.

"Then start showing it," Evangeline replied, her tone softening. "You're not the only one who lost someone, Harry. She lost her mother. Don't make her lose her father to a ghost chase."

In the quiet that followed, the ticking of the mantle clock filled the space between them, marking time against the weight of everything said and unsaid.

He sat rigid, the muscles in his shoulders taut, as he struggled to contain the whirlwind of emotions churning within him. The suggestion that he should let this go and stop searching, even for Julia's benefit, sent a surge of stubborn denial coursing through his veins.

"Evangeline, I...." His voice faltered before regaining strength. "I can't just abandon the pursuit of justice. It's all I have left of her." His words hung in the air between them. "And if I don't catch those men, if I don't stop them from doing it again, to someone else." He paused and swallowed hard, forcing the rest of it out. "They almost killed a baby. The only thing I know is they came to take something, but what? And when they didn't find it, why did they take off with a defenseless mother and child? No. We don't know what they are after but what we can be sure of is these are men without morals. I have to bring them to justice before they can do more harm to others."

That sounded right, but he knew, and he knew that Evangeline knew, that more than that, he wanted to see the men who had stolen his wife from him in a jail cell.

"Justice won't put food on the table or kiss Julia goodnight," Evangeline countered gently, yet with a firmness that brooked no argument. "She needs a present parent, Harry. A home without fear of losing another. As you say, they have no morals. That means they will not hesitate to kill you, too, should it come to that."

Her gaze held his, unyielding. "You're chasing phantoms at the expense of the living. She's growing up, Harry. She should be learning to read, to play, not worrying whether her papa will come back from the wilds of the open plains."

He wanted to keep arguing, to defend his choices and make her see the rightness in what he was doing, but the image of Julia's face, wide-eyed and hopeful each time he returned, rose into his mind unbidden.

"Maybe you're right," he conceded, the admission tasting bitter on his tongue. "But moving on, it feels like giving up. Like I'm betraying her memory."

"Moving on isn't forgetting; it's allowing for healing—yours and Julia's. She deserves to grow up without ghosts haunting every step she takes, don't you think?"

Harry's resolve wavered as he considered the full scope of what lay ahead. The path of retribution had grown thorny and isolated, its once-clear direction now shrouded in doubt. Evangeline's words carved out a space in his mind, a space where the possibility of a different future for Julia—and for himself—could take root.

"Perhaps," he said, the word less a commitment than an acknowledgment of the crossroads before him.

Evangeline rose from her chair, the wooden legs scraping against the floorboards as she moved toward an end table. She retrieved a folded newspaper and carried it back to where Harry sat, his hands resting heavily on his knees.

"Here," she said, extending the paper toward him. "Take a look at this."

Harry eyed the newspaper with curiosity, noting the deliberate circle Evangeline had drawn in pencil around one of the advertisements. He hesitated for a moment, unsure what she intended, but took the paper and unfolded it. The creases were sharp, betraying the many times she must have reviewed whatever lay within that circle.

He scanned the page quickly. As he began to read, his eyes widened ever so slightly, a flicker of recognition igniting.

"May Allen," Harry murmured under his breath. The name was familiar. Why?

"I knew her parents," Evangeline said. "She's a good girl, and that ranch...well, it's a pretty piece of land." She leaned in close, catching his eye. "She lost her parents in a carriage accident just a few months ago, and now she's looking for a husband to come help her run things."

"You want me—" His throat was so dry it clicked as he tried to swallow. "To marry? That's what this is all about?"

He had assumed she had wanted to convince them to move into her home, to live together so that she had constant access to her beloved granddaughter. He had not expected...*this*.

"It pains me to admit it, but I'm struggling to keep up with her. I'm old. I can't run and move like I used to. Even if I could, Julia needs more than a grandmother. If she's going to have a chance in this world, she needs a mother figure." Evangeline nodded to the page. "That's how you make that happen. You marry May, and you give our girl a safe place to live, money, protection, and land. A future."

Harry couldn't be sure in the dim light but thought he saw the sheen of tears in her eyes.

He shifted in his seat and cleared his throat.

Evangeline took a deep breath and patted his knee, the largest display of affection that existed between the two of them these days. She stood and drew her dressing gown tight across herself. "I'm headed to bed. It's been a long day. You think on what I've said, and we can speak more about it in the morning. You'll sleep here?"

He nodded, seeing how he had been outplayed once again. He wouldn't be taking Julia home tonight after all.

"Good night, Harry," she said, lifting a candle and taking it with her down the hall.

He stared after her as the flickering light grew smaller and then disappeared, his mind racing.

There had been times that he had thought about settling down, slowing down the chase so that he could spend more time with Julia. He knew she missed him, and he knew he was missing the small, important moments of her life. But he had never, not once, considered remarrying. The thought, even all these years later, felt like a betrayal of Beth.

31

His eyes scanned the room once more, the memories flashing. If he could speak with her now, what advice would she give him?

It didn't take long to come to a conclusion. As much as he wanted to find the men who had ruined their lives, he knew that Beth's focus would have been on one thing and one thing alone: giving Julia the life she deserved.

He read the advertisement again, something about that name hooking his brain. What was it?

And then it came to him.

And he realized that maybe there was a way he could give Julia the life of stability and comfort she needed while still ensuring justice was served.

Folding the newspaper with care, he slid it into his pocket and stood, his mouth a grim line, the path forward clear.

Chapter Three

Today was the day her husband arrived.

She fluttered around the ranch, making sure everything was just so. There was a midday meal prepared, a separate room cleaned and prepared for him, and all of the ranch hands and servants were lined up along the entrance to the house, ready to greet him and introduce themselves.

She mumbled aloud, ticking tasks off on her fingers to be sure nothing had been forgotten.

Willa caught her hand. "Quit it already. This Harold sounds like a kind man, a decent one. Nothing like that no-good cousin of yours."

"Harold," May said, trying out the name of the man who would be her husband.

She shook her head at the strangeness of it. In all of the rush and preparation, she had been able to forget about the reality of what this day would bring. A man. A man she didn't know, in her home.

A cold shiver of goosebumps trailed across her arms despite the heat of the day. She rubbed her arms beneath the thin cotton of her dress sleeves and busied herself retying her apron and pulling her curls to the front of her shoulders.

Willa tsked, leaning over and pulling the apron tighter, then flashing a quick wink. "Can't have you looking like you're wearing a potato sack, can we?"

May started to argue and fix it, but one of the ranch hands called out.

"He's here!"

Everyone stood at attention, all eyes on the dusty road curving through the red cedar trees her great-grandfather had planted, eager to catch the first sight.

Time seemed to be moving in slow motion, the carriage taking forever to come through the shade of the trees.

Overcome with anxiety, she shot her hand out and gripped Willa's. Willa squeezed back, leaning in to whisper, "Remember, this is your best option. And think how nice he sounded in those letters."

May grimaced. "He said he was a successful sheriff. Shouldn't he be married by now? There must be something wrong with him that he answered my advertisement."

"Well, when I said *best*, what I meant was only." Willa dropped May's hand and nudged her forward right as the carriage broke past the tree line and thundered closer, passing the arching front gates. "Now, go meet your husband."

"Thanks for the reminder," May muttered to herself, but she smoothed her skirts one last time and stepped forward, in front of the servants and ranch hands and stood tall and straight-backed as her mother had taught her, bringing her hands together in front of her and hoping he wouldn't notice the whiteness of her knuckles.

The carriage came to a stop, and the whole world seemed to stop as she watched the door open and Harold step out.

He ducked low through the doorway, then stretched to his full height. As she took him in, her stomach lurched.

She had assumed an unmarried sheriff would be physically undesirable in some way. She had hoped that, in the best case, he would simply be old. Worst case, there had been a few dark of the night fears of a man covered in boils, or a skin decaying disease, or....

In any case, she had been wrong.

Harold stood tall and broad-shouldered, his hair glinting gold in the sunlight, eyes so brightly blue she could feel their cold burn even from this distance. Her heart beat a quick tattoo against her chest, and she swallowed, her mouth suddenly dry.

Harold scanned the area, then turned back to the door of the carriage, reaching one hand in. When that hand reappeared, it was holding another small hand. A little girl climbed out behind him, her eyes, his same bright blue, alight with interest as they took in everything around her.

Who...?

May didn't have time to finish the question in her head. Harold had scooped the girl into his (broad, bronze) arms and was moving toward her with purpose. He nodded to the ranch hands and the servants, and then they stood just a foot apart.

She sternly reminded herself that she was the hostess and had a job to do.

"Welcome," she said, proud of the strength and clarity of her voice. "I'm May Allen, and this is my family's ranch."

"Hello." Harold's voice came out rusty, and he cleared his throat and started again.

She realized with a flash that he, too, was nervous, and something inside her relaxed a touch. Her father had taught her to be wary of confident men, to approach them with caution as one might a dog, and it was a lesson she had seen him proven right on. A man who showed nerves...well, it put her more at ease.

"Hi," a little voice squeaked, this one full of a genuine confidence only attainable by a small child. May couldn't stop herself from smiling at the little girl in Harold's arms, even as she wondered who she could be and why she was here. "I'm Julia, and this is my papa. He says you're famous!"

The words stopped her short, and not just the part about "Papa." There had been no mention of a child in Harold's letters. May frowned, but her concern won out.

"Do you know my family?" she asked Harold, who winced slightly—an admission?

Her mind raced. Had he answered her advertisement because he had known her family name? Possibilities rolled through her brain: He knew she had money, he wanted something her family had—

Her thoughts caught up shortly at the feeling of the eyes on her, eyes from every side. The weight of the attention of the household staff, her new family (?), and Willa. This was not how her mother had raised her.

Drawing herself to her full height, she pushed the worries aside for now. There was little that could be done right then; they were here, she was out of time, and Edward would be back any day now, so she could not send them away.

"Come," she said. "Let's speak more inside. I'm sure you could use a cold drink and some rest after your journey."

As they obediently followed on her heels inside, the staff scattering back to their duties, she could only hope that her questions would be answered and she would know what to do next.

Chapter Four

Harry hesitated on the threshold of the grand house, his boots scuffing the polished wood floor as he followed May Allen inside. The late afternoon sunlight streaming through the windows caught the lustrous waves of her long, brown hair, turning them into cascades of molten chocolate. She moved with a grace that seemed to command the very air around her, and Harry felt the weight of his own rough-hewn presence— like a weathered barn standing beside a stately manor.

Her every step was confident and elegant, a kind of woman different from any he had encountered. Harry's hands, calloused from years of labor, clenched at his sides as if trying to hide themselves from the judgment he imagined in the elegant lines of the room. His heart hammered a rhythm of inadequacy; he was a simple man with dirt beneath his nails, standing amidst finery that whispered of a life far beyond his reach.

Julia shared no such compunctions.

They were hardly through the front door before she straightened, slipping right through the circle of his arms and landing on the fine wooden floors with a thump and running ahead of him, her wild, unruly curls, so in contrast with the sleek, shining ones of his would-be bride's, blurring as she rushed up to the lady without reservation.

"Miss May!" she exclaimed, one small hand reaching up.

May stopped in the doorway of the parlor, looking down at his little girl.

He was no fool. Years of sheriff work in the small, wild towns of the West had given him razor-sharp instincts and the ability to read people, and upon their meeting, he had seen doubt in the woman's face. Now, however, it softened, and without hesitation, her smooth, lily-pale hand enveloped Julia's, a smile blooming across her features as natural as the roses planted along the boundaries of the front fence.

"Your house is so big!" Julia said, her grip tightening with earnest enthusiasm.

"Would you like to explore it together?" May offered, bending slightly to bring herself to the young girl's level.

Harry watched the interaction, a knot of emotion tightening in his chest. Perhaps May, with all her wealth and breeding, would accept the two of them. The connection between her and Julia—a bridge built in an instant—offered a glimmer of hope that maybe, just maybe, they could create a life here.

The air was filled with the rich aroma of baking when a robust figure, aproned and dusted in flour, crossed the threshold from the adjoining kitchen. The cook—a woman whose hands spoke of years kneading dough—beamed at Julia with a grandmotherly warmth.

"Come along, young miss," she beckoned, her voice as welcoming as the scent of her culinary creations. "I've got a batch of cookies just waitin' for a taste tester."

Julia turned her head, seeking out Harry's gaze. Her small brow furrowed ever so slightly, a silent, hopeful petition for his consent.

Harry nodded once.

Julia scampered after the cook, questions already bursting at the poor woman as they went.

With Julia's departure, the parlor settled into a sudden hush, leaving Harry and May enclosed within its wallpapered walls.

Harry cleared his throat. He knew he owed her an explanation.

"I ought to explain—"

"Harold, I must ask—" May's voice interjected.

They both stopped, eyeing one another uncertainly.

"Please, call me Harry," Harry said, stepping back, both physically and conversationally.

He watched as May gathered her thoughts, her fingers brushing against the locket at her neck.

May's eyes, warm and soft in the sunlight, now narrowed as she considered Harry. "I chose you because you seemed different," she began, the edges of her words sharp. "I believed you valued honesty and integrity above all else." She took a step closer, her presence as commanding as it was graceful. "In fact, I believe those are characteristics you specifically mentioned in your letters. And yet, here you are, knowing full well who I am—knowing the weight my name carries in Chambers, though that was something you never mentioned. And on top of that, you bring a child you never mentioned into my house without a word of warning."

Harry recoiled from the anger in her voice. The rawness of his surprise left him grappling for a response, his mind racing to assemble the scattered pieces of explanation.

"May, I—" he stumbled, the conflict within rendering his voice uncertain. He sought the right words, but they seemed to scatter like leaves. This was not how he envisioned their meeting unfolding.

He could see it there, in the tilt of her head, the expectation of an explanation he owed her but hadn't yet found the ability to voice. How could he reconcile the image she had constructed of him—a man of straightforward dealings—with the complexities of his reality? Harry was caught in the crossfire of his intentions and her perceptions, struggling to bridge the chasm that had opened up between them.

May's gaze, sharp as polished steel, bore into Harry as she folded her arms across her chest. "I should send you away now, shouldn't I?" Her voice was a mix of ice and fire, clearly articulating her distrust. "You come into my home, knowing who I am, yet you say nothing of your daughter. How do I not see this as an attempt to ensnare me with emotional ploys? For all I know, you could be just another fortune hunter."

Harry felt the weight of her accusation like a physical blow. Each word she spoke seemed to pull the air from the room, leaving him struggling to breathe. He had anticipated skepticism but not the force of her conviction that he might be one of the many schemers drawn by the allure of the Allen wealth.

"May," he began, his voice rough, his hands reaching out then pulling back. "It's not what you think." He swallowed hard, steadying himself against the storm of her suspicions. "I knew that a child would complicate your opinion, but if you met her, you would see how wonderful she is and understand the fear of a father looking out for his daughter." There was more he wanted to say to explain himself, but May got there first.

"Complicate things?" May interjected, the words slicing through his attempted explanation. "Or perhaps sweeten the deal for you?"

"No!" The denial burst from him, raw and earnest. "I swear on my life, that's not it. I would never use my child as a tool in some...some deceitful game."

He took a breath, scrubbing a hand across his face, and then squared his shoulders. He was dancing around, barefoot at a fire, but it was time to walk straight through.

"I should have told you about her. But I couldn't take the risk that you would turn me away because I did not come alone." His knuckles tightened around the brim of his hat. "If you'd like us to leave, we will. I won't stay where we're not wanted."

The silence that followed was thick with tension, as if the very walls of the house were holding their breath, awaiting May's verdict.

Her pink lips parted to speak, but a new sound broke through, this one clearly at odds with the atmosphere of the home.

The heavy thud of boots, the slamming of the front door, and without a word of warning, with a force that suggested neither patience nor politeness, a man rounded into the parlor, as if his welcome were assured.

"Well?" the man drawled. "Where's this husband I've heard so little about?"

May's face tightened just as the man's eye caught Harry's.

The man was a dust storm personified. A dark hat sat atop his head, shadowing keen eyes that rested above large, fleshy cheeks. He was tall and wide, and his stance blocked out the gentle afternoon light, casting a gloom over the room.

Harry felt the instinctive urge to protect flare up within him, and though he remained silent, he stepped closer to May, prepared to stand his ground. May, for all her poise, seemed to shrink for an infinitesimal moment before regaining her composure. Her lips pressed into a thin line, the only outward sign of her distress in the face of the stranger.

May turned her head slightly toward Harry. Their eyes met— a fleeting moment where the question in her eyes was as clear to him as if she had spoken it aloud. He nodded infinitesimally. In the span of a heartbeat, they understood each other: Their ruse would continue. The charade they had clumsily stepped into now became their lifeline.

"Edward," May began, her voice a calm that belied the fear he was sure he had seen in her face just a moment before, "you seem to be under some distress." She took a step forward, the hem of her skirt whispering against the polished wood floor. Her approach was deliberate.

The man's impatience faltered at May's unexpected composure, his brow creasing as if he were reevaluating the situation before him. Harry remained silent by her side, letting her lead.

He was never one to charge unknowing into a situation he didn't understand, but his body was tense and ready to strike if need be.

The man's—Edward's, he supposed— eyes narrowed, a hawkish glint targeting Harry as if he were prey. His gaze swept over Harry from head to toe, lingering on the dust of travel still clinging to his coat, the wear of his boots, and the frayed edges of his much-worn hat.

"Your husband, is he?" The man's voice was edged with skepticism, his words slicing through the quiet of the room. Harry met the man's scrutiny without flinching.

May's hand twitched at her side, but she maintained her composure.

Harry decided he had allowed this to continue long enough. He took another step forward, glad to now be between this man and May, and introduced himself. "Harry Danvers," he said, his voice hard. "And you are?"

Chapter Five

May's heart was racing. Edward had come back so quickly, and she could see him sizing up this man, sizing up the two of them together. She could only be thankful he had not arrived a day before, or worse, in the minutes before Harold—Harry, she corrected herself—and his daughter arrived.

Willa entered then, bustling through the door as calmly as if it were any other day, but May knew her friend. She had been watching and waiting. She would not have wanted May alone with a strange man, but it turned out it wasn't Harry she needed protection from.

"Ah, you've met Mr. Danvers, then," she said brightly, as if the room weren't drowning in leaden silence. "Too bad it's not a good time for a visit, right, May?" Brazenly, she winked, and despite her anxiety, May had to keep herself from rolling her eyes back at her.

"Am I being denied hospitality in my aunt and uncle's home?" Edward sneered.

"Your aunt and uncle aren't here, are they?" Willa responded cheerily. "And these two newlyweds need time to themselves. Now, you came to see the husband, and you've seen him. On your way."

May was behind Harry still but could see from the small movements of the back of his head that he was looking between Willa and Edward, likely attempting to put pieces together with no information. She bit her lip and hoped he would wait to ask questions until Edward had gone.

"Harry Danvers, you said?" Edward turned his attention away from Willa, as if she hadn't spoken. "Why is it I've never heard of you? Where are your people from? Not Chambers, I am quite sure of that much."

Before Harry could respond, Julia burst into the room, clutching fistfuls of cookies, a dusting of sugar across both cheeks.

Edward jumped as if a rat had entered. "Who the hell is that?"

"Julia Danvers, sir," Julia answered sweetly. "And you ought not to curse. Grandmother says it's unladylike."

Edward looked at May questioningly, and she realized with panic she had no answers to his questions.

Harry spoke up, his voice unruffled as he swept the girl into his arms and brushed the sugar from her cheeks. "Julia's my girl from my first marriage." He kissed her forehead and set her on the ground, whispering something to her that set her skipping from the room, before he straightened and continued speaking. "Her mother was killed."

Edward looked as if his curiosity was not satisfied by that short explanation, but May was glad for even that much new information.

Her heart twinged at the thought of the motherless little girl, so young, and she wondered how old she had been when she had lost her. The thought helped her understand the choice Harry had made, though she would not tell him that. He had been alone, trying to do the best he could for her.

"Any other rude demands, Edward? Or shall you take your leave before it gets dark?" Willa chirped.

Edward shot her a murderous look, but he knew he had lost.

He grunted. "I'll want to talk to you about the carrying on of the ranch. This is my family's legacy, after all. The Allen name is an important one around here. I won't see it sullied by," his gaze swept Harry once more, "new additions to the family." He leaned into the hall, calling for coffee. "We can speak in Uncle's office. I believe that's where the files are all kept."

Harry shook his head. "We won't be doing any such thing," he said easily, as if he were declining an invitation to the pub and nothing more. "My daughter and I have had a long journey and have work to do to get settled into our new home. All of that will have to wait."

May knew Edward wouldn't like that—he was never a patient man—but he had sized up Harry and knew better than to try and push him.

He nodded begrudgingly, straightening his hat atop his head, and made for the door. "I'll be back then. You won't put me off forever," he said warningly.

"Until next time," Harry said.

They all watched Edward go, and it wasn't until the door swung shut that the three relaxed and the tension in the room eased.

Willa extended a hand to Harry, a smile on her face. "That was well played," she said. "Harold Danvers."

"Harry," he said again, smiling at her. "And if I may ask, you are?"

"Willa," she said. "May's best friend. Couldn't live without me. You'll get used to me; I'm here all the time. My father, too. He has a personal interest in May's safety, you know. Chambers may not be as small as some towns, but we're tight-knit. We look after each other."

All of this was said conversationally, completely friendly, but the warning in each word rang clear as a bell.

To May's surprise, Harry's smile was genuine. "I would expect nothing less. I hope my daughter and I will be welcome here."

Willa looked between Harry and May and then nodded. "I'll leave you two for now, but I'll be back tomorrow for breakfast. With Father." She kissed May's cheek and nodded to Harry before sweeping from the room.

After she had gone, May sighed and sank into the sofa. "Well," she said wearily. "I suppose I owe you an apology." The weight of the world felt so heavy on her shoulders at that moment. "And an explanation."

Harry sat in the brocaded armchair across from her, shifting as he sat and keeping from resting against the carved wooden arms, as if he were afraid to damage it.

"I owe you the same, it secms," he said, a small smile twitching at his lips.

She looked at him in surprise, taking him in once more. Her brain was refitting the pieces together of the image she had created of this man in her head prior to meeting him, widow, father, protector now sliding into place. He was not at all what she expected.

"That was my cousin, Edward. He believes he has some rights to this place, although my parents did not care for him. There was one incident that I know about, perhaps others I was too young to be told. There is no truth to this idea he has that he has rights to our ranch; in fact, my parents are sure to be rolling in their graves at the mere thought."

The words came out easily, but the meaning, and the reminder that her parents were gone, buried, and unable to help, struck her anew. It was a constant bell ringing inside her, a bell that never silenced, only quieted before being struck again by something that reminded her of them. She wanted to pull herself into a ball to lessen the pain, but she had so many things to do, and they had raised her to be strong.

She forced herself to sit up and pull her shoulders back to meet Harry's eyes. The sunlight streamed through the windows, lighting up their blue. She had never seen the ocean, but she imagined its color to look the same.

Harry looked as if he were putting pieces of his own together. "Ah, so that is the reason for the marriage?"

She looked at him, startled. "Well, yes. You put that together quickly."

He smiled ruefully. "Part of the job."

"Former job," she corrected, but as gently as she could.

He nodded. "I was a sheriff, but the loss of my wife shook me. I need to focus on my daughter, on bringing her up right. I can't do it alone."

"And apparently I can't run the ranch alone," she added.

Their eyes met in the silence that fell, and just like before, in that moment with Edward's demanding presence, an understanding passed between them.

"I apologize for questioning your intentions," she said.

"And I apologize to you for showing up with a daughter you knew nothing about."

"It looks like we need one another. So," she stood, extending one hand, "let's move forward, shall we?"

He stood as well and took her hand in his. His palms were rough with callouses, his grip strong but gentle.

As their hands touched, something sparked between them, so bright and hot she nearly pulled away. Had his boots dragged across the carpet? But when she looked down, they both stood on the smooth wooden floorboards. Fighting to keep her face unperturbed, she pushed the confusing feeling aside. She was a grown woman with no time for foolishness.

They shook.

Chapter Six

Harry and May rode into town first thing the next morning and had the town preacher marry them. There were no decorative touches, and they did not exchange secret looks. It was as plain and simple as a business transaction.

Harry had one brief, fleeting memory of Beth, wildflowers tucked into her waterfall of dark curls, walking toward him in the sunlight.

But he shoved the thought away. It was time to focus on the here and now, not get lost in memories of what was or past dreams of what could have been.

A few coins, a quick ride in and out of town, and that was it; they were married. They both wore plainclothes, though May's were decidedly finer than even his nicest, and her hair was carefully combed and curled in what he assumed to be her usual way, and they were back at the ranch in time to share lunch with Julia.

Julia helped Cook lay out the food on the table, proudly displaying the biscuits she had helped to make. They were knobbly and small, the size of her little fists, and May and Harry shared a quick smile over her curly head before enjoying them.

After lunch, Cook took Julia back to the kitchen with her—she insisted on helping prepare supper, and Cook said she was happy for the company—and May sent for the foreman.

"This is Adam," she introduced the tall, rangy man, his skin so brown and wrinkled from the sun he resembled nothing if not a walnut. "He'll show you around the land, the house, the property. Adam, make sure he knows what he needs to know. He's to have access to all the buildings, anything he needs."

Adam nodded gamely, and the two took off over the gently sloping fields of the ranch. For the first few hundred yards, the two men walked in a companionable silence, Harry enjoying the warmth of the sun on his face and the sweet smell of hay.

They paused at the outcropping of the barn, a stable, and two other buildings.

Harry adjusted his hat against the afternoon sun and listened as Adam talked him through the animals that were part of the ranch, the number of staff that were employed to work the land, and the work they did on a usual day, his boots sinking slightly into the dry Nebraska earth. Past the buildings, the land stretched wide, golden fields rolling like waves, broken only by the sturdy wooden fences and the occasional silhouette of grazing cattle. A cool wind carried the scent of hay and dust, a smell he was used to but hadn't called his own in a long time.

He hadn't been at the ranch long, but already, he felt the pull of responsibility. Not just for Julia, though she was always first in his mind, but for this land, for the people who called it home. For May.

That thought crept in before he could push it away.

He had no right to feel protective over a woman he barely knew, but something about her had settled deep inside him like a burr under the saddle.

Knowing Julia was safely tucked away in the beautiful house, playing with her hands and guided by the matronly cook, allowed the tension always tight in Harry's neck to ease some as he and Adam walked the property, to get a feel for the land, to start mapping it out in his head. He wasn't a rancher, not in the way May was, but he understood land, understood its weaknesses and strengths. And if trouble was going to find them, he wanted to be ready for it.

He had learned never to discount the fact that trouble could find any person, anywhere, at any time.

His boots crunched over the packed dirt as he made his way toward the corral, where a man was tightening a saddle strap on a bay gelding. He was tall and lean, with a weathered face that had seen its fair share of hard days. The man straightened when he saw Harry and Adam approaching, wiping his hands on his trousers.

"Afternoon," Harry said, nodding.

Adam introduced the man as their head horse trainer.

As they met other workers and toured the stables, Harry didn't miss the careful way Adam was watching him, measuring him the same way a man sized up a horse he wasn't sure about yet. He couldn't blame him. May had built this place up, kept it running against odds that would have broken lesser folks. And now, here Harry was, a man she barely knew, stepping into her world.

"She runs a fine operation," Harry said, his voice even.

Adam's mouth twitched into something close to a smile. "That she does. Her folks built it, but she's the one who kept it from fallin' apart after they passed."

Harry leaned against the fence, watching a pair of horses trotting near the far side of the corral. "I heard they died suddenly."

Adam's jaw tightened. "They did. Accident. Wasn't much anyone could do."

Harry nodded slowly, feeling a pang of sympathy. He knew loss well enough. "That must've been hard on her."

Adam exhaled, crossing his arms. "May don't like folks feeling sorry for her. She got up the next morning and kept on working, same as always. Didn't ask for help, didn't let anyone treat her different. Just put her head down and did what needed doin'."

That didn't surprise Harry, even considering the little time he had known her. There was a steel in May's spine, an independence he recognized. But it made him wonder—why had she advertised for a husband? A woman as capable as she was, as strong-willed, didn't seem the type to go looking for help, especially not in a stranger.

He glanced back at Adam. "Then why the ad?" He had met Edward and seen the issue the man had created for May, but still, her reasoning wasn't quite clear to him. A woman as strong as she seemed to be surely could have found another way out of that mess.

Adam shrugged. "Don't know. She didn't tell me, and I didn't ask. Figured she had her reasons."

Harry filed that away. Maybe it was just business. A practical arrangement, like she'd said. Maybe it was something more. Either way, he intended to find out.

"You had much trouble out this way?" Harry asked, shifting the subject.

Adam sighed, glancing toward the road leading into town. "Some. Nothing too bad, but cattle rustlin's been on the rise. Few strangers hanging around who don't have much business bein' here. May's got a good reputation, but that don't stop folks from thinkin' they can take what ain't theirs."

Harry's jaw clenched. That was what he'd feared. He didn't doubt May could handle herself, but running a ranch and fighting off outlaws were two different things. And if someone thought her being unmarried made her an easy target, well— he aimed to make sure they learned otherwise.

"What about the sheriff?" he asked. "He reliable?"

Adam hesitated, then gave a slow nod. "Sheriff Taylor is Chambers through and through. Been sheriff for longer than most people can remember. He knows everyone, knows everything that happens."

Harry grunted. He couldn't be sure, not knowing Adam very well, but his vague answer gave him an idea of what to expect from the sheriff. Harry would ride out and introduce himself to the man in the next few days, get a measure of him. If trouble came, he wanted to know exactly what kind of backup he could expect—or if he'd be better off handling it himself.

He pushed away from the fence, glancing back toward the house. The light spilling through the windows was warm, welcoming. Julia was safe inside, probably listening to the cook's stories with wide-eyed fascination. And somewhere in there was May, strong and sharp, with mysterious reasonings and plans for the future that he didn't know about yet.

He hadn't come here to get involved. He hadn't come here to care. But standing there, feeling the weight of the land, the pull of something he couldn't quite name, he wondered if it was already too late for that.

Chapter Seven

May stood in the doorway of the dining room, her fingers twisting the edge of her apron. Harry was at the table, maps and papers spread before him, his brow furrowed in thought. The flickering lamplight cast deep shadows across his face, making him look even more serious than he usually did.

She wasn't sure what he was working on, and she didn't think she could ask. Instead, she studied him from afar, taking in the strong line of his jaw, the way his dark hair curled slightly at his temple. He was handsome—more than she wanted to admit. And yet, there was something guarded about him, something closed-off.

She wondered about his first wife. He said she was killed, but she didn't know how, and it didn't seem like a question one could ask without breaking every rule of general etiquette.

Still, she wanted to know.

It was a strange thing, being married to a man she knew nothing about. All her life, she had loved stories with happy endings, a fact her parents had teased her mercilessly about. After her mother had bought a dime-store copy of *Portrait of a Lady*, May had read it over and over, so much that the pages loosened from the spine and the cover had crumbled nearly to dust, never growing old of the way Isabel and Gilbert fell in love.

She had always imagined marriage to be building a family and home atop the foundation of a rich, merciless love like theirs, one that turned both parties nearly mad and led them to forget everything else aside from each other.

Instead, she had married into a family that already existed apart from her, one that she had had no hand in creating, and to a man whom she did not even know how to hold a conversation with.

Well, that was one small thing she could change.

She backed away and went into the kitchen.

Cook was preparing a turkey for the next day's meal and was happy to share a cup of coffee from her pot. She poured it into two heavy ceramic mugs, the rich, nutty aroma filling the room.

May took them and returned to the dining room, coming up behind Harry to place the mug in front of him at the table.

"I thought you might—"

Harry shot to his feet, chair scraping against the wooden floor. His hand flew to the gun at his hip, eyes wild.

May froze.

The second cup slipped from her fingers, shattering against the floor.

A cry came from upstairs.

Julia.

Harry scowled, his face still tense with whatever ghost had just gripped him. He didn't say a word to May. Instead, he turned and strode toward the stairs, boots heavy on the wood.

May let out a breath. She knelt to pick up the broken porcelain, her hands trembling slightly. Whatever had just happened, it wasn't about her. It was about him. And now, she wanted to know why.

She took her time cleaning up, using it as an excuse to gather her thoughts. She was no stranger to men with tempers, but this wasn't anger—it was something else. Fear, maybe. Or memories that refused to stay buried. She knew better than to pry, but that didn't stop her from wondering.

Her hands moved mechanically, but her mind was restless. Her face burned, embarrassment and frustration mingling. This was her home, and yet she felt like a stranger in it.

Cook came down the hall, wiping her hands with a cloth. "I'll get that," she began, moving forward to take the broom.

May waved her away. "You have enough on your plate, and we've kept you busy with Julia. Don't worry."

Cook hesitated before disappearing back into the kitchen.

After sweeping up the shards and wiping the floor clean, she set the broom aside and returned to the dining room.

The papers on the table were still scattered, the maps half-unrolled. She hesitated before stepping closer, her eyes scanning the markings.

The maps were those of the ranch. He had marked out fences and natural borders, boundaries that crossed into open territory. There were question marks and circles over open spots on the map.

The markings were heavy, breaking through the thin, soft paper in places, but they were precise and even.

This was the work of a man who wanted to protect someone from something. But what? She couldn't imagine. It wasn't something she remembered her father speaking much about. They had the ranch hands, Adam, the fences. There were always issues to be concerned with, but Chambers was small enough and far enough from any real city that they didn't bother themselves with worries about safety too often.

She pulled out a chair and sat, folding her hands in her lap. The house was too quiet now, save for the occasional creak of the wooden beams settling in the night. She could hear the faint murmur of Harry's voice upstairs, low and soothing. Whatever fear had startled Julia awake, he was tending to it. That, at least, spoke well of his character. He might be an enigma, but he was a father first. That much was plain.

Minutes passed, and when Harry finally returned, his expression was unreadable. He looked at her, then at the clean floor where the broken cup had been, before sighing. He took a breath and rubbed the back of his neck.

"I apologize," he said, his voice formal. "I didn't mean to snap at you."

"It's fine. My mother always said I walked as quietly as a cat." She hesitated, then met his gaze. "Are you always that on edge?"

He glanced away. "I haven't been sleeping much lately. I suppose that does set me on edge. I've just gotten used to the feeling of always needing to be ready."

She wanted to ask why, but something in his face warned her not to push. It was closed and tight, not a hint of openness or vulnerability to be found. Still, she couldn't stop herself. "What happened to make you this way?"

For a moment, he didn't answer. Then, quietly, he said, "I'll tell you someday."

It wasn't much, but it wasn't nothing, either. Something about the way he frowned as he said it, the tiredness in his eyes, made her heart ache for him.

Wanting to break the tension, she gestured at the broom. "I suppose I should invest in sturdier cups if I'm going to keep spooking you."

To her surprise, he let out a small chuckle—the first she'd heard from him. It was brief, but it softened something between them.

And that, May thought, was something.

May hesitated, then leaned over the table, nodding at his work. She didn't want him to think her nosy, but this was her house, her land, after all. She had a right to know what he was thinking or planning. "You're mapping the land." It wasn't a question.

Harry glanced at the papers before nodding. "Getting a sense of what we've got to defend, if it comes to that."

She frowned. "Do you expect some sort of trouble?"

His eyes met hers, steady and unwavering. "Always."

That sent a chill down her spine. She wasn't naïve—she knew the risks of running a ranch alone. Knew that men with greed in their hearts saw women like her as easy prey. But she'd handled things just fine before Harry arrived. She wasn't sure how she felt about him stepping in like this, as if it were his burden now.

Still, there was something reassuring about it, as much as she hated to admit it.

She crossed her arms. "I can take care of myself, you know. Chambers is a safe place. People here look out for one another. And I've been tending to this ranch since I lost my parents."

"I don't doubt your capabilities," he said, taking his seat and leaning back in his chair. "But that doesn't mean I'll stand by and do nothing. It's not in my nature to be passive and allow bad things to happen."

There it was again—that quiet, unyielding protectiveness. May didn't know what to make of it, what to make of *him*.

Silence stretched between them before she finally sighed. "I'll fetch us more coffee."

This time, when she returned with the cup, he took it without flinching.

When May went to bed that evening, she didn't have answers to her questions. There were still so many things she wanted— no, needed—to know. About Harry, about his past, his family, all of it.

They hadn't talked about anything, really, sitting at the long dining room table her parents had had made in town from the trees on the ranch. She had not broached any of the subjects that were pressing, had not asked him any real questions at all.

Instead, they had sat together, across that table, hands wrapped around the warm ceramic of their mugs. The candles had burnt down and flickered low and soft across the room, sending his face in and out of the shadows as the wax dripped lower and the flame slowly burned down until it went out.

May pulled on her nightgown and sat at the vanity that had been her mother's. Thoughtfully, she pulled the boar's hair brush through her long hair. One hundred strokes, every night, just like she had always done.

She brushed her hair, splashed water on her face, pulled on her thickest wool socks, and climbed into bed. All the while, with each step of her nightly routine, the thoughts that thrummed over and over in her head were not the questions she wanted answered.

All she could think about was how safe she had felt, how comfortable it had been, to share the evening with him. To watch the glint of the flame flicker in his blue eyes.

That was the last image in her head as she drifted off to sleep.

***

The next morning, Willa, her father, and her husband were in her kitchen just moments after she had made it out of her bedroom.

"Joseph is eager to meet Harry," Willa said, grabbing May's arm the instant she came around the corner. "Where is he?"

It was barely light out, the pink glow of dawn just stretching past the plains and beginning to turn gold. May looked in the dining room and the kitchen, but both were quiet, save for the servants hard at work.

She shrugged. "Perhaps he's still sleeping."

Willa's father frowned.

As her father's best friend, James Keene had known May all of her life, had watched her and Willa learn to walk together, fall and play and tackle life together, and she knew it was natural that he was being protective now. Still, she bristled when he said, "A layabout, then? May, what's all this about?"

"I'm not sure it's fair to call him a layabout," May said stiffly, looking down the hall to be sure Harry wouldn't overhear James's booming voice. "It's barely daylight outside."

"Best time of day to be out in the fields," Joseph, Willa's husband, noted.

When Willa had told May she was marrying the son of the dairy farmer, May had worried about losing her to the toils of marriage. Joseph, however, was a man constantly in demand, always mending fences for widows or catching stray livestock for his neighbors. His kind heart and need to be busy left Willa with more free time than ever, and their friendship had not suffered a bit since their marriage.

"You're right about that," Harry said as he came through the front door.

All four of them snapped their attention his way, watching as he kicked off his muddied boots and hung his hat on the peg by the door. He ran a hand through his thick hair and strode forward, nothing but ease and confidence showing on his face as he stretched out a hand to James.

"You must be Mr. Keene, then?" he asked, gripping James's hand firmly. "Good to meet you. You've raised a hell of a girl there."

James stuttered as he began to respond, his overwhelming pride for his daughter battling against his inclination to dislike the interloper.

Harry didn't seem to notice, turning to introduce himself to Joseph. "I suppose you're a farmer too?"

"Dairy cows," Joseph confirmed. "About three hundred head, all told."

Harry whistled. "You know, I met a fellow who got to see that mechanical milking matching they've got in New Jersey in action."

Joseph's face lit up. "You never," he gasped, leaning forward. "What do they call it? The glover?"

"Glove milker, I think he said. I tell you, the lengths people will go to to avoid working with their hands." Harry shook his head.

Joseph's eyes grew even brighter. "That's what I said when I heard about it. Just imagine the gall of farming that way. Now, I'm dying to know—"

He was still talking, but Willa and May had stopped listening.

Rolling their eyes at each other, they ducked into the kitchen.

"He's got Joseph's approval; that's for certain," Willa said. She was acting calm, but May knew the prospect of their husbands getting along was hugely important—to the both of them.

"I have a feeling your dad will be coming along before too long as well," she said with a smile.

Willa laughed, grabbing a tray and beginning to stack cups and saucers to lay out coffee for all of them.

"So," she prompted, "tell me. What do you think?"

It was a simple enough question, but loaded all the same.

May thought about it as she spooned sugar into the bowl, positioning a tiny silver spoon in its center.

"It's hard to say for sure," she said thoughtfully. "He's not very forthcoming. As of yet, at least."

Willa nodded. "He's awful quiet, for sure," she mused. "It'll be hard to get anything out of him, I'd say." She pulled a glass jar of milk from their farm out of her basket and poured it, thick and creamy, into a serving cup, adding it to the tray. "But he seems like a good man, don't you think?"

"I feel safe," May said. "Last night, I slept without waking up, no nightmares. It was the first time since…." She trailed off.

Willa had spent many nights with her friend, warding off the nightmares and holding May when she woke, damp with sweat and shaking with an unnamed, all-consuming fear she could not explain.

Willa's eyes widened.

Before she could respond, May lifted the tray. She didn't feel ready to examine this information with Willa yet. It all felt too overwhelming, too difficult to process. She would take it a day at a time for now.

They entered the parlor together, setting down the tray, pouring mugs of steaming coffee, and passing them around before sitting down together. By the time they all stood and Joseph, James, and Willa took their leave, May could see in their faces that Harry had passed some sort of test.

As he made to leave, James hung back, allowing the others to file ahead. He leaned in close to May. "I have always thought myself to be a good judge of character. This Mr. Danvers of yours seems like a fine fellow, but I wanted to ask you plainly. Do you feel safe?" His eyes were steady and piercing as he looked into hers.

She gave the question the thoughtfulness it deserved. "I do. But if something changes...."

He nodded, smiling, and squeezed her hand. "We are here for you any time, dear girl."

She and Harry stood side by side, waving goodbye to the trio as they rattled in their carriage down the drive, the tall wooden wheels kicking up dust that glittered in the setting sun.

It was an odd thing, to be hosting alongside a man she didn't know, but the morning had gone well, and she was glad for it. She lifted a hand, shading her eyes from the bright sun, and felt the wind tug at her curls. It was a beautiful day, not a hint in the soft, sweet-smelling breeze that winter was on its way.

She turned back to the house, and that was when she noticed Harry's eyes on her. She smiled a little, questioningly, but as soon as she looked at him, he cleared his throat and turned away.

"Better go find Julia," he said, his voice oddly gruff. "Can't have her making herself a nuisance all day to your poor cook."

She followed him inside, wondering what he had been thinking.

Chapter Eight

Harry left right at first light to introduce himself to the sheriff. After the past three years of hunting the men responsible for the murder of his wife, he had gotten to know most of the sheriffs across the eastern side of Nebraska, but he'd never made it to Chambers, so he didn't know what to expect of the man.

Still, in his experience, sheriffs tended to fall into one of three types. The ones who had had the position foisted on them because they were known to be good, honest men who could be trusted to lead the town. The ones who sought the position to prove to themselves and the people around them that they were real men and were constantly holding up the image of the men they wanted to be. And the men who craved power.

As he walked into Sheriff Mitchell Taylor's office, he received his second clue about which type the man was likely to be, the first being the non-answer that he had received from Adam.

When Harry had been Sheriff of Columbus, he had kept a clean, tidy office. Wood floorboards, one long counter at the entrance, two simple jail cells that were positioned so he could see them from his office.

Sheriff Taylor had gone a different way.

Heavy rugs lined the entrance of the office, the imported ones that no general person out West was buying from the general store. A large, imposing desk sat in the center of the room, behind which sat a thin man with an even thinner mustache, scrawling busily onto a piece of paper. The windows were covered with heavy velvet curtains, and jutting from the walls were ivory tusks, antlers, and some sort of exotic animal head, the name of which Harry couldn't even guess at.

The man looked up as the door slammed behind Harry. As soon as it did, the office darkened, all of the natural light blocked out by the curtains and the heavy wooden door. It gave the room an oppressive feel, not much helped by the flicker of the two gas lanterns.

An odd choice, Harry thought, for a sheriff to close himself off to the town. Harry had liked to be able to see the road outside, but that had been the way he liked to do things. He tried to keep an open mind.

"Can I help you?" the man asked, and his voice oozed judgment, his eyes raking across Harry, apparently unimpressed with what he saw.

"I'd like to speak to Sheriff Taylor."

"And have you made an appointment?"

"An...appointment?"

The man smiled tightly, pulling a sheet of paper from his desk and turning it with the pad of his finger so that it faced Harry. He scanned it. It was a calendar, blocks with some sort of coded lettering marking out the majority of each day.

"As you can see, Sheriff Taylor is a busy man. There are appointments available, but they must be scheduled in advance. We can't have him bothered by every Tom, Dick, or Harry who enters."

Harry fought not to react to the irony of this statement, being that he himself was a Harry. He looked at the calendar once more, then at the clock. "I may be a simple man, sir, but it appears to me that the sheriff has an open slot of time right about now."

The man's brows drew together in consternation, and he snatched back the paper, glaring at it as if it had betrayed him.

"Be that as it may—"

"I'll just step back and see for myself," Harry said. "As you said, his calendar seems to be open."

"Wait just one minute!" he shouted, but Harry was already down the hall and making his way to the open doorway through which hushed voices could be heard as he approached.

If the entrance had been dark and austere, the man's actual office was a different sort of beast altogether.

Flooded with light from gleaming glass windows, the sheriff sat behind a desk so large it stretched nearly end to end across the walls. Atop his desk sat a heavy marble base, a thin stand holding up one obscenely large nugget of gold. Hanging on each of the two side walls were seven-shot repeating rifles, their oiled barrels gleaming.

Harry fought to keep his expression passive, but his mind was racing.

Though the windows covered the back wall, the sheriff had set his desk so that his back was to them, another odd choice in Harry's opinion.

Out of all the many sheriff offices he had visited across the state of Nebraska, never before had he seen one like this.

But even more surprising than the office was the man hunched in the seat across from the sheriff, talking in a low, urgent tone.

It was Edward, May's overbearing and demanding cousin.

Harry stepped in the office, leaning one hip against the doorjamb and clearing his throat.

Both men straightened and looked at him in surprise. The sheriff recovered first.

"Well, now," Mitchell Taylor drawled, hooking one thumb in the chest pocket of his jacket. "Seeing as you've made yourself welcome into my office without an appointment, you had better introduce yourself."

"That's him," Edward said, standing. "That's Danner."

"Harry Danvers," Harry corrected, tipping his hat. "I've come to meet the sheriff. What a surprise to find my new cousin already here."

The air in the room was tinged with a sense of danger he couldn't understand. Though he couldn't determine why, it was clear that he needed to be on his guard here.

Still, he continued on. "I married May Allen and am living out on her ranch now. As a former sheriff myself, I wanted to introduce myself to you and let you know that I'm happy to be of service if you ever need assistance."

"Your job is to run the ranch," Edward spat. "And Sheriff Taylor is no amateur; he's not likely to need help from an out-of-towner."

"Now, now, Edward." Taylor stood, hooking one thumb into the chest pocket of his (finely made, expensive-looking) coat. "I find this to be a precipitous meeting. Were we not just discussing the profitable business arrangement we have for sweet little May's new husband?"

Harry couldn't resist lifting an eyebrow at that. Though he was still new around here, he would not have thought to describe May as "sweet" or "little" and could only imagine the look she might have made had she heard it. "And what might that be?"

Edward shot a glance at Taylor but stood, one hand resting on the gleaming wood of the desk. "It's a good arrangement for all of us."

Taylor pulled out a wooden box of cigars and lit one, offering it out to Harry. Harry raised a hand to decline. Edward reached out for it instead, but Taylor ignored him, chomping it between his teeth and puffing. Edward dropped his hand to his side, cheeks pinkening, and returned his attention to Harry.

"As I was saying," he said. "It's something we all win on."

"You had better tell me what it is." Harry was growing impatient. There was nothing he hated more than men tripping over one another to prove something and playing petty games like children.

"There's a farm, nothing special. Just a little one down the road from here. Sad story, really. It's been run down, falling apart at the seams since the owner died of fever a few months back. It needs a man at the helm to get it back into shape, and once it is, it'll turn a tidy little profit for everyone involved."

"And how does that involve me?" Harry asked, though he was beginning to get an idea of what they were asking him for.

"I want you to buy it," Edward said bluntly. "Buy it. It doesn't cost much, not in the scheme of the Allen fortune, and let me run it. It's the least you could do, the least May could do, considering I don't get to run the ranch."

Even if Edward had presented the proposition humbly and asked for help, Harry would not have been inclined to agree. Besides the fact that the ranch and the fortune in question were May's and these decisions were ones he would leave to her, it was a big ask to make of a man you had just met. However, the look Edward turned on him was so spoiled, so petulant, and so reminiscent of a toddler who had been denied a treat they felt was rightfully theirs that Harry could not even make himself agree to bring the proposition to May to consider at all.

"I'm in no position to be making business dealings right now," he said flatly. "Nor handing out money that is not my own."

"Be reasonable, Harry." The sheriff laughed. "You pay for that farm upfront, and Edward will give you a percentage of the profits once they start to accrue. What, shall we say thirty percent?"

Edward shot a glare at Taylor. "Thirty—"

"And there'll be my own thirty percent, of course," Taylor considered, talking right over Edward as if he hadn't tried to say a word. "The farm is guaranteed to make a profit. Old man Carlson has fields on fields of wheat, corn, and potatoes. There's a stable full of good hogs, and he'd managed to get himself one of those steel plows before he passed, Lord knows how. Won't take but a season to start bringing the money in."

"As I said," Harry said slowly, "I'm in no position. You are welcome to approach May with this sort of thing, however."

The sheriff let out a bark of a laugh. "Now, boy, I don't know what it's like where you come from, but 'round here, once a man and a woman are married, everything becomes shared. You've as much of a right to every penny in that fortune as Miss May does. I'm the lawman, aren't I? Law says it's yours, and even if Miss May doesn't agree, well, I'll back you up, sure enough."

Harry felt the hot flush of fury rise in his chest at the sheriff's words, and he flexed his hands, attempting to remain in control of his temper. "Law or no, I don't find it right for a man to come in and start spending money he didn't earn," he said tightly.

"You afraid of your wife?" Taylor shot an amused look at Edward. "Her parents were a bit unorthodox, sure, but they raised her well enough. She knows what's what. You're the head of the household. You'll have to stand up to her now or later, 'less you want her to run roughshod over you the rest of your life."

"I'll thank you to keep your opinions of my wife and our marriage to yourself," Harry said, the fury so hot he could taste it on his tongue.

There was a time in his life when he wouldn't have been able to stop himself from hitting Mitchell Taylor, but he was older now, with land, a wife, and a little girl relying on him. So, he dug his nails into his palms and forced out the last thing he needed to ask before he could get away from these two odious men. The office, with all its fine trappings and haze of cigar smoke, felt like it was closing in on him, and he was suddenly desperate to get outside and away from the absurdity of all of it.

"Before I go, I need to ask about robberies around town. Have you had any recently? Any gang activity I should know about?"

The sheriff still looked amused. "Why should you know about gangs, Mr. Danvers?"

Harry stared back at him, his gaze hard, until the smirk faded from the sheriff's face. "There's not anything you need to know about. Good day, sir."

"Good day."

Harry turned and walked quickly from the office, not liking the two men being behind his back, and ignored the daggers from the front desk man as he pushed out of the dark entryway and into the open, bright air of the street.

He took a deep breath, striding to his horse and leaping into the saddle. His mind worked through everything he had learned as he clicked at the mare and turned her nose toward the ranch. His shoulders started to loosen as he left the main part of town and put more distance between him and that office.

For some reason, he found himself oddly eager to lay eyes on May, and without questioning that, he shoved the thought aside but dug his heels into the horse's side, spurring her forward.

Chapter Nine

"How about this one?" Willa lifted an old day dress of May's mother's.

May touched the hem. "It's in bad shape. Let's set that one aside to turn into cleaning rags."

"Bad shape?" Willa took the dress back from her. "They don't need to be in perfect shape; it's for charity."

May frowned at her. "I'm not giving them anything I wouldn't wear myself, and that is something I would not wear. There's plenty here to fill their needs, I'm sure."

Willa pursed her lips, staring at the piles and piles of clothes on the dining room table, and then nodded in agreement. "That's true enough."

They were gathering clothes for a church drive for a family in town who had lost everything after a fire. May didn't know them well, but she wanted to give them clothes that they would be happy to receive. While they were sorting through them, she had decided to clean out the older pieces of her parents' as well.

It was a more daunting task than she had imagined, not only because her parents had loved fine clothes and had more things made than they could have ever worn. Every now and then, she would come across a piece that had been worn often—her mother's favorite dress, her father's most loved hat—and touching the familiar pieces made her heart ache. She was still new to grief, but it seemed that as the days went by, the pain did not lessen; it only grew further away. And as things were now, her grief had hardly made it down the driveway.

"You know," mused Willa. "Some of these things of your father's would look quite nice on Harry." She slid a sly glance at May. "He's handsome."

"Is he?" May kept her voice deliberately cool. "I hadn't noticed."

Willa dropped the button-up shirt in her hands to the table, her mouth dropping open in delighted glee. "May Allen, you could have said anything else, and I might have believed you, but saying you simply *had not noticed* is too much!"

May rolled her eyes and continued sorting the clothes.

"So, you haven't noticed those broad shoulders, then?" Willa poked her. "Those bright blue eyes? That hair!" she trilled. "I love Joseph desperately, but what I wouldn't give for the man to have kept at least some of his hair." She sighed wistfully and dropped her chin into one hand. "It used to be so luscious."

"Willa, really!" May said, scandalized. "Joseph is a good man. You shouldn't say things like that about him!"

"A good man," Willa agreed. "Without hair."

May snapped a tea towel at her. "Enough of that! Your idea was fine. We will set aside a few things of Father's for Harry. He might like that."

She sorted a few more pieces, now thinking of what would look best on Harry. Her mind drifted to what might fit those broad shoulders, his wide chest.... She shook her head firmly and focused back on the task in front of her, ignoring the amused look on Willa's face, as if she knew precisely what May was thinking.

"Fine, Harry is handsome," May admitted, after the two had been sorting quietly for a few minutes.

Willa's head jerked up, and she grinned devilishly. "I knew it!" she shrieked. "Besides, it only makes you look foolish to deny what's as plain as the nose on your face."

May restrained herself from rolling her eyes. She tried to limit herself to doing it just three times per visit with Willa, partly out of respect for her mother's rules of etiquette, but mostly because if she didn't, her eyes might just roll out of her head.

"He's handsome, sure enough, but it doesn't matter. He's only here to make sure the ranch doesn't fall into Edward's hands."

"Even so, he's your husband now. Why not make a go of a real union?" Willa's question was nosy, but her face was genuine.

May bit her lip. "I don't know if I can trust him. He spends hours checking fences, walking and riding the perimeters of the land, and studying maps to find weak points in the property. He's always making notes, listing out things to do, but I don't know what he's up to."

Willa considered this. "So, he's trying to protect the land and his family. That doesn't seem so bad."

"He knew my name before he married me. I think that's why he answered my advertisement in the first place."

"Your family is well-known," Willa countered, but her voice had lost its edge of assuredness now.

"I just don't know. I usually feel so sure of myself, but with him, nothing feels certain."

"Nothing you can do for now but wait and see, I guess," Willa conceded. "We'll just keep an eye on him, that's all. We'll work everything out together."

May leaned over and squeezed her friend's hand gratefully, and they moved on to other, lighter topics.

They continued on to the next pile, and right away, May's eyes filled with tears as she looked at the leather and sheepskin jacket on top. Willa's face went soft as well, and the two women shared a look, years of memories passing between them in an instant. Her father had worn this jacket every winter. It was passed down from his father, and the decades of wear had turned the leather buttery soft, the sheepskin still as thick and warm as the day it had been made, she was sure.

May pressed the collar to her nose, inhaling the woody, tobacco leaf scent of her father. Her heart felt like it was cracking open, and for a moment, she was not sure how she could continue to carry on with her life without the two of them.

All of the decisions that had led her here were because she had lost them. Sometimes, in moments like these, she cursed the people who had caused the accident, cursed her parents for riding together, though they had done everything together, cursed the world for being so cruel.

But this was her life now, and no amount of anger and hatred could change any of it at all.

Willa pulled May into her arms and hugged her tightly, and the two rocked together. May sank into her friend, closing her eyes in gratitude. It wasn't her parents' embrace, but it did make her feel less alone.

A sudden cry from the open front door set them both to their feet and running out to the yard. They had kept the door open to keep an ear out for Julia as she played. Harry was working in the barn and had said she could play so long as she stayed in the front yard.

Heart in her throat, May passed Willa in her rush and ran as quickly as she could to the little girl, crumpled on the ground beside the fence.

"Julia!" she cried, dropping beside the little girl. "What happened?"

Julia lifted a tear-stained face to her and pointed to her knee. Her dress had ripped, exposing the little bony knee beneath. May kept her sigh of relief at the minor of the injury to herself, smiling and taking Julia's hand.

"Oh, my, what an injury! We can't have that! Come, dear girl, let's get you all fixed up."

Julia didn't move, so May scooped her into her arms as she wailed, dropping her head into the crook of May's shoulder.

"Shh, shh," she crooned, carrying her up the stairs and into the house.

Willa ran ahead to fetch their home medical kit.

May took Julia to the dining room and set her on the table, keeping one hand on her back as the other gently tugged at her leg to straighten it so she could see the small wound clearly.

"There now. You're doing beautifully," May said, taking the warm, wet cloth Willa had returned with and wiping at the area as gently as possible.

"It stings."

"I know, sweetheart. But we have to clean it so it won't hurt later. I promise, it'll be over in just a second." As she removed the dirt, it became clear that it was only a small scrape, nothing to be concerned about, and her heartbeat finally began to slow. She started to sing a little melody her mother had once sang her as she worked, and slowly, Julia's cries slowed, turning into gasps and then sniffles until she stopped.

"Here," came a voice from the doorway. She looked up to see Harry moving toward them, chest heaving as if he had run into the house, bringing the scent of sunshine, hay, and horses into the dining room. "Let me."

Chapter Ten

The cry sliced through the air like the crack of a whip, high and sharp enough to make Harry's blood run cold.

He was in the barn, bent over a broken rein, but the sound yanked him upright before he could think.

Julia.

His heartbeat thundered in his ears as he bolted toward the house, boots pounding against the packed earth. His mind was a slate wiped clean of everything except the memory of that long-ago night, that cry Julia had made as she was dropped from the horse into the mud.

He took the porch steps in two strides and shoved open the door, barely managing to stop himself from throwing it open so that it slammed against the wall.

His daughter sat on the kitchen table, her tiny face scrunched up in distress, tears welling in her big blue eyes. A scrape marred her chubby knee, an angry red streak with a single bead of blood welling at the surface.

But she wasn't alone.

May knelt beside her, dabbing the wound with a damp cloth, her movements slow and precise as she sang a sweet tune he had never heard before.

"It stings," Julia sniffled, her lip trembling.

"I know, sweetheart." May's voice was low and soothing, a stark contrast to the sharp hitch in Julia's breathing. "But we have to clean it so it won't hurt later. I promise, it'll be over in just a second."

Harry hesitated in the doorway, catching his breath. He'd been ready to find Julia wailing, needing him, but the way May held her focus—calm, steady—was something else entirely. His daughter's hands clenched into fists, her little shoulders tensed, but she wasn't flinching away.

May had a way of working, soft but firm, her free hand resting lightly on Julia's shin as if anchoring her there. Harry's own mother had done the same when he was a boy, tending to his scrapes without an ounce of fuss, always making him feel safe and cared for.

He exhaled, shoulders lowering from where they'd bunched near his ears. Julia was in good hands.

Still, the protective instinct in him wouldn't let him stay put, even as he still struggled to catch his breath from the headlong sprint in from the barn. He stepped forward, clearing his throat. "Here, let me—"

May glanced up, and for the first time since he'd met her, there was no distance in her gaze. No guarded edge. Just warmth. She shifted slightly to make room, handing him the cloth.

Their fingers brushed.

It was barely a touch—just the barest skim of skin against skin—but it sent a jolt through him. He felt the way her breath hitched, saw the way the hollow of her throat moved with a quick swallow.

Something about that moment unsettled him, like stepping into warm water only to realize it ran far deeper than expected.

Still, he focused on Julia. "You all right, honey?"

She nodded, though her sniffles hadn't entirely faded. "It hurt, Papa."

"I know, baby." He smoothed her wild curls, pressing a kiss to her temple. "You were brave."

May's lips curved into a sweet smile. "She sure was."

"What happened?"

Julia's eyes slid sideways, a sure sign she had been doing something that she had been specifically told not to.

Harry folded his arms. "Julia Marie, you tell me right now what happened, or there will be no supper for you tonight. It'll be straight to bed, and no more playing outside without me either."

Julia grimaced, and she muttered something so quietly he couldn't make it out.

"Speak up now," Harry said, leaning in and putting one finger under her chin and lifting it so she was looking him in the eye. He softened his voice. "You won't be in trouble. Just tell me what happened so we can make sure you don't get hurt like that again."

"I was climbing the fenceposts," she said and then burst into tears once more. "I'm sorry, Papa. You said not to, but I did, and I fell, and I'm sorry!" The last word stretched out into a long, dramatic wail. Funny, because he couldn't see a hint of wetness in her eyes.

May and Harry exchanged amused looks over her head, biting back smiles as they waited for her to calm down.

Harry rubbed a hand through her hair, thankful she hadn't been hurt worse.

Julia perked up at that, scrubbing at her damp cheeks with the back of her hand.

May sat back, tapping a finger to her chin in exaggerated thoughtfulness. "You know," she mused, "I've heard something that I think might be relevant right about now."

Julia blinked at her, curiosity taking over. "What?"

"I've heard," May said, lowering her voice to a conspiratorial whisper, "that cookies have magical healing powers."

Harry nearly laughed at the way Julia's entire expression transformed. Her brows lifted, her mouth forming a tiny "o" of delight. "Really?"

May nodded solemnly. "Absolutely. But only if you eat one right after getting hurt. Otherwise, the magic wears off."

Julia gasped. "I need one!"

Harry chuckled, shaking his head. "That so?" he asked May, arching an eyebrow.

She smiled back at him, the picture of innocence, only the tiny twinkle in her eye giving anything away. "Would I lie to a little girl?"

Julia giggled, all traces of distress forgotten. Harry felt something loosen in his chest, a warmth unfurling in his ribs.

May pushed to her feet. "One cookie coming up," she declared, moving toward the pantry.

Harry scooped Julia into his arms, her tiny hands resting on his shoulders. She was still warm from crying, her breath soft against his neck. He savored the weight of her against him—small, safe. For a moment, he closed his eyes and buried his nose into her hair, thankful that she was right where she belonged.

Just as May returned with a treat, her gaze lifted to his, and for the briefest of moments, time seemed to pause.

She held the cookie out, and as he reached to take it, their fingers brushed again.

There it was, that strange, fleeting sensation. Something unspoken, something unfamiliar.

"Thank you," he said quietly.

May nodded, though something unreadable flickered across her expression.

Before either of them could say another word, Willa clapped her hands together.

"Well, isn't this a sight to behold?" she said, grinning. "You three look like a real family."

The words hit like a slap.

Harry stiffened.

The warmth, the ease of the moment—all of it shattered in an instant.

A family.

That wasn't what he was here for.

He saw the way May's smile faltered, the way her cheeks flushed deeper. She glanced away, suddenly busy dusting flour from her hands onto her white cotton apron.

Harry swallowed hard. "Come on, Jules," he murmured, adjusting Julia in his arms. "Help Papa in the barn, will you?"

Without another glance, he turned and strode out of the house, out into the open air where he could breathe.

But as he walked, his chest still tight with something he didn't quite understand, he could feel May's touch lingering against his own.

And that unsettled him more than anything.

Chapter Eleven

The sun hung low in the sky, casting long golden streaks across the pasture as May made her way along the fence line. She had been up since dawn, as always, but today, her work took her out of the house and onto the land. Her father had never kept hard tasks from her simply because she was a girl.

"It'll be yours one day, and you'll need to know how to run it. And running it starts with getting your hands dirty."

He had taught her that she could only leave so much to hired help, even the ones who had been there the longest. It was her ranch, and she was responsible for it.

It still felt strange to call it her ranch, even now.

It had been their family line that had built it, and her parents' judgment had guided every decision. But now, the weight of it all sat squarely on her shoulders.

And she carried it.

She tightened her grip on the leather gloves she had tucked into her belt, surveying the land with a keen eye. The cattle were in good condition, grazing lazily beyond the barn. The fences were holding, at least for now, though she made a mental note to have someone reinforce the east side before the next storm rolled in.

Thinking that now, she wondered if she would say that to Adam later only to learn that Harry had already said the same thing. If there was one thing he was not going to let slide, it was their fences.

Maybe she wasn't holding as much of the weight alone as she thought.

The thought made her shoulders loosen just a touch—that and seeing that everything was as it should be.

It was then that a movement in the distance caught her attention.

A lone rider was approaching, leading two horses behind him. May narrowed her eyes against the glare of the sun, taking in the unfamiliar figure. He was broad-shouldered, wearing a dust-covered hat that shadowed his face, and his posture was easy but confident.

She didn't recognize him, and that alone was enough to set her on edge. The fact that it was just past dawn didn't help matters either.

She stiffened, hand drifting to her side as she watched him approach.

Turning on her heel, she strode toward the front of the property, intercepting him before he got too close to the house. As she neared, the man pulled up his horse and tipped his hat in greeting.

"Morning, ma'am." His voice was smooth, practiced. "I'm looking for your husband."

May didn't so much as blink. "For what reason?"

The man straightened in the saddle, seeming slightly surprised by the directness of her question. "Business."

She folded her arms across her chest, tilting her head slightly. "This ranch is mine to run. You can talk business with me."

The man let out a low chuckle, shaking his head. "Beggin' your pardon, ma'am, but this ain't the kind of business a lady needs to trouble herself over."

May arched a brow, her patience thinning. "Is that so?"

"I've got two fine horses here, real prize stock. Lookin' to make a sale, but only with the man of the house. No offense, but you wouldn't understand the value of 'em."

A flicker of movement beyond the barn caught her eye.

Harry.

He was standing just outside the open doorway, arms crossed, watching. He made no move to intervene, no indication that he would take over the conversation.

May turned back to the man, offering him a polite smile that didn't quite reach her eyes. "If you've got prize horses, then I suppose I'll be the judge of that."

He scoffed, scratching one finger down the length of a whiskered cheek. Then, a thought appeared to occur to him, and a sly smile spread across his face.

"Well, then," he drawled, dismounting and stepping forward. "Nice to meet ya, missus. Pony Joe is what they call me, seeing as I know all there is to know 'bout ponies, horses, and anything with hooves and hair, as I like to say." He laughed at himself as he stuck a hand out her way.

May dismounted from her own horse, sidestepping his outstretched hand and approaching the horses tied to the back of his own.

"A lady who gets right down to business! I like you already. Now, these here horses you're looking at, missus—now, they're about the finest you'll find in our grand state of Wyoming. None better. That's the Pony Joe guarantee."

"Nebraska," May said, running one hand lightly down the flank of a horse.

"What's that, now?"

She didn't respond right away, bringing her hand all the way down to the horse's hoof, ensuring she wasn't in reach of a sudden kick. Then, she straightened and looked back at him. "We're in Nebraska. Not Wyoming. How old are these horses?"

He didn't miss a beat. "All yearlings there, not a one over two years old. Got a male and two fine-lookin' females."

"Hm," May said, lifting the lips of the second horse and peering in at its teeth. "Not over two, you say?" She patted the horse's face and walked back to her saddlebags, pulling carrots and apple slices from it and passing them out to each of the three, then to the man's own horse.

"Not a single day," he said. "And thank you kindly for your hospitality." He moved closer to her so that she could smell the stink of drink emanating from his pores, and she did not fight the urge to wrinkle her nose, moving closer to the horses as she did one last circle around them.

When she stopped to look in the mouth of the second, he cleared his throat. "Although it's not a certain science, is it, birthdays? Hard to say for exact how old they are."

She leveled him with a hard gaze. "I have not found that to be true."

He shrugged easily, gesturing around them at the well-tended land, the picturesque barn, and the open fields. "Lady of a manor like this, sure. I'd imagine our life experiences have been mighty different." He clapped his hands together. "Now, what do you say? We've gotta deal? You'll be wantin' that male, I bet."

"You bet wrong," she said coldly. "These horses are, to a one, undernourished. Not a single one is a yearling. You've got a colt and two fillies who have had hard years of life. You are quite right that we have different life experiences, but a two-year age gap is one that I would imagine anyone could get right, or at least closer to." She sniffed. "Their hooves and coats are in very poor shape; even a fool could see that. You aren't feeding them enough, or you aren't feeding them right. Which is it?"

"Hey, now," he protested, the slick veneer slipping from him like a coat into the dirt. "That ain't true. These here are fine yearlings, and you don't know a—"

"You're only making yourself look more the fool." She folded her arms and fought the urge to check if Harry was still watching. From the heat at her back, she felt certain he was. "We have no interest in purchasing these horses."

His face reddened, and she saw something hard in his eyes, but it flashed by as he looked behind her, his eyes catching on the front of the barn. "Uh-huh," he said, mounting his horse. "As lovely as this here conversation with you has been, missus, I finally see a man around, and he's sure to know a good horse when he sees one." He spurred his horse toward the barn, clicking back at the horses in his train so that they picked up the pace. "There's who I'm needing to be speaking to, right there."

Fury flashed in May's belly as he rode past her, the horses' hooves' kicking up a cloud of dust that settled around her. She swung onto her own saddle and followed him at a trot.

Harry moved out of the doorway of the barn, and though she had not known him very long, she could have sworn he looked like a different person, a version of himself that she had not yet met. The lines of his body were hard, and his mouth a tight line. She had the flash of a thought that this was not a man to fool with, and that this unfolding scene would not go well for "Pony Joe."

The man's faux charisma was back on display as he approached Harry, pulling off his hat with a flourish and dropping back down onto the ground.

"Greetings, sir," he called out, all vim and vigor. "Mighty fine day to buy a beautiful horse, wouldn't ya say?"

May had to wonder at him. Was he so stupid to think a husband would greet a man kindly who had just nearly rode down his wife not twenty yards away from him? Or did so many of the men he met not spare a thought to their wives' dignity so long as their own was tended to?

She could not answer that question for sure, but she did know that it was not an action her father would have stood for, nor would Willa's father or her husband. And she had a fairly good feeling, based on the tightness of Harry's jaw, that he was not about to stand for it either.

"You don't want to come one step closer," Harry growled, his voice so low and menacing that the horses' ears pricked back, and they eased back anxiously.

"What was that?" Pony Joe seemed determined to make his pitch no matter how many signs of danger shone in front of him.

"If you value your life, you had better stop right there."

The horses balked back now, themselves much more attuned to the signs of danger, and finally, Pony Joe seemed to understand. He looked back at May and then at Harry, scowling. "Some kinda welcome out here. Guess I shoulda assumed Podunk people out here wouldn't know a good thing when they saw it."

"My wife was clear with you, and yet you remain on our land. She knows horses better than I ever will. You have overstayed your welcome, and I'm itching for a reason to test out my shotgun."

Pony Joe was back on his horse like a shot. But before he could go, May had one last thing to handle with him.

"Ride up the road a ways, and you'll see a pasture with broken down fences. That's the Smiths' old place, but no one lives there now. You wait there, and our men will deliver a few salt licks and some hay cubes for these horses. If you want a hope of selling them, take better care of them, and for heaven's sake, be honest with potential buyers."

Pony Joe opened his mouth, his face twisted with an unspoken retort, but Harry had had enough.

"You heard the lady," he snapped. "Go on, get!"

As the man made a wide circle to get all his horses turned around, spurring into the side beneath his saddle, Harry called after him, "And don't think those men won't be armed when they come! You feed your horses and stay away from here. I see you again, I'm shooting on sight!"

Harry and May stood side by side, watching the man ride off as quickly as the four horses could go without a word or turning to look back.

There was nothing more to be said after that.

Chapter Twelve

Harry watched the fly-by-night salesman ride clumsily down the road until he disappeared through the front gate around the bend, his veins on fire with fury. He squeezed his hands together, cracking his knuckles in front of him in an attempt to remain calm.

It would do no good to shout at May, but it was taking everything he had in him to swallow the urge to do so.

"Well," she said with satisfaction. "That was well done. I appreciate your assistance." She turned to face him, her pretty smile light and easy, and it was too much. The dam inside him broke.

"Do you think a strange man being able to just ride up and approach you on your land in the near dark is something to joke about?" he snarled.

The humor in her face disappeared, replaced by anger sparking from her eyes. "Excuse me?"

"What should be excused? The only thing I can think of is the poor excuse for security you have on your land!" he shouted. "You could have been out here, entirely alone, too early even for the men to be working in the fields."

"I wasn't, though, was I?" she shot back. "And even if I had been, you might have noticed that I know how to take care of myself." She lifted her pert little nose into the air, and he had to bite back a roar.

"He could have hurt you. Hell, he could have killed you, May. I'm wearing myself thin trying to keep you and this land safe, and here, a strange man just waltzes on the property without you batting an eye!"

"I would hardly call that a fair summary of what just happened," she scoffed. "Besides, what am I to do? Do you know how many acres of land we have here? What, shall we erect a fence across the length of it? Perhaps a height of fifteen feet would work?" Her sharply dismissive tone sent spikes of irritation rolling down his skin.

She needed to take this seriously.

He fought to keep control of himself, to find a way to explain to her why this mattered—why it was so important. But her flippancy, the lack of tension in her shoulders where his felt like they were tied up with wire, made him crazy. He couldn't hold himself back.

"You can't say what might have happened because you don't know. You don't know what can happen because you haven't seen it like I have. You live here, in this pretty little bubble, in your big manor, with your servants, and you think that you know anything about the world?" When he laughed, it came out mean and ugly. He was on a runaway train, and though he knew he should stop, he found that he could not. "You're a rich girl thinking she can buy safety, and that's the most foolish kind of person there is."

She reared back as if she had been slapped, her cheeks going white. He waited for her to yell back at him, but when she responded, it was worse than that.

Her voice was quiet, so quiet he had to lean forward to hear her words. That and the lack of emotion made him think of the way the worst storms would send giant gray clouds creeping along the skyline, no other sign of impending damage, just that quiet appearance until you were soaked through to the bone.

"You know what, Harold?" she said, her gaze on him steady. "I believe I've heard enough of your opinions for today."

He couldn't resist one last attempt to make her understand. He was sorry she was angry, but her safety was more important to him than her feelings. "I am your husband and—"

Her hand shot up, held out to him so firmly she did not have to say a word to get him to stop speaking. "Don't finish that sentence."

Her cheeks were still white, but now anger flared hot in her eyes, and he could not help but think that in her anger, she was stunning. Like how he might have imagined the image of some sort of vengeful Greek goddess with her cold glare, the line of her aquiline nose, the perfect symmetry of her curls, not a single hair out of place, and her eyes gleaming sharp in the sunlight.

"I may have been raised rich, in a bubble"—*rich* and *bubble* both hit with staccato bursts, and he flinched with each—"but I was not raised to be a shrinking violet. My parents were partners, and I was raised to be a partner in this ranch and in my own life." Here, her voice wavered for the first time, a watery edge to her words, but she regained her composure again quickly. "I will not be told what to do simply because it is a man doing the telling, no matter if that man is my husband or not. I apologize if that is not the life you wanted, but the facts are the facts, and I cannot and will not pretend to be someone I am not. I married you to avoid the control my cousin tried to have over me and my life, and hoped to find you were a different sort of man."

This felt unfair. He could not abide being compared to Edward, of all people.

"I am the face of this ranch and its business and will remain so. I appreciate your work, but do not think you will tell me what to do with it or with my own life."

Before he could respond, she turned sharply on one heel and walked, back straight and head held high, into the house.

He watched her go. Watched the door close resolutely behind her and then turned to stare up into the clear blue sky, overcome. After a moment, he looked back down at the ground, ripped his hat from his head, and tossed it into the dirt with a curse.

He could have handled that better, but for the life of him, in this moment, he could not figure out how. The image of her standing in front of a strange man, a crook, in the dim morning light haunted him. When he stepped out of the barn, all he could see was the man scooping her onto his horse and riding away, off into the plains.

Not a day went by that he didn't fall asleep trying to picture the last hour of his late wife's life. Had Beth fought them? Had they convinced her to mount the horse or forced her to do so? Had they used Julia to force her compliance? His mind would race, putting pieces together, imagining scenarios, picturing the way the house had been when he had returned to it—the covers in a wild, tangled mess on the floor, the child's sleeping basket tipped onto its side, the back door standing open.

He had drawn sketches of the tracks of the horses, hoping some explanation or clarity would emerge from them, and often found himself peering over them even now. But it didn't matter. All of the imagining, the questioning, the hunting he had done. The years spent searching for clues and answers. It had gotten him nothing and nowhere.

This, here, with this (infuriating) woman—this was the first step forward he had made since losing Beth.

He wondered if it wasn't time to stop holding so tightly onto those fears from his past.

In that moment, surrounded by fierce sunshine, with the echo of a fierce woman's words echoing, it felt possible.

And yet, did he not now just stand to have more to lose?

Chapter Thirteen

When Julia ran down the stairs for breakfast that morning, May eyed the length of her sleeves.

"Come here, sweet girl," she said, stepping closer to her.

Julia obliged with a smile.

"Can you lift your arms for me?"

Julia threw her arms up gleefully.

May squinted and leaned closer. "Now bend down like you need to pick something up off the floor?"

"I like this game!" Julia chirped, following instructions. "What should I do next?"

May smiled at her, running her fingers through her soft curls, stopping when her fingers snagged in several tangles. She carefully withdrew her hand. "Go fetch me a comb and the spray bottle from my dresser now, will you?"

Julia took off, and as she ran, May noted the way the legs of her linen one piece pulled at her round little thighs.

By the time Julia met her at the dining room table with the requested items, May had drafted out a list of things the girl needed.

"'s that?" she lisped, staring at the paper on the table as she passed over the brush and bottle.

May pulled her into her lap and spritzed her hair, gently tracing her fingers through the curls to work the mixture into the tangled curls in front of her. "It's a list," she said. "Of things you need."

"Things for me?" Julia perked up. "Like presents?"

May laughed. "Sure, like presents. But these are presents that you need." The mixture worked in, she began to brush, keeping her touch light and gentle as she navigated the tangles. "You're growing and getting older, and it's time you start dressing like a little girl."

Julia looked down at her clothing, perplexed. "I'm not dressed like a little girl?"

"Well, right now, you're dressed like a toddler. You see how your outfit is just one piece, pants and shirt all together? Now look at mine. See how I have a dress? I think it's time for you to get some dresses of your own."

Julia whipped her head around so quickly that it was all May could do to lift the brush away in time. When she spoke, her voice was reverent. "A dress?" She smoothed one soft hand down the skirt of May's dress. "Pretty like this one?"

Looking down at her dress, May considered it. It was pale blue gingham, the blue still bright, the white clean and unmarred. After some wear, the cotton had turned soft, making it one of her favorites. "Pretty like this one, yes. But we will pick out some fabric designs that you like. What's your favorite color?"

Julia might have been considering the answer to widespread farm debt, her little face turned so serious. Brow furrowed, she looked off into the distance, and then, like the sun breaking through the clouds, her face cleared, and she smiled up at May. "Yellow," she said decisively.

May cupped the girl's cheek, overcome with her sweetness. "Yellow is a lovely color for you. We will get lots and lots of yellow fabric and make you some beautiful dresses that I am sure you will love."

"When?" Julia began to bounce in her seat as May set back to work on her hair. "When can we go?"

"Why not today?" May's habit each morning was to sit down with her coffee and plan out her day, a bit of life advice her father had passed down to her. She was caught up on her tasks and had only planned to discuss the upcoming week's menu with Cook, a task Cook would do just as well without her assistance, and to sort through the mountain of paperwork in her father's office, a task she would be very happy to put off for another day.

Julia leaped from the chair, jumping up and down and clapping. "Today? Really? We can go today?"

That was when Harry entered the dining room, the newspaper folded and tucked underneath one arm, and May was quite sure she did not imagine the way the air cooled as he did. They had not spoken a word since their argument the prior day. She had hoped he would come to his senses and approach her to make things right, but instead, they had resorted to cordial nods when they passed one another and chilly silences that crept across the table, so that she had begun to wear an extra sweater to dinner in the evenings.

"Going where?" he asked as he slid into his seat at the table and poured himself a cup of coffee.

"Into town," May said, her voice cool.

She focused on the comb in her hand; his mere presence at the table had her heart rate elevated. The fact that he could sit there, so easy and unbothered, sipping the rich coffee Cook made while apparently thinking the women around him were incapable of managing themselves—her fingers on the comb tightened, and she forced herself to stop thinking about him. And to stop looking at him. Now was not the time to notice the way his skin had turned gold from the work outside, making his eyes even brighter.

The comb.

She took a breath and returned to her work.

Harry seemingly did not have the same understanding regarding the status of their relationship. His eyes sharpened on them as he repeated. "What do you mean, into town?"

"I believe it's a simple enough statement. I'm taking Julia into town to pick up some fabric. It's high time we put away these toddler clothes and get her dressed properly, like the little girl she's becoming." May squeezed Julia's shoulder gently, and the girl turned to face her, smiling excitedly. "All set, sweetheart," she said, setting the comb on the table.

Julia shook her hair out and hopped from the chair, dancing in a circle. "Going to town! Making a dress! A dress for Julia!"

But Harry's face did not soften as he watched her celebration. "That's not happening," he said shortly, unfolding the newspaper and taking a drink of his coffee as if he hadn't said anything strange at all.

May and Julia stared at him in quiet astonishment.

Julia recovered first.

"Papa!" she shrieked, her face crumpling. "May promised!"

He didn't look up. "She had no right to promise you something like that. You're my daughter, and this is my say-so. Neither of you is going into town today."

Julia began to cry, the showy wailing of a child who was not yet truly crying but wanted to be sure all the adults understood there was a problem.

Harry caught her eye, and he said in a tone that brooked no argument, "Do you want to keep crying, or do you want to talk to me like a little girl? Because it seems to me you're arguing to be treated like a little girl, but you're acting like a toddler."

Julia's face flashed a series of emotions as she struggled through this, and if May weren't so irritated, she might have laughed at the resolute consternation that finally won out.

With a shriek, the little girl threw herself onto the polished wooden floorboards and began to kick her bare heels and fists against the ground. Harry leveled a look at May, and she had to bite back her retort at his audacity. Was he blaming her? When she was doing the work necessary to take care of his daughter?

She found herself empathizing with the wave of emotions Julia was feeling and wished she had the luxury of letting them take over.

Harry set down his coffee, wiped his mouth with the edges of the linen napkin, and stood, taking his time as he walked slowly over to Julia, seemingly unaffected by her ear-piercing shrieks and the fat crocodile tears pouring down her cheeks— the real thing now.

He crouched down beside her and then, to May's surprise, lay a gentle hand on his daughter's back. "All right now, hon." His voice was soft and soothing, like one might use with a particularly spirited horse.

Julia sat up, still crying, and he pulled her into his arms, where she melted against him at once.

"'s not fair, Papa," she cried into the front of his shirt.

"I know, baby." He rocked her back and forth, his large, muscled arms swallowing her so that she looked impossibly small against him. He leaned away and made eye contact with her, rubbing a thumb under her eyes to brush away the tears. She sniffled but had begun to calm. "What do we say about feelings?"

She sniffled, the words coming out watery as she answered. "We are stronger than our feelings."

He smiled, the tender look on his face easing years of hard labor and sun from his face, and May was struck anew by how handsome this strange man she had married was. He was made even more so by his softness toward Julia, so at odds with his tough, impenetrable exterior.

"Why don't you take a minute to yourself while I talk to Miss May, and come back down here when you're ready to talk, too, hm?"

Julia nodded, hiccupping and rubbing at her face.

Harry kissed her cheeks, then her nose, then her temples, until she began to giggle and wriggle away from her. "Papa, your whiskers!" He nuzzled at her cheeks until the only shrieks were her laughter, and she ran down the hall, the sounds trailing behind her.

The silence that followed was heavy, and once more, May could feel that cold rush of air as she and Harry eyed one another, like two prize bulls in a ring.

Finally, May broke the silence, though she found herself struggling to regain the irritation from before after watching the way he handled his daughter. Even her father, who had been known across town as a patient and kind man, would never have had such a calm and reasonable response to one of her tantrums as a child. Their relationship had grown as she had, with him enjoying time with her more as she had matured. Still, good father or no, she would not abide by his dictating how she spent her days.

"I tell you now, and I hope you hear me, that I will not allow you to control how I spend my days. If I want to go into town, then I shall do so."

Harry looked at her, his face giving away nothing. After a moment, he strode back to the table and picked up the paper, turning its surface around to face her and sliding it across the table. "Read that."

She huffed in annoyance. "Read what?"

He came around and tapped one long, callused finger at a section in the lower left. She tried to ignore the way he smelled, like sweet green hay and sunshine, and something deeper, more manly, peppery, just beneath.

She scanned the short article and then looked up at him in bemusement. "A barn caught fire? It's a shame, sure, but what does that one thing have to do with another? The general store will still be open, and that barn isn't even on our way into town; it's clear on the other side of town."

He didn't answer, just tapped another part of the front page, the ink smearing beneath his fingertip.

She read that as well. This section was a bit longer, and a bit more relevant. "The tavern was robbed?"

Two men, tall and wearing bandanas across their faces and tall black boots, robbed the tavern at gunpoint on Friday evening. No witnesses, but owners of the general store stated they heard shouting. They did not call the police, citing that the general noise of the tavern is always high. A two-dollar reward is offered for information aiding in the arrest of the two bandits.

She considered this, but still, no connection made itself immediately obvious. She looked up at him with a questioning frown. "I don't understand."

"There is activity happening in this town that I don't like. Maybe it's nothing, but in my experience, where there's smoke, there's fire." He took the paper back, folding it carefully and tucking it into his chest pocket. "I don't want you and Julia in danger, and right now, I can't be sure that sending you both into town would be safe."

His experience as a sheriff hung between them, unsaid but obvious all the same.

"Be that as it may, all I see here are a few isolated incidents of misfortune. Do you intend to keep us all in the house every time ill befalls a person in a ten-mile area?"

She could have sworn the corners of his lips twitched in a hidden smile before he answered. "No, but until I know more, I ask that you stay at the ranch, and I will not allow Julia to go in on errands without me."

It was a compromise, subtly offered, but it did appease her. They were like two cats, stepping lightly around one another, watching and making more wrong steps than right. At times, she thought if he would just speak to her openly, if she could understand him, maybe their union could be easier. But she looked at him now, his face so tightly closed, so protective of— what? If he would tell her, she could ease his burden, could share it with him like a true partner, the way her parents had been.

He interrupted her thoughts with a surprising compromise. "If you'll go first thing tomorrow morning with Adam and be back before lunch, I suppose that should be safe enough."

She lifted her eyebrows but didn't argue. "All right, then."

Julia peeped around the edge of the doorway then, her face cleared of its earlier emotion. At once, the room lightened, and May felt like she could breathe again. She couldn't resist the smile that took over her face at Julia's entrance.

Julia walked formally up to her father, hands clasped behind her back, head down in contrition. "Papa?" she said.

Harry was smiling, too, as he placed one hand on her head. "Yes?"

"I'm calm now." She looked up at him, grinning toothily. "I'm stronger than my emotions."

He grinned back at her, crouching down in front of her. "I'm proud of you. And I have good news. Miss May and Mr. Adam are going to take you into town tomorrow and get you some things to make dresses. How's that sound?"

In answer, she threw her arms around him and squealed. Over the top of her head, the curls now smooth and shining, May and Harry's eyes met. For a moment, the only thing that rested between them was amusement. Amusement and fondness for one little girl.

The next morning, the sun still rising above the flat gold horizon, Harry watched them load up in the carriage, Adam at the head. Before they left, Harry pulled Adam aside, and May watched Adam open his coat, showing Harry something inside at his hip, something she knew to be the gun he carried on cattle drives and overnight rides. Harry clapped Adam on the back and said something, low and serious, that she couldn't make out from this distance. Adam nodded, and they shook hands before he hopped easily in the front of the carriage.

"All ready back there?" he called back, his tone jovial.

"Ready!" Julia cried, bouncing eagerly in her seat.

He looked at May, who nodded at him with an absent smile, thinking about Harry. When she turned back, he had walked to the end of the drive, watching them bump and clatter down the long drive, his face so openly concerned she was overtaken by the desire to tell Adam to turn around and bring them back, that they would go to town another day.

But then she shook the feeling off. He was dealing with fears she couldn't understand. He had seen things as a sheriff, and from the way he spoke, she imagined he had been well respected and good at his job. So sure, he would see fears that she couldn't imagine.

But that didn't mean she would spend her life in fear, hiding out on the ranch.

She sat up straight, turning decisively to face the road ahead, and squeezed Julia's hand. "What colors are you thinking for your dresses?"

This conversation topic lasted them the entire trip, the two debating colors, designs, and other things they needed from the general store—Cook had sent along a list, including a request for beets if they had them in so that they could make pink-colored cookies for Julia, who was possibly more excited about this than she was about her dresses, although it was close.

It was such a rush of excitement and small child emotions, so much catching up with the other women shopping that day and introducing Julia to the many curious people, such a whirl of colorful fabrics and careful ribbon choices and picking the perfect beets, that by the time they had purchased everything and Adam had loaded up the carriage with their sacks and baskets, May had forgotten to even think about the supposed dangers lurking in town.

She and Julia collapsed onto the bench in the carriage after sharing a slice of Mrs. Margaret's famous vinegar pie, Julia delighting in the tartness of it, which had, in turn, delighted Mrs. Margaret. May laughed as she took in the sight of the child, cheeks flushed, clothing marked with flakes of pie crust, a dab of custard on each cheek.

She leaned across, pulled her handkerchief from her apron pocket, and wiped the custard from Julia's face, Julia squinting and flinching away from her as she did.

"Ah, ah, now," May chided. "If you're to be a big girl in pretty new dresses, you'll have to keep them tidy, now won't you?"

Julia conceded and allowed herself to be cleaned up.

They had barely made it back onto the long road that left town and curved out to the ranch when a horse thundered up behind them, the sound triggering a chain of events that happened at once.

Adam stood, whirling around, his hand disappearing into his coat and then reappearing with his pistol, one thumb cocking back the hammer, as he snapped the whip into the air to speed up the horses, who jerked forward, sending May and Julia sliding into one another across their benches. Julia clutched at May, fear washing over her face, and May pulled her into her side, tucking her behind her back as much as she could in the small, limited space.

And then the horse pulled up alongside them, and a snarky, oily laugh boomed into the panicked space between them, and May relaxed even as irritation overtook her.

Edward.

"Don't recognize a man of the family? I ought to call the sheriff on you!" Edward said.

Adam's face did not relax, but he did remove his thumb from the hammer, releasing it and returning it back beneath his coat. He clicked at the horses, soothing them, and sat back down, pulling them into an easier pace. Edward and his horse fell alongside them, walking evenly so that they were only a foot or two apart.

It was a long, empty stretch of road from here to the ranch, only a few neighboring farms with homes set back a mile or two from the road and a few abandoned farms, but they were not likely to see another soul on this road at this time of day.

Edward had no reason to be here, considering he was staying in the saloon in town, no reason at all except to be looking for them.

"Not afraid of the sheriff? He doesn't stand for men pointing guns at their employers, you know. Not our sheriff. Some of these may be softer. You hear about these sheriffs in other towns, letting bandits and crooks in and out doing whatever they like. Sheriff Mitchell is tough. If I were you, I'd be apologizing to make sure no one told him about that little show right there." Edward's tone was mocking, like he was playing for laughs, but his eyes and mouth were hard, and May could see that having the gun pointed at him had scared him.

"You won't be doing any such thing," she said coolly. "And even if you did, his employer was right here and saw the whole thing. A fool riding up on a carriage with a woman and a child, no greeting or warning, and a man who was ready to protect them if need be."

She didn't allow Edward time to respond. "What are you doing out here, Edward? We've had a long morning and a full day ahead of us and no time for one of your games."

Edward cast one last petulant look at Adam before facing her, pulling his horse back a pace so they were right next to each other. "Maybe I came out to meet this little girl you've made part of our family." He smiled, oily, snakelike, at Julia, who smiled back at him uncertainly. "What's your name?"

"I'm Julia. What's yours?"

May didn't like the two of them talking. The proximity of Edward to Julia made the hair on the back of her neck stand up, but for no real reason she could distinguish.

"I'm your Uncle Edward, sweetheart." His tone dripped faux sweetness. "I'm sorry we haven't met yet. We are all very happy to have you in the family."

Julia regarded him seriously, then said, "Miss May bought me two red ribbons."

"Isn't that lovely?" Edward shot May a look she could not identify. "Two, you say?"

But Julia had lost interest and was staring at his horse.

"What do you want?" May asked him. This was her cousin, and there was Adam just ahead of her, who, by the set of his shoulders, had clearly not relaxed either, but something about this long, empty stretch of road, just Julia and May and Adam and Edward, was making her heart beat more quickly. She wanted this encounter to end; she wanted to be back at the ranch.

She wished Harry were there with them.

An odd thought, one that took her by surprise, but she did not have time to parse her feelings right now.

"I came to give my dear cousin important news about the man she married. I would have thought that might grant me a more kindly reception."

"What news?" she asked sharply.

"Oh, so you would like to hear from me now? How—" Edward could smell when he had an advantage and had never once missed a chance to use that any way that served him.

"Enough of your games, Edward. If you have something to say, then say it. Otherwise, I'll ask Adam to speed the horses up so we can get home."

They looked at each other, both trying to read the bluff in the other's eyes, but May had grown quite skilled at hiding her true emotions, and finally, Edward conceded. The sarcasm left his voice as he said, "I don't trust this Harry fellow. What sort of man shows up on a doorstep and marries? A man the rest of the family knows nothing about? A man not even from this corner of the state?" Edward shook his head. "I didn't trust any of this, not even for a moment. So, I did some searching. I talked to a few people I know, sent out some requests for information from that knothole town he comes from, and do you want to know what I learned?"

"What?" May asked, fighting to hide the breathlessness from her voice. If he tried to stop now, she would throttle him.

"He was dismissed from his position as sheriff back in Columbus," Edward said smugly. "Dismissed! How shameful! Aunt Vivian would be horrified, her daughter marrying a man like that. Uncle William never would have stood for it."

The rage in May at hearing him speak for her parents, who hadn't been able to stand him, was so strong she nearly did not even process what his words meant.

"Dismissed?" This was surprising. Harry had seemed like the quintessential sheriff type, a man made for that sort of job. She couldn't imagine him doing it poorly. Still, she didn't want to give Edward any further ammunition. This was something she could ponder at another time and in another place.

"That's what they said," Edward said cheerfully. "Now, listen here, cousin. It's not too late to send this man packing. We can speak with the preacher about sort of a...what do they call them? Those Catholics? An annulment?" The practiced uncertainty with which he said this made it clear it was a front, that he knew exactly what the word was and might even have already spoken with the preacher.

May's skin began to crawl.

"Adam?" she called.

Adam turned to face her at once, his own face tight.

"It's past time we get on home. Please pick up the pace. Julia is looking tired."

"I'm not tired!" Julia, whose head had begun to droop during the conversation, protested.

May patted her knee. "Thank you, Edward, but it's time for us to go." Edward started to speak, but she interrupted him. "Adam?"

Adam needed no further urging. "Yah!" he called, striking the whip into the air above the horses, and the clatter of their hooves and the rattling of the wheels drowned out Edward's words.

As Julia's eyes began to close, her head lolling forward and then finally coming to rest on May's shoulder, May pulled her into her lap and ran her fingers through her hair until she fell asleep properly. She forced her body to relax so that Julia would not pick up on her stress, but her mind was racing.

It wasn't until they crossed through the front gate, until she saw the ranch hands (were there more out than usual today? And closer to the road than they might normally have been?), until she saw Harry working ostentatiously on the front post gates, that she felt herself truly relax and felt safe once more.

Chapter Fourteen

Harry's relief at seeing Julia and May return safely to the ranch was so overwhelming he thought he might drown in it. The rush of feelings was so strong he did not trust himself to greet them; instead, as soon as he laid eyes on them, Julia sleeping sweetly in May's lap, the carriage laden with their purchases, he found a reason to ride out into one of the far fields and gave himself the rest of the day to get back under control.

It scared him sometimes, this fear, this overwhelming drowning need to protcct Julia. And now, May. That just added a salt of confusion into the mixture, creating a churning in his inner self, which he had not even the slightest idea how to handle. And so, instead, he buried it down as deep as he could and lost himself in the pleasure of completing tasks.

He rode hard down the fences, pleased whenever he found something that needed doing, throwing himself into each task until his hat brim dampened with sweat and he stripped out of his jacket, warm in the autumn sun, and rolled up his shirt sleeves.

By the time he made it back to the main house, darkness was falling, and he was worn out. He hadn't had a bite to eat the whole day, too keyed up that morning to think about breakfast or even a cup of Cook's good coffee, and in his rush to get out to the fields, he hadn't brought any lunch with him.

He left his horse with one of the ranch hands. "Give her a little extra tonight," he said as he passed over the reins. "She did good work today." He ran a hand over her soft snout and then went inside, eager to lay eyes on Julia. Eager to lay eyes on May.

She had a habit, he had noticed, of cleaning up before supper. It wasn't something he'd seen other women in his life do, besides hand washing or maybe retying their apron. Beth had embraced chaos and was more likely to show up to supper with flour in her hair and singed sleeves than she was to worry about freshening up.

May, on the other hand, changed into an entirely new dress. Washed her face, if he was right, and combed her hair, sometimes tying it back with a ribbon, sometimes putting something on that made her smell like vanilla.

It wasn't better. It was just...different.

There was one dress she wore every week or so to dinner. Gold, with cornflower blue flowers embroidered along the waist. The gold made her eyes, so deep brown they looked to him like chocolate, brighten with flecks of gold.

He really liked when she wore that dress.

All that to say, by the time he strolled into the dining room, he had a bit of a pep in his step. The sight of May in the gold dress, a gold ribbon tying back her long, dark curls so that they cascaded down her back, and Julia with a red ribbon tying back her own hair and her face alight with the joy of the day, only added to that. The table, nearly groaning beneath the weight of Cook's incredible dishes—beans and bacon, jalapeno studded cornbread, and beef glistening with freshly churned butter—had him feeling like he might actually float into the room instead of walking.

"My girl!" he said, sweeping Julia into his arms. "Look at that beautiful ribbon and your shiny hair. Aren't you a sight?"

Julia blushed and giggled as he brushed his face against her cheek.

He set her down, and she scampered to the table, taking her seat. He took his, as well, and May joined them, her graceful movements heightened in the flickering glow of the candles set amidst the plates of food, and as she sat, he caught a whiff of vanilla.

He couldn't stop himself from smiling broadly at her, breaking the cold truce they had set, and she looked back at him in surprise before smiling back, a bit tentatively, but it looked genuine enough.

They said grace, and then the maid served up their plates.

"Can I have my pink cookies?" Julia pleaded, spotting them at the end of the table.

"Not yet," Harry said. "Clean your plate first."

Julia lifted her napkin and wiped its edges industriously, then turned to face him with a grin that was all mischief. "Okay, now?"

He laughed aloud and nodded. "All right, grab yourself a half of one—a half! Not that big! Good, but you better eat everything else on that plate tonight!"

She nodded at him, mouth stuffed full of the cookie, and he winked at her. When Harry glanced up, he caught May's eyes on them, and the look there could almost be described as tender.

Harry loaded his fork with beef, beans, and bacon and had just taken a huge bite—relishing the salty juices, the tender meat, and thick stew of the beans—when Julia swallowed and said, "Papa, what's dismissed mean?"

Harry looked at her quizzically as he chewed.

"Uncle Edward says you were 'dismissed' from your job. What's that mean?" Her voice was guileless, almost disinterested, and she was already sneaking peeks at the pile of pink cookies, oblivious to the effect of her words on her father.

The food turned to ash in his mouth, and he nearly choked as he forced himself to swallow it down.

"I—who said what?" he asked, his hands suddenly cold.

"Uncle Edward," Julia said. "He said dismissed. Right, Miss May? Dis-miss-ed?"

May's face, now nowhere near in the vicinity of what one might call "tender," flushed as she turned to him. "That's right, Harry," she said, and he could hear the danger lurking beneath the deceptive calm of her tone. "We did hear a bit of news on our way back into town today." She placed her hands in her lap and cocked her head at him, one long curl escaping and falling down her shoulder.

"*Uncle* Edward?" he snagged for a moment on that detail, and May nodded.

"I agree on that front. He intercepted us today on our way home; it was not pleasant. However, perhaps we could focus on the more important detail."

She was right; it was a nothing detail, something small and inconsequential in this moment, with May's eyes hard and questioning and Julia's beginning to show concern as she awaited the answer. And yet, it was the first time he had thought of the connection of that odious man to his daughter, of the way his choices had led to a situation where Julia was stopped on the road by a man introducing himself as her uncle and bearing harmful information about her father.

He would have to work through those thoughts later, however, because May had grown even more irritated in his silence.

She placed her hands flat on the surface of the table. "Answer me, Harry. Your silence is only making me question everything. Why are you no longer a sheriff? I suppose I'm a fool for not asking you this question sooner, for assuming all was fine and nothing was amiss with that part of your mysterious past. Is that what brought you here? You saw a rich woman in distress and thought you would tap into her fortune like some sort of…" she cast around for the right words, her breath coming quick, her chest heaving, "disgraced fortune hunter?"

The questions peppered him, shot out like bullets, and he had to stop himself from physically ducking to avoid them. He took a dccp breath and pushed his plate away, then turned to Julia. It was clear there was only one thing for him to do at this point, and he wanted her somewhere else for this.

"Hon, let me answer your question. It's a good one, and I'm proud of you for remembering that word and asking me what it means." He fought to push everything from his voice besides warmth and affection. The last thing he wanted was for her to think that this argument was her fault. "Dismissed means to send away or ask to leave. It can be in a situation like this or in a job. For example, if I dismissed you from the table, I would be saying you can leave and go somewhere else. Does that make sense?"

Julia nodded thoughtfully, and he could see the series of questions this spawned begin to gather in her brain. Attempting to head those off, he said, "Now, let's practice it, yeah? Would you like to take a few pink cookies and be dismissed?"

Her face brightened, all questions and concerns disappearing. "Yes, please, Papa!"

He rose, wrapped three cookies and an apple in one of the linen napkins, and passed it to her. Kissing her on her temple, he nudged her back. "Miss May and I are going to have a little grown-up time. You go play in your room, okay? Papa will come get you in a bit."

She nodded and skipped from the room, pink cookie crumbs trailing behind her as she went.

Harry sat back at the table, noticing something unreadable in May's dark eyes as they faced one another once more.

He took a deep breath and cracked the knuckles on his hand. "You're right. It's not fair that I haven't told you more about these things. It's...difficult for me to talk about, and we don't know each other very well. I suppose I hoped to handle everything myself and not burden you with the knowledge." He looked down at the table, eyes tracing the delicate inlay on its surface, before looking back up at her. "But you deserve the truth."

She sat perfectly still, an oil painting in the soft glow of the candles, and waited. It was another thing he had come to appreciate about her. She did not speak without thinking, and was not so impatient to be heard that she couldn't wait and listen. It was something he admired, but in this moment, he would give a fortune to know what she was thinking.

"There was a gang, back in Columbus. We knew about them, but we were always two steps behind them. To my great shame, I had decided they were mostly harmless. I knew things were ramping up—they were pushing limits and getting rowdier— but I was certain we would catch them. Most of their work was silly, small. Vandalism, hell-raising, cattle scares. A little thieving, here and there. I was doing all I could, but it was just me, and I had other work to tend to as well." He looked at May, but she gave away nothing. He sighed and dropped his eyes back to the table, rubbing a thumb between his eyebrows. "Then they killed my wife."

He heard her sharp intake of breath but did not look up. "I worked with some other nearby town sheriffs, and we think they were looking for prize horses. I still don't know why they thought there would be any on my land. We just had a small farm, nothing like this. Nothing special at all."

His throat closed on the last few words because it had been special, just not in a way that would attract thieves. He remembered the way their home had always smelled like cinnamon and cloves, the way it had felt so full when Julia had been born.

He swallowed hard, shoving the memories away. "I tracked them for three years. I was gone all day, every day, working with other towns, chasing leads, tracking down every single clue I could find. They were always a few steps ahead of me."

May stood then, and he looked up at her in surprise. He continued speaking as she turned to the low shelf in the corner of the room and grabbed two glasses from the shelf above it.

"When I saw your advertisement in the paper, I wondered about them finding out about a woman living alone on a ranch known for its horses. I didn't come here hunting your fortune, but from a desire to solve both of our problems. My mother-in-law—Beth's mother—she told me I was doing Julia a disservice by not giving her a real family. It was time for me to build a life for her, and your advertisement was just in time for me to realize that." It was mostly the truth, just missing one other detail, but he couldn't share that with her, not now. Not yet.

She returned to the table, holding two glasses with an amber liquid. One glass had just a few sips worth, the other about a two-finger pour. She placed the second in front of him and then cupped the first in her own hands as she sat back down across from him, tucking her legs beneath her as she did so. Her face was pale, the gold in her eyes no longer anywhere to be seen, both dark and unreadable, even as she leaned back into the light.

He was overtaken by the strangest urge to pull her into his arms, to ease into an embrace and feel himself relax against her, and for her, in turn, to relax into him.

He shook it away.

He thought if he touched her right now, she was liable to balk like a horse, away from him, and in this moment, he couldn't bear the thought of putting more distance between them.

"There would have been no one to dismiss me from my role as sheriff, but I did it to myself. I couldn't focus on keeping the town safe because I had one goal and one goal alone: to find those bandits and bring them to justice by any means necessary. All I could think about was revenge. It wasn't fair to the rest of the town. I left my job, I left my town, I left it all behind."

He took a sip of the whiskey she had poured him. It was smooth, rich, and the hot burn down his throat helped him to focus on the here and now, rather than all the would'ves and could'ves that haunted his past.

Could he tell her now, that since his arrival, he had felt something else between them? That though he had come here for the reasons he had admitted to her, and some that he had not, he had found something that had surprised him?

He looked at her.

He thought about it, about bearing his soul completely, about reaching for her and seeing what she would do to respond. But as he searched for the words, he could not find what he might say. What—*I like the way your hair falls down your back? Sometimes, your eyes look gold, and I can't look away from them? I think about you, wonder what you're doing, what you're thinking, try to picture where you are in the house at any given moment, as I work out on the ranch?*

He would sound like nothing but a fool, and besides, surely now was not the time to further burden her.

He sighed again, downing the rest of the whiskey and putting both hands flat on his knees as he leaned toward her. There was still one more thing he needed to say.

"I'm sorry," he said to her plainly. "Can you forgive me for not being honest with you from the beginning? Can we move forward together?"

Chapter Fifteen

"Can we move forward together? Now that you know the truth, I will answer any question that you ask me with total honesty; I swear it."

Harry's face was full of promises, his eyes sincere and more open than she had ever seen them, and she was quite sure this was not a trick of the light; still, there were shadows lurking in that bright, brilliant blue.

She searched his face as she searched her own feelings. One of the most valuable lessons her mother had ever taught her, one that she had never needed more than right in this exact moment, was to wait. Wait, listen to your feelings, and then question them. Only when you decide that you can answer should you speak.

There was a roaring in her ears, and as she sipped her own drink, welcoming the hot fire that steadied her, she noticed the trembling in her hands.

That thought, that physical reaction he had caused, brought one emotion surfacing—anger. She had always prided herself on her strength, her ability to take the difficulties—the many, many difficulties that life had thrown at her—and continue moving forward. Get the work done on the ranch that needed doing and take care of the animals and her employees, and now, take care of little Julia as well. Julia, the daughter of a woman who, it had just been made very clear to her, Harry would never be able to move past.

"May?" he asked, his voice soft. He leaned even closer, the hair on his arms glinting white-gold in the candlelight.

She stood so abruptly that she had to grab the back of the heavy wooden chair to stop it from toppling to the floor.

"I—" She sucked in a breath but found there did not seem to be any in this warm room so thick with the smell of Cook's best meals, of Harry's light, spicy scent, of all of the silly, stupid things she had been thinking. "I need some air."

Her throat was tight, but she managed to croak out the words, and with one last look at him, she fled out through the front door and into the yard.

Out in the moonlight, in the soft grass, she bent forward, putting her hands on her knees, and sucked greedily at the cool night air. What a fool she had been, thinking that there was anything between them except the cool partnership that they had created together. What a fool to think that he had been ready to move past the woman who had borne him his child, who he had married in entirely different circumstances.

What was she to him? A rich ranch owner with resources and a home to raise Julia in, a step closer to the revenge he sought from the men who had taken his own life away from him. And the worst part was she could not even hate him for it because this had never been anything but a partnership from the beginning. She had needed protection from Edward's advances and any other who might see her and think, *rich, vulnerable, alone.* And didn't he work hard, doing everything and more that she could expect from a husband?

The sky above her stretched vast and indifferent, smeared with brilliant starlight. May wrapped her arms around herself, suddenly aware of how the temperature had dropped while they'd been inside, how the day had slipped away while she'd listened to Harry reveal his true purpose for being here.

May pressed her palms against her eyes, trying to block the words he'd spoken. Her breath came in sharp bursts that threatened to become something worse. She'd been a fool. A desperate, lonely fool who'd let herself imagine things that weren't there.

The main barn loomed ahead, a dark, hulking shape against the moonlight. May aimed for it blindly, needing walls around her, needing somewhere to hide while she pieced herself back together. The familiar smell of hay and horse greeted her as she slipped inside. She leaned against a post, feeling the rough wood dig into her back, a physical discomfort to ground her.

"This is what happens," she whispered to herself, "when you let a stranger in."

She could have waited, gone for the known quantities, and stood stronger against Edward instead of appealing for help from some stranger who wasn't even from this town.

She sank to the ground, stretching her legs long in front of her, digging her heels into the dirt, and cupping her chin in her hand as she looked up at the stars. He had done nothing wrong, not really, but kept back information that didn't really impact her at all. His reasons for coming here—what business was that of hers? Of course, he wanted somewhere for Julia, and of course, they all benefited from her family's wealth.

Things had never been easy between them; they were not always on the same page, but she had thought she had sensed something growing between them, something more than just two strangers building a life. Their shared affection for Julia, the way he'd looked at her sometimes when he thought she wasn't paying attention, the ease with which he had taken on everything she had asked of him. She'd felt a stirring she hadn't ever experienced before, had allowed herself to imagine possibilities beyond the isolated life she'd carved out.

What a joke. He wasn't seeing her at all. He was seeing an opportunity, a means to an end. A stepping stone on his path to vengeance.

His shape appeared in the shadows, the wooden floorboards creaking as Harry's weight settled beside her. She stiffened, keeping her eyes on the stars.

"May?" Harry's voice was tentative, gentle in a way that made her throat tighten further.

She had to respond to him, but the thought of admitting what she was actually feeling first and foremost made her skin turn cold with mortification. Instead, she reached for something else, another justifiable response.

"You lied to me." She did hate being lied to.

"I didn't lie." His voice was steady, but his hands fidgeted with the brim of his hat. "I just didn't tell you everything."

"A lie of omission is still a lie, Harry." May pushed herself to her feet, finding strength in her anger. "You came here under false pretenses. You're just using this place, using me, to get to those men. Is that why you're always looking at the maps? Are you still trying to hunt them down, even now?"

"I haven't been searching for them," he said, and she did believe him. But should she? "I look at the maps because I'm afraid of our vulnerabilities here and want to be prepared. I'm trying to protect Julia. Trying to protect you."

The last word sent a zing through her, but she shoved the feeling down. It was time to get more answers, not to become that fool again, looking for something that wasn't there. Harry was a good man, and good men didn't allow their wives to be hurt. It wasn't necessarily personal.

His eyes met hers, stark with honesty. "I let it go too far. I didn't even recognize myself. I wasn't the father that Julia needed. It took Beth's mother pointing out to me all the ways that I was failing Julia to get me to see the truth and make a change. I'm not searching for them, not anymore. But I won't let our new home become a target."

"What would you have done? If you found them?" She couldn't help but ask.

Harry looked down at his hands, as if seeing something there that disturbed him. "At first, I thought only about making them pay. Eye for an eye. But somewhere along the way, I realized that wouldn't bring Beth back. It wouldn't make me feel whole again."

"So, what do you want now?"

"Justice. Real justice. I want them arrested, tried, and locked away where they can't hurt anyone else." He lifted his gaze to hers. "I used to care about protecting a whole community. What was important to me used to be keeping everyone safe and doing what was best for the town, not just what I wanted. I want to be that man again."

"You still should have told me," she said, but the edge had dulled in her voice.

"I know." Harry shifted on the step, making room beside him. After a moment's hesitation, May took the offered seat, though she maintained a careful distance between them. "I'm sorry for that. I've kept more things from you than I should have."

"Why did you never tell me any of this?" She thought she could guess, but still wanted to hear his explanation.

"I didn't want to scare you. I didn't want you to think a pack of bandits was likely to show up here and try and hurt you. The truth is, May, I still don't know what exactly they were after, if it was personal or just bad luck, why they were trying to take my wife and child from me, and what they had planned to do with them if I hadn't returned when I had." She could hear something haunted in this statement, and it made her heart ache for him. He turned to face her, head on, so close she could smell the sweet scent of whiskey on his breath, could lean in and touch him. "Because there is a danger, that maybe they're looking for me, maybe they aren't finished with me." He sighed, started again.

He turned to look out, his profile cutting a sharp line against the darkening barn. "I was afraid. Afraid you'd ask me to leave if you knew the truth. Afraid these men might come back through here, and if they did—" He stopped abruptly.

"If they did, what?" May pressed.

Harry's expression hardened. "If they came here and found me, they wouldn't hesitate to hurt anyone in their way. Including you."

"I can take care of myself." The words came automatically, a mantra she'd repeated through years of independence.

"I know you can," Harry said, surprising her. "But these men, May—they're not like the troubles you've faced before. They're killers who don't think twice about who they harm."

A chill worked its way down May's spine that had nothing to do with the cooling night air. She thought of her isolated ranch, miles from the nearest neighbor. Of the evenings she spent alone on the porch, an easy target. Of the unlocked doors because who would come all the way out here?

"At first," Harry continued, his voice lowering, "finding them was all I cared about. But now—" He looked at her directly, his gaze intense. "Now, there's another reason I need to stop them."

May's heartbeat quickened. "What reason?"

"You." The word hung between them, simple and complex all at once. "The thought of them coming here, of them hurting you or destroying what you've built—" He shook his head, as if trying to dislodge the image. "I can't let that happen."

"Why?" The question was barely audible. Her heart had begun to lift again, questioning, hopeful, wondering—

Harry's expression softened, vulnerability replacing the hardness that had been there moments before. "Because I care about you, May. I didn't plan to. God knows I didn't come here looking for that. But somewhere between fixing fence posts and listening to you talk about your horses, between the way you are with my girl and watching you face down every challenge this place throws at you—somewhere in all that, you started to matter to me."

May felt as though the ground beneath her had shifted. She'd been prepared for more excuses, more justifications. Not this raw honesty that demanded an equally honest response.

"I trusted you," she said finally. "But you were never honest with me, even from the very beginning." She couldn't let it go, even though she felt like maybe she already had, maybe she believed that they could move past this and build something different, something new, together.

"I know." Regret colored his voice. "And I'm not asking you to trust me again right away. Just to understand that whatever my reasons were for coming here, they're not why I stayed."

The barn had grown dark around them, their faces now just shapes in the gloom. Outside, a coyote called, the sound drifting across the open land. May thought about the loneliness of that cry, how it had once seemed to echo her own isolation. How lately, with Harry and Julia around, she'd noticed it less.

"These men," she said after a long pause. "Are they really likely to come back through here?"

Harry hesitated. "I don't know. But they follow a pattern, hitting small, isolated communities where law enforcement is spread thin. Your ranch would be an easy target if they needed a place to lie low."

May nodded slowly, processing this. "And if they did come, what would you do?"

"Alert the sheriff. Use the evidence I've gathered to make sure they're arrested properly." His voice firmed. "I'm not looking to be judge and executioner, May. Not anymore."

She studied what she could see of his face in the darkness, trying to read the truth there. "And then? After they're caught?"

The question seemed to catch him off guard. "I haven't thought that far ahead," he admitted. "For so long, finding them has been everything. I'm not sure who I am without that purpose."

There was something painfully honest in that confession. May recognized in it her own journey—how, after losing her parents, surviving had been her only goal. How strange and frightening it had been when she'd finally lifted her head and realized she needed to build something more than just a hiding place for her grief.

"It's hard," she said softly, "finding yourself again after loss."

Harry nodded, the movement just visible in the darkness. "Yes."

They sat in silence for a while, the horses shifting occasionally in their stalls, the night deepening around them. May felt the anger that had propelled her out of the house ebbing away, replaced by something more complicated. Not trust, not yet. But understanding, perhaps. And beneath that, a reluctant recognition of the feeling that had been growing in her own heart these past months.

"I'm not saying I forgive you," she said finally. "Or that everything just goes back to how it was."

"I wouldn't expect that."

She turned to face him. "But I do understand better now. And I—" She hesitated, searching for the right words. "I'm not indifferent to you either, Harry. That's what made finding out the truth so painful."

In the darkness, she felt rather than saw him shift toward her. His hand moved across the space between them, finding hers where it rested on the hay bale. His fingers were warm against her skin, slightly rough with calluses earned from months of ranch work.

The touch sent a jolt through May that had nothing to do with static electricity and everything to do with the walls she'd built around herself crumbling just a little. She looked down at their hands, his covering hers, and felt a strange mixture of fear and possibility.

"I don't know what happens next," Harry said, his voice low and close. "But I'd like to find out. If you'll let me stay, let us both stay."

She couldn't stop herself from shooting him a quick smile, "Ah, using my affection for Julia against me?"

He laughed, shaking his head, but she turned serious again.

May didn't pull her hand away. The simple contact anchored her somehow, even as everything else felt uncertain. "I'm not making any promises," she warned.

"I'm not asking for any." His fingers tightened slightly around hers. "Just a chance."

Outside, the coyote called again, and this time another answered—the lonely sound transformed into something like conversation. May thought about isolation and connection, about the risks of trusting and the cost of not trusting at all. About the man beside her, whose presence had somehow shifted from threat to comfort in the span of a single conversation.

"A chance," she repeated, and felt something inside her unlock, a door opening to a room she'd kept sealed for far too long. "I think I can manage that."

His hand remained on hers, neither of them moving to break the tentative connection. Around them, the barn settled into night sounds—horses breathing, wind finding cracks in the old wood, hay rustling as mice went about their business. May sat still, aware of each breath, each heartbeat, each moment stretching between what had been and what might be.

She didn't know if she could trust Harry completely. She did not know if his presence would bring danger to her door or healing to her heart. But as they sat together in the darkness, their hands still touching, so lightly, so sweetly, so uncertainly, May found herself willing to wait and see.

Chapter Sixteen

Harry stood in the wide open fields and watched the heavy clouds gather, darkening the horizon like a bruise. The wind picked up, carrying with it the smell of rain and an uneasy tension. The hair on his arms lifted from his skin, a humid, staticky feeling pressing down on him.

He worried about tornadoes, about wind, hail, about the horses getting spooked. About all of them if Julia were trapped inside for longer than a few hours.

The sound of hoofbeats pounding toward him made him turn quickly to see Adam riding up to him, his face drawn and serious. Harry watched, forcing himself not to guess what could be causing Adam's concern. It could be a sick cow, a bug-infested crop.

Adam pulled up a few feet from him and slid from his horse. The rain had started, pebbling their hats, the wind kicking up red dust.

"The Wilson place got hit last night," Adam said, lifting his hat and pushing damp hair off his forehead. "I was in town getting supplies, and the whole town's talking about it."

Harry felt a familiar knot tighten in his stomach. The Wilson place was their nearest neighbor. They had a long fence line that split their two properties, nothing else. "What happened?"

"A gang of men, from what I heard. They broke in, tied up the Wilsons, stole half a dozen horses, and left the Wilsons tied in those chairs in the house. Luckily they had a visitor this morning who found them and untied them." Adam frowned and then continued. "I stopped by on my way back, spoke to them myself. They're shook up, house is a wreck. Just waiting on the sheriff to come out now."

Harry glanced at the sky, then back at Adam. He didn't miss the way Adam shifted from foot to foot, like he was afraid of what Harry might say next.

"Show me," Harry said, his decision made with a quiet certainty. Adam nodded, looking unsurprised.

When Harry had first asked Adam to fill him in on what he knew of robberies, particularly those involving horses, in the area, Adam had simply agreed. But Harry had learned that Adam was a man who never asked a question he could answer himself, and so it was not until Harry had had Adam bring him maps of the ranch and the neighboring farms, the roads leading out and in, and a list of any vulnerable areas around the outer limits of the ranch, that Adam started pressing.

After speaking with May, Harry found that it was easier to tell Adam about his past, and he found Adam to be a better listener than just about anyone he had ever encountered.

As he prepared his horse for the short ride, he made a note to thank Adam later, for bringing this information directly to him.

They made their way to the farm together, the wind at their backs. Harry felt the air grow heavier with each step, the promise of real rain hanging above them. He hadn't been sure if he should come, but the thought of doing nothing had gnawed at him too much to wait for more idle gossip to answer his questions. He knew what he was looking for, and he couldn't waste a minute.

As they approached, Harry saw the broken fence first, a gaping wound in the enclosure. The Wilson farm was a mess of trampled ground and farm work detritus, though there wasn't another person in sight.

Harry knelt by the fence, examining the splintered wood. "They used an ax to split this open," he said, mostly to himself.

Adam stayed a step behind, watching Harry with a mix of concern and uncertainty. "Does it look the same? As those men from before?"

Harry didn't answer. He was already moving along the fence line, studying the ground, looking for anything the men might have left behind. His boots sank into the mud, and he felt a stubborn resolve settle in his chest. He knew what it was like to have something stolen from you.

He found a length of rope, frayed at one end, and held it up for Adam to see. "Used this to tie the horses."

Adam nodded, his expression lightening for a moment. "Maybe you can help, then."

Harry didn't say what they both were thinking: *Maybe they'll let you help.*

He spotted a set of tracks moving west and got down to the ground quickly, looking for any similarities to those tracks he had memorized years ago, the ones he could still picture perfectly in his mind even now.

He was leaning in closer, careful not to disturb the marks, when the front door of the Wilson house opened with an echoing creek.

"What do you think you're doing?" Sheriff Mitchell's voice was loud and aggressive as he pounded toward them.

Harry turned to see Mitchell standing with his hands on his hips, his gaze hard and unyielding. "I'm lending a hand to a neighbor," Harry said steadily, holding Mitchell's stare. "The fence was broken from the outside with an ax. They came here prepared, and they knew what they were doing."

Mitchell's scowl deepened. "I don't need you telling me what I already know."

Harry took a breath, trying to keep his voice steady. "I just thought—"

"I know what you thought," Mitchell cut him off. "But in this town, we do things the right way. I don't know you from Adam, and no one asked you to show up here and poke around where you aren't wanted. One thing we don't need? The help of a fired sheriff."

Mitchell's words were nearly spat at him, and though Harry's first reaction was shame, his investigative brain had already begun turning, had started the moment he mounted his horse at the ranch and made his way here, and so he did not let himself linger on the feeling.

A few deputies rounded the far edge of the house, and Harry knew he did not imagine the smirks or weight of their judgment as they approached. Mitchell shot Harry one last look before turning to join them, leaning close as they conferred.

What had they been doing in the back east side of the house? The barn was up ahead, and the fence the bandits had broken through was right where Harry was standing. There was nothing on that side except the land that bordered the next neighbor, whose property was at least a mile out.

Harry leaned in close to Adam. "Would you have thought to spend much time searching on that side of the house?"

Adam, eyes narrowed, shook his head. "Not for a second."

More men rounded the side of the house again, and Adam and Harry watched as Edward appeared among them.

Harry wondered why Edward would be a part of this group. From what he knew of the man, he didn't live in Chambers, and the only claim he had to town was the one he wished he had of May's ranch. Yet he seemed to always be around when Mitchell was somewhere.

Edward shot Harry a glare so strong he could feel it from across the yard, but Harry didn't have time to lose playing the man's petty games. Shooting a glance up at the darkening sky, he jogged up to Mitchell, falling in step with him as he approached the other men.

"Listen, I know you have this under control," he forced himself to say, forced himself not to question the man's motives, or the way he seemed more worried about talking than he did about tracking the bandits before the rain started and made the job impossible to do. "But my town was hit similarly to this, and though it looked at first like a one-off, like a few bad men just making trouble, it escalated. I may not be a sheriff anymore, but I know what to look for. Let me help. At least just hear me out. Let me tell you what I learned about these men and the calling cards they tended to leave."

Mitchell stopped and turned to face him. "I think I was clear. I don't need any help from a man who couldn't do the job he was entrusted with and had to go running to another town and marry a rich woman. You're nothing but a fortune hunter taking advantage. Now get out of here before I have my men run you off." Gone was the jovial, respectful man he met in his office.

They paused, standing toe to toe, both assessing the other. This close, Harry could see the way the man's buttons gleamed, as if this jacket had never spent much time outside that luxurious office and in the dust of the plains. Harry stood nearly a head taller, but Mitchell's barrel pressed was so puffed out that it was clear he felt that he was the bigger man.

"I'm just trying to help," Harry said, keeping his voice calm. "That's all I'm trying to do."

Mitchell turned away, dismissing him with a shrug. "We've got it under control."

The men circled around Mitchell, closing around him as he approached, and Harry went back to Adam and the fence line, casting another anxious glance up at the sky. He could taste the impending rain now, could feel the grit in the wind. They had minutes now, if that.

"What do you need from me?" Adam asked quietly as he approached him.

"I don't have time to recreate these tracks," Harry said. "Do what you can to remember them so I can try later."

Harry crouched, scanning the area. He saw drag marks where the horses had resisted, muddy footprints leading toward the barn.

He moved quickly, following them as they exited the barn.

A rumble of thunder sounded in the distance, and the first drops of rain began to fall.

"You take the rear," Harry called over the wind to Adam, who disappeared immediately around the back of the barn, eyes intent on the ground.

From the house, he heard mocking laughter.

"We said we didn't need your help!" Edward shouted, but Mitchell waved him off.

"Let him look," he said. "What does it matter?"

The rain fell in fat droplets, and a strike of lightning cracked in the distance. His skin was damp with humidity.

He moved quickly, doing all that he could do, ignoring the men behind him, hoping Adam would know how to describe what he was seeing.

The sky opened, and a torrent of rain began. They had seconds, if that.

Harry wiped his face, calling out to Mitchell over the rain. "The tracks are fading. Are you and your men going to look?"

Mitchell smirked and said something to Edward, whose eyes, furious, did not leave Harry.

Thunder rolled across the plain, another crack of lightning. Harry's breath was coming quickly; they were too late. He called out one more time. "Are you going to do your job or not, Mitchell?"

But Mitchell was already walking toward the other men, leaving Harry standing alone in the rain. "Let's move," Mitchell called to them, ignoring Harry's words.

The men mounted their horses and, with a few last shouts, began to ride in the direction of town. As they went, two or three veered deliberately, their horses pounding the already fading tracks into indecipherable mud.

Harry watched them go, rain hitting the brim of his hat and soaking through his jacket, fists clenched. Adam appeared at his side, his face set. The horses disappeared off down the road as they stood in the rain, watching the last of the tracks disappear beneath growing puddles.

At last, they mounted their horses, riding side by side back to the ranch, the farm disappearing behind them, the storm raging above.

Chapter Seventeen

May watched the rain strike the windows, the violence surprising. The parlor grew dark as the light outside dimmed beneath the clouds and pouring rain, and she moved to light the lamps around the room, pulling her sweater closer against the chill.

Upstairs, she could hear pounding footsteps as Julia ran the length of the hall with an old hoop of May's she had found in the attic for her. The sounds of her laughter and energy kept the house from growing too gloomy from the storm.

When the front door slammed open, she jumped, peering out into the hall to see Harry enter, soaked to the bone.

"My God, Harry, were you out working in this?" May rushed to help him remove his jacket, closing the door against the wind, the front entrance already covered in water.

He snatched his hat off his head, hanging it on the hook and running a hand through his hair. He was dripping, not one part of him dry.

"I'll ask Cook to make you some tea," she said, worried he would catch a chill, and rushed to do so, grabbing a cotton towel on her way back. He stood in the doorway, eyes far away, the water softly dripping from him onto the floor.

She paused at the end of the hall, noticing the rain had soaked through his white shirt so that she could clearly see the shape of his chest and the long, hard plane of his stomach beneath it, and her skin burned hot.

Clearing her throat, she forced herself to walk to him, passing him the towel and then pressing a cool hand to her burning cheek, averting her eyes as he toweled off.

"Thank you," he said, his voice gravelly.

The rain and wind rattled the exterior of the house, and she led him into the parlor, gesturing for him to sit in the armchair in front of the fire.

Cook delivered two steaming mugs of tea, and they both took them in a silence that did not feel like silence, with the elements roaring around them and the fire crackling between them.

"I appreciate your industriousness, but I would rather you not die of pneumonia just to get a little work done on a day like this," she said with a small smile.

He looked up at her, and she drew back from the open anger in his eyes. He noticed at once, swiping a hand over his face and shaking his head. "Sorry," he muttered, taking a long drink of the tea and rubbing the towel into his hair. "I'm not.... This isn't because of you. I just left your neighbor's. The Wilson place. They were robbed yesterday, and a pack of men made off with their horses."

She stiffened at the news. "Do you...." She swallowed, her mouth suddenly dry. "Do you think it's them?" She knew it was foolish to think men would be out in weather like this, whatever the reason, but she couldn't help but look out the large bay windows, as if they would appear against the glass.

"I can't say," he said, his voice tinged with frustration. "Adam and I got there right before the storm began, and Mitchell was already there." He shot her a quick look. "So was Edward. A few other men from town as well, it looked like. But they weren't looking at the tracks or the damage, and they left without letting me talk or looking at anything. Now all that evidence is gone." He gestured at the storm. "Erased."

She stared out the window, her brow furrowed. "What would Edward be doing there?"

"He doesn't live here in town, does he?" Harry asked.

She shook her head. "No, he lives in a small place a few towns over. About a two-day ride, not so far. But Willa told me she had heard he rented a place above the saloon. She asked the innkeeper, and they told her he was paid up for another month."

Harry frowned. "What's keeping him here? He wanted the ranch, but you've made it clear that he can't have it. Why doesn't he go?"

"If he's here, it's because he wants something and expects to get it."

"He and Mitchell tried to talk me into giving him money to buy a little rundown farm on the edge of town," Harry said.

She raised her eyebrows. "And you said?"

"I said it wasn't my money to promise to anyone," he said.

She nodded. The thought of keeping Edward closer, of having him just on the other side of town where he could come by the ranch as he wished, or she would have to see him randomly in town, made her stomach twist.

"He must be planning something. Does he want the ranch so badly?"

May thought on this. "He has always thought he was entitled to it," she mused. "When it became clear my parents were only going to have me, no boys in sight, he was certain that they would leave it all to him. But as far as I know, that was never the plan. My father always planned to leave the ranch to me; he raised me to know how to run it. I'm sure he knew there would be a husband one day to help, but he was never going to pass me over for Edward."

"Did they ever think to marry the two of you?" Harry asked. "A tidy solution for everyone."

She laughed shortly. "Maybe they did, but he made sure that was never a real consideration."

"What do you mean?"

"They used to write, my father and Edward. And one summer, when I was seven and he was twelve, my parents invited him out to stay with us. Maybe that was their intention, to consider him as a marriage partner for me. I can't say for sure. But I do know my mother was already worrying about the lack of eligible men in town and what my prospects would look like." She stopped, looking at Harry for a moment, and then stood. "Here," she said. "Let me show you something."

The task of clearing out her father's office had been slow going, not only because she wanted to read it all, to learn those things about him she had not had the time to learn herself, but also because he had been a meticulous record keeper.

She returned with a thin sheaf of papers and passed them to Harry. "I knew that they had sent Edward home after Mother found him tampering with the food of the ranch hands, but I found this the other day and learned there was even more to it than just that."

Harry scanned the pages quickly, then he looked up. "This is the year he stayed with you?" He gestured to the date, carefully noted at the top of the page.

She nodded.

"Ah," he said. It was a record of accounts, week by week, with the final monthly total tallied at the end of the tidy columns. At the bottom of the final page was a large red circle, denoting a difference in the expected total and the final one, a difference of two hundred dollars. Beside it, in all capital letters, in her father's hand, it said: EDWARD.

Harry looked up at her, frowning.

"Flip it over," she nodded to the pages, and he did.

On the back was a list of things her father had written, from what she could tell, an account of how Edward might have managed to steal this money.

Hay delivery, $1, ten deliveries

General store supply run, $5, eight trips

Ranch hand salary envelope, $20

The list continued that way, some items punctuated with question marks, some more exact, as her father tallied the numbers and the ways that Edward had stolen from them.

Harry lifted his gaze to meet hers, eyebrows raised. "Brazen, isn't he? To not only have done this to begin with, but then to come back now and act as if he is entitled to any of this...." He trailed off, but she could see his fists clench against the pages.

She nodded. "When I found it, I was furious. How dare he? The nerve! I'm quite sure my father would have wanted to press charges, no matter how young he was and how unlikely the law would have been to actually prosecute him, but my mother would have held him back. Out of loyalty to her sister, of course, though they weren't close by that time. But also because that was just the way she did things. Her style was direct and to the point. I imagine she told Edward what they had discovered and to keep the money he had helped himself to, to consider that a final parting gift from this side of the family, and to never come back."

"And he would assume you were too young to know about any of it," Harry said thoughtfully.

"When you put all these pieces together, it shows you what kind of man he is. He has no honor, no desire to build a community or be a valuable part of one."

"He wants what he can't have," Harry said grimly.

"And he'll do anything—anything but work hard to earn it honestly—to get it," she agreed.

"We need him away from here." Harry stood, striding to the window and staring out at the storm, the lightning and thunder had finally passed, leaving behind only heavy, thudding rain. "How do we make him see there's nothing to be gained by him here?"

She joined him at the window. The rain streamed down the glass, but out ahead was a glimpse of lightening sky, a small sign that the storm would soon pass. It was her turn now to place a hand on his, and she did so lightly, carefully, like she would approach a horse who was prone to spook.

"We will figure out a way," she said, not looking at him as he accepted her touch. "We will get him out of here and out of our lives for good, somehow."

Chapter Eighteen

Harry ran his knife along the envelope's edge, splitting the wax seal with a careful hand. The letter inside was brief, just a few lines written in a steady, deliberate hand. Sheriff Walters was a man he had gotten to know over the years, a sharp old-timer with decades of experience and, most of all, a man who always got directly to the point.

Harry,

Mitchell's been noted in five counties in the last eight years. Every place he's been, there's been trouble—robberies, violence, men turning up dead who shouldn't have. Each time, he's returned to Chambers just before folks started asking too many questions. I'd keep your distance.

Harry exhaled sharply through his nose, folding the letter tight and tucking it into his vest pocket. He already knew Mitchell was bad news—he didn't need another sheriff to tell him that. But the fact that trouble had been on Mitchell's heels for years, always slipping away before the noose could tighten.... That meant he was clever. Worse, it meant he was dangerous.

What would send the man working in other towns, making himself known in faraway counties and places when he had a seat and power right here in Chambers?

Harry could only think of a few things that pushed a man like that.

A floorboard creaked behind him.

Harry stiffened, his hand dropping instinctively to the revolver at his hip as he turned.

May stood in the open doorway of the barn, the last light of evening catching the fine stitching on her riding skirt. Her hat sat neatly atop her pinned hair, not a single strand out of place. The sight of her—so composed, so proper—always set something uneasy in him. They had made strides lately, more strides than he would have thought possible, but there was still so much unsaid between them, even now with their honesty on the table.

Whenever he noticed something about her, like the way the skirt cinched in at her waist, the guilt surged up right after, the reminders of Beth.

Even though May could not have been more different from Beth.

She studied him with that sharp, assessing gaze of hers, her gloved hands folded neatly in front of her. "You seem troubled," she observed.

Harry grunted, stepping past the stall where his bay gelding nosed at a feed bucket. "Just a letter."

She didn't move. "From whom?"

He hesitated. She was from here and had likely known Sheriff Mitchell all her life. Adam had described him as a fixture here. Interesting, that the man could maintain such a strong presence here while also being attached to so much trouble elsewhere. Could he trust that May would take his word for it, that there was something wrong with this man? He had a letter that helped validate his concerns, but she didn't know the man who had written it.

"A friend," he said finally. "Sheriff Walters, down in Kansas."

Her brows rose. "Is it about our situation?"

"Not in the way you're meaning."

"What's the purpose of telling me things if you still don't tell me everything?" she asked, exasperation breaking through her controlled exterior.

"I'll tell you what you need to know when you need to know it."

As soon as the words left his mouth, he regretted it. It was a door slamming in her face, and she didn't deserve that. But he was so tired of always being calculating, always trying to stay two steps ahead, never feeling like he could rest easy. He wanted to tell her about Mitchell, but they had just made a slightly uneasy truce. He wasn't ready to wreck that.

She was quiet for a moment, watching him as he grabbed a brush and ran it along the gelding's side, movements brisk, controlled. He could feel her weighing something, calculating. That, too, set something uneasy in him.

His skin prickled, and he wished he was alone in the barn once more. He wasn't fit for company right then. But no matter how hard he worked on this ranch, it still wasn't his home, his property. For a moment, he ached for his little home back east, a place that was all his, where there was nothing to confuse him like this.

Where he could miss his wife in peace.

Where he could take out her memory and hold it tenderly, and miss her without battling the guilt that he was noticing the way another woman looked, or dressed, or laughed, or furrowed her pretty brow when she was thinking about something.

"I came to speak with you about Edward," she said at last.

Harry kept brushing. "What about him?" He was glad for the change in subject. He was tired of oscillating between guilt and longing, frustration and temptation.

146

"I believe we need to take a firmer stance," she said. "Make it clear to him that he has no claim to this ranch, and that he never will."

"Do you have an idea for how to do that?" He was just as eager to get that man out of their lives but had come up with no ideas for how to do so without having a sheriff friend arrest him and lock him up far away. Tempting, but not his style. Not really.

"Yes," she said. "I've been thinking, about what you said about what type of man he is. Men like Edward don't listen to words. They will always be looking for ways to weasel past the rules or sneak through. What they do respond to is strength."

Harry finally turned to look at her. "And what do you propose?"

She lifted her chin, a little glimmer in her eyes that he wasn't sure he liked. "A party."

He frowned. "A what?"

"A party," she repeated. "For Julia. Her birthday is next Sunday, isn't it? I believe we should make an event of it. We can invite the whole town, do the party the way my family used to do parties." She swallowed. "Before. We will show them all how very happy we are here, how solid this marriage is. Edward will see he is outnumbered. That there is no path forward for him here."

Something cold crept up Harry's spine, and his jaw tightened.

"No," he said.

May blinked. "No?"

He turned back to the horse, running the brush down its flank. "We're not bringing the whole town onto the ranch."

"And why not?" she asked, her voice calm but edged with steel. The irritation sparked between them like one of those strikes of lightning from the other day, blue-hot and just as quick to burn you as it was to brighten the world.

"Because it isn't safe," he said shortly. "Not with these bandits sniffing around. Not with Edward scheming in the dark. I won't put you or Julia in danger just to make a statement. We're just as liable to cause a problem as we are to solve this one with your fool cousin."

May tilted her head slightly, regarding him. "Harry," she said evenly, "this is my home. My ranch. My father left it to me, and I will not be told what I may or may not do with it."

"You've made that clear enough," he said. Finally, he turned, stepping closer. His voice lowered. "Not on that day."

A flicker of confusion crossed her face. Then, something like the beginning of understanding began to show on her face.

Her lips parted slightly, and for the first time since he'd met her, she looked unsure.

Harry's hands curled into fists at his sides.

It had been three years—almost four—but the day still remained sharp, a shred of a bullet left inside him, one he could never dig out. Even Evangeline, who had never once dodged a difficult topic, retreated from him on that day.

He shook his head. "I won't have a celebration on the anniversary of my wife's death."

May was silent.

For a long moment, the only sound in the barn was the slow, steady shifting of the horses in their stalls.

Then, Harry turned on his heel and strode past her, out into the evening air, leaving her standing in the dust.

Chapter Nineteen

May stood in the dusty barn, the weight of Harry's words settling over her like a thick, suffocating blanket.

The anniversary of my wife's death.

She had seen many iterations of Harry—strong, stubborn, frustratingly silent. But this was something else. This was grief.

Guilt twisted in her stomach.

She had pressed him, thinking only of Edward, of appearances, of strategy. She had wanted control over a situation that had been slipping further and further from her grasp since the day she agreed to this marriage. But she hadn't considered—hadn't even thought—that there might be something more behind his refusal.

She drew in a slow breath, smoothing her hands over her skirts as she gathered

herself.

Then she turned and stepped out of the barn.

Harry was easy to find.

He sat on the porch steps, forearms resting on his knees, gaze fixed somewhere in the distance. The sky was deepening into dusk, streaked with fading gold and violet. A breeze stirred the dust along the path, ruffling the edges of his shirt.

May hesitated. She had never been good at this—at comforting people. That had always been someone else's job. Hers had been to manage, to oversee, to keep things running smoothly. It was always her mother, or Willa, doing the fluttering and the patting and the soothing. But this wasn't something she could control or fix. It was something she had to face, and neither of them could do it for her.

She stepped onto the porch, the wood creaking beneath her.

Harry didn't move.

"I didn't know," she said softly.

His jaw tightened, but he didn't look at her.

She sat down beside him, leaving enough space between them so as not to crowd him. "If I had known...I wouldn't have suggested it." She bit her lip, one part of this discovery pinching her heart. "And I didn't realize—how soon, how quickly after Julia, she...." The words escaped her, and she lost patience with herself, trailing off as he stared out into the brilliant colors of the evening sky over the plains.

Silence stretched between them.

She clasped her hands in her lap, choosing her words carefully. "Edward has been asking to be invited to dinner." She glanced at him. "I can't keep pushing him away. A gathering with our friends and family might be the only thing that convinces him to leave."

Harry let out a slow breath, shaking his head. "Edward's not the type to take a hint."

"No," she agreed. "But if he's alone in this—if he sees the town standing with us—it might be enough."

Harry didn't answer right away. He sat there, staring out over the land, his hands clasped loosely together. Finally, he exhaled, running a hand over his face.

"I should've been there," he said. His voice was quiet. Rough. "I should've been home."

May frowned slightly. "When?"

He hesitated, then looked at her for the first time since he had stormed out of the barn. There was something raw in his expression, something that made her chest tighten.

"The day Beth died."

She held still, waiting. She had never heard him say her name before, and it struck her, along with the raw pain in his voice.

Harry leaned forward, resting his elbows on his knees. "Back in Columbus, things were pretty peaceful, for the most part," he said, his voice low. "We had trouble now and then, but nothing real bad, nothing like the bigger towns. Mostly, it was just me, and that was more than enough for the work that needed doing. That day, the owner of the general store insisted we talk, saying there'd been vandalism in his store. He told me he was sure they'd be back in his store that night. They were breaking windows, destroying his supplies." His knuckles were white as bone. "So I went. I left her." He swallowed hard, and when he spoke again, his voice was rough. "I left both of them."

May's breath caught.

"It was a trick," he said bitterly. "There was nothing wrong in town. They just wanted me gone. By the time I got back, it was too late."

A chill ran through her. "Julia?" she asked.

"I got back in time for her." His voice was hoarse. "Barely."

May pressed a hand to her throat. "Harry—"

"I was a fool," he said, cutting her off. "I should've known. Should've seen it coming. I was so damn sure I was doing my job, keeping order, protecting people. But I left *her* unprotected." He shook his head. "She paid the price for it."

May's fingers curled in her skirts. The grief in his voice was deep and heavy, years old but still alive beneath the surface. She understood guilt. She understood the weight of choices, the way regret could carve itself into a person.

It wasn't his fault. She was no lawman, but that much was very clear to her. She couldn't find the words to say it, to make him see. "You couldn't have known," she said softly. It wasn't quite right, didn't express what she wanted to say, but it was the best she could come up with in the moment.

Harry let out a short, humorless laugh. "That doesn't change anything."

"No," she admitted. "But blaming yourself doesn't either."

He was quiet for a long moment.

Then, slowly, he exhaled.

May hesitated, then reached out, resting her hand lightly on his forearm. He stiffened slightly at the contact but didn't pull away.

"You were doing your job," she said. "You were trying to protect your town, your people. There is no shame in that. I can't imagine that Beth would have blamed you for doing the job you were dedicated to."

She stumbled slightly over the name but hoped he did not notice. What right did she have to conjure the woman she had never met and speak for her? But still, knowing him, knowing Julia, she knew it to be true.

He turned his head slightly, looking at her. For the first time, she thought he really *saw* her—not as a stranger, not as someone he was responsible for keeping safe, but the real, actual woman she was.

A long breath left his chest.

He nodded once.

If this was the first time he had truly seen her, she was sure this was the first time she had seen the lines in his face ease. Something let go of its hold on him, just a touch.

May released his arm, straightening. "We will have the party," she said. "Not as a celebration of what was lost, but as a way forward. Edward will see that he has no place here, and then we will be done with him."

Harry exhaled again, rubbing a hand over his face. Then, finally, he nodded.

"All right," he said.

May stood. "I'll start making arrangements."

He didn't say anything, but as she stepped back into the house, she could feel the shift between them. It was small, almost imperceptible.

But it was there.

Chapter Twenty

Julia's birthday dawned bright and beautiful, the sun so strong it illuminated and sharpened everything around them, making colors more brilliant. Harry rode out to the far fields before she woke up, mounting his horse while the moon was just beginning to descend.

He had noted a place out west on the ranch that was exploding with wildflowers. He made it out there as the sun rose, spreading golden rays across the dew-dipped heads of flowers of all different types.

Tying up the horse on a low tree branch, giving her room to graze the sweet grass, he patted her nose absently before steeling himself to enter the field.

The smell overwhelmed him at once, instantly, irrevocably bringing Beth to mind. Beth's favorite thing in the world had been flowers. She had worked tirelessly on their little garden, tenderly growing flowers of more types than he could ever keep straight. Wooden cups of blooms sat on every free space in their home, and she would drop petals into her bath and the water she used to wash their clothes.

The scent and sight of flowers had been a foundational part of their home, and he had always kept an eye out for unique blooms when he was away from the farm, loving to bring some home and watch the joy and delight on her face.

Since her death, he had hidden from flowers like a coward, averting his eyes when he passed some at the roadside, flinching when the smell hit him unexpectedly.

But he knew now that it was time to move past that. He needed to, for Julia.

The realization of the ways he was failing Julia had begun with Evangeline, but his conversation with May about Julia's birthday had shown him how, once again, he was letting her down, ruining her childhood, and keeping the precious memories of her mother away from her.

Because what kind of childhood had gone three years without a single birthday celebration?

He screwed his eyes shut, pain and guilt shooting through his gut in equal measure.

But determination won out. He forced himself to take one deep, long breath, filling his nose and lungs with the sweet, overwhelming smell of flowers. Then, he opened his eyes, squaring his shoulders and marching determinedly (but carefully—watching the flowers) through the field. He knew exactly what he was looking for.

Western Wild Roses had been Beth's favorite. She would tuck one of the pink blooms in her hair, and he could picture it so well, even now. Watching the thorns, he picked a small bouquet, tucking them carefully into a flour sack, tying it off with twine, and setting it aside.

Next, Bush Morning Glory. He collected these gently, careful of the delicate petals. While Beth was pregnant, she had talked endlessly about what flowers she wanted to use to celebrate their baby. She had been certain that they were having a girl, and after months of deliberation, she had looked up at him when he had entered the room, still sweaty from birth, holding their tiny, newborn child, and said, "Bush Morning Glory. That's her flower. Deep roots, can grow in the toughest conditions, and so bright and beautiful."

He had nodded, tears in his eyes, barely registering her words as he took in the sight of their baby girl.

They had never had time to collect the flowers for their daughter together, and so he would have to do that now in Beth's place. He should have done it years ago. Her words rang in his ears as he gathered them, oddly prescient and spot-on accurate. Bright, beautiful, adaptive, strong. Those all described their little girl to a tee.

Closing a larger, fuller sack with those, he then turned to one final task. Cowboy's Delight. For May.

He glanced up at the sky. It was brightening, and birds were singing. He needed to get back. Carefully attaching his bags to the horse, he untied her and mounted, staring out once more over the field.

"By God, Bethie," he whispered aloud. "Would you have loved this place."

For a moment, he let all of the pain and longing in, let it wash over him, flood him with all of the feelings he always tried so hard to hide from, until he felt he might drown beneath the weight of it.

Then, he dug his nails into his palms, bringing him out of it and focusing on the day ahead.

"I won't let her down any longer," he said, hoping that Beth could hear him. "It's a new day, a new year for our girl, and we're going to start it off right. We love you, Beth."

Straightening, he scrubbed the emotion from his face, put his hat firmly atop his head, and rode back to the house.

He made it back before Julia had woken, and, stepping lightly, snuck into her room, sitting at the edge of her bed, her bunch of flowers in his hands.

Her hair, wild and unruly curls just like Beth's, fanned around her small head on the pillow beneath her. She looked so relaxed, utterly peaceful, dark eyelashes fluttering as she dreamt. His heart ached with twin feelings of joy and pain. She was growing up so quickly, but she was doing it so very well.

He lifted a finger and brushed her soft, round cheek. Her eyelashes fluttered, and then, her eyes opened. She blinked blearily, and then, as she saw him, her eyes lit up.

"Papa?" she asked, her voice croaky. Then, her eyes fell to the flowers. "Flowers!" She rubbed at her eyes with chubby little fists, bolting upright, her hair a cloud of chaos around her.

"Happy birthday, sweetheart." He proffered the bouquet. For one moment, they both looked at the flowers. Soft, lavender blossoms with long, bright green stems, as he looked at them so close to her, his heart warmed. Beth had been so very right about this.

"For me?" Julia asked in a whisper, looking back up at him.

"For you."

She took them carefully from him and then buried her face in them, smiling in delight before throwing her arms around him. "I love them, Papa."

He pressed his face into her hair, breathing in the scent of her intermingled with the flowers' perfume. "Your mother picked these out for you, way back, before you were even born," he whispered to her, his voice husky. "She knew you would love them, and look, wasn't she right?"

"Right," she agreed, pulling back to stare down at them.

They went down to breakfast together, after Harry tucked one of the blooms behind her ear. May hadn't come down yet, so Julia helped him arrange May's bouquet in a jelly jar at her place setting at the table and then they sat together, digging into the special breakfast Cook had prepared for Julia with gusto.

"My, my, are those pink Johnny cakes?" an amused voice came from behind them.

Harry turned around to see May in the doorway, backlit by the morning sun. She was wearing a dress he had never seen before, a soft yellow with a pink bow tying in at her waist. "Papa, you've got food sitting in your mouth," Julia giggled, pointing her fork at him.

He swallowed hurriedly, coughing a little, as May crossed the room and sat gracefully at her place. She noticed the flowers and raised her eyebrows.

"And what are these?" she asked.

"Papa got some flowers for you too!" May chirped, and then gestured to the one that had tumbled from her ear into one of her riotous curls. "Just like me!"

May's look changed to one of surprise as she turned to Harry. His cheeks heated as he quickly looked back at his plate of food, shoving it around with his fork. "Saw those and thought of you," he said, a bit grumbly if he had to admit. He cleared his throat, took a drink of his coffee, and made eye contact with her. "I hoped they might make you smile."

A smile stretched across her face then, so pure and sweet it made his breath catch in his throat.

"What a lovely surprise." She reached out a hand and touched the edge of one of the petals. "A lovely surprise," she repeated, as if to herself.

The rest of the morning was a blur of party preparation. Harry was sent with strict instructions to ensure the barn was clean, a task he assumed was really meant to get him out from under their feet. He watched from the barn as Willa and May whisked in and out, overseeing the cleaning and the cooking and then disappearing inside to get dressed.

He took that as his own cue to do the same and headed inside, dressing in his nicest coat and hat, shaving carefully in the clean glass mirror in his room, and running a brush through his hair. When he left his room, he ran into Julia leaving hers, dressed in a pink dress with a matching ribbon tying back her now-shining curls. He grinned and tugged at one of them, making Julia giggle.

"Who did your hair?" he asked. "Where's my bedhead Betty?"

"Ms. May did," she said, twirling to show him the small blooms he had chosen for her threaded in the braids.

May had done a good job. Julia's hair was beautiful but still wild, not forced into submission or tugged tightly to be tamed. He chucked her on the chin, and they went downstairs just in time for the first guest to arrive.

An hour later, the front yard of the manor was packed, neighbors from all over Chambers drinking, talking, and laughing. Julia was running around with a pack of kids of all different ages, looking as if she had never had a better day in her life. Lining the porch were baskets and bags, presents on presents, so many he couldn't imagine how they would manage to thank the givers of them all. Amongst all of this, May flitted, freshening glasses, starting conversations, and passing out plates of food.

Harry stayed mostly on the porch, nursing a lemonade and watching the fun. It did his heart good, to hear Julia shriek with laughter, to watch her charm the residents of the town, to watch their children enjoy playing with her. Evangeline had been right; she had needed this.

When his eyes weren't on Julia, they were on May.

The sun tinged her hair gold, and the pink bow around her waist matched the pink flush in her cheeks. She was the consummate hostess, but more than that, she was incredibly beautiful.

He was so focused on May, in fact, that it wasn't until their guests began to leave that he realized Edward had never made an appearance. He stood at the thought, frowning as he scanned the crowd of people.

The butcher's family was calling out happy goodbyes as they made their way down the drive. Willa was crouched in front of May, presenting her with a stack of shadow puppets in the shapes of various animals and people.

"Did you make these?" May asked her over Julia's head.

"Made them myself," Willa boasted, sounding pleased. "Look, here's one of your Papa, and Ms. May, and even one of me!"

Julia crowed over each as she lifted them one by one.

No Edward.

Adam approached then, a bit shyly, and handed over a sweater. "Wife made it," he grunted. "Hope it fits."

The sweater was pink wool, and when Julia tugged it over her head, it fit her perfectly. She jumped up and gave Adam a hug that made his cheeks turn about the same color. He squeezed her back, patted her head, and disappeared quickly into the barn.

Still, no Edward.

They had gone to such pains to make this day mean something not just for Julia, but also for Edward to see. May had said he had been badgering her for an invitation, and yet when he received one, he didn't bother to show? Harry didn't like it. He hadn't thought one party would solve all of their Edward-related problems, but he hadn't anticipated the man to not show up either.

As if his thoughts had conjured him, Edward came flying down the drive atop his horse, one hand holding his hat atop his head as he galloped past a family making their way out on foot, spraying them with a cloud of dust. They coughed and waved their hands in front of their faces, but he didn't spare them a glance, not slowing until he entered the front gate, where he dismounted and strode directly to Julia.

Watching the man approach his daughter set Harry's teeth on edge. Though he had just been looking for Edward and waiting for him to arrive, now all he wanted was the man to be gone. He gritted his teeth, reminding himself that this was the purpose, they just had to get to that point.

"Sorry I'm late," he boomed, as if everyone had been just waiting to hear from him. Heads in all directions turned, conversations coming to a halt. "I had a meeting with my lawyer."

It seemed both threatening and designed to spark questions. Either way, Harry didn't like it.

"Did you bring me a present?" Julia got right to the most important question, and though Harry knew he should chide her, he was too busy biting back a smile.

"Call me Uncle Edward and give me a hug, and we'll just see," Edward said, kneeling down and opening his arms.

Harry's fists tightened, and it was all he could do to keep himself from shoving Edward back. Instead, he watched, breath coming in short, tight gasps, as Julia gave him a thankfully quick, perfunctory hug and said, "Uncle Edward, present, please," with a wide smile.

162

Edward chuckled, ruffling her hair so that the flowers were knocked askew, and then turned back to his horse, rifling in a saddle bag until he lifted out a small wooden box. Julia's eyes went round as she took it from him. Every other gift had been swaddled in a bit of burlap, tied up with simple twine, or not wrapped at all.

This box was well made, the wood thick and heavy, and the sides fitting together so that Julia could remove the top in one easy, fluid motion. Harry, unable to help himself, leaned forward and peered inside.

Julia lifted out a small, intricately made horse. Carved of smooth, deep black wood, it had shining green pebbles for eyes, what looked to be real horsehair woven for its mane and tail, and laid across its back, a perfect miniature saddle blanket with a red and blue crisscrossed design.

Harry's breath caught in his throat at the sight. The blanket, the horse, the eyes. For a moment, the very earth beneath him rocked, and he had to put out a hand on the fencepost to keep himself from staggering back away from it.

It was, to an inch, an exact replica of Beth's favorite mare.

The sound of Julia squealing with delight and thanking Edward came to him as if he were underwater, muffled and far away.

Edward, still kneeling down in front of Julia, looked slowly up at Harry, and as the two men made eye contact, a wide, malicious grin stretched across the length of his face. His eyes danced with the look of a successful prankster, a man who had accomplished what he had set out to do.

Could he—

Harry would not even finish the thought. He turned quickly, striding back inside the manor, closing the front door with care and scrubbing at his face with his hands until the world righted itself once more.

He dragged in a deep breath. Edward was the worst type of fool, but to even think he had modeled a toy horse after Harry's dead wife was madness. Surely, it wasn't even possible that he would know such a thing. How could he have learned? Unless he had seen it somehow. But no, that was impossible. Harry had let himself slip today, leaning into the past, thinking of Beth, remembering her, instead of keeping it all shut up tight inside of him. This was what he got for the effort—memories bombarding him from all over.

He dug his nails into his palms and shook it off.

Whatever Edward was up to, he wasn't about to leave him alone with Julia and May. He pulled himself together and stepped back outside into the thick of it.

Chapter Twenty-One

Even once Harry stepped back outside after presumably gathering himself, he looked pale and hunted. May stepped forward, placing a hand on his arm.

"Will you come help me gather a few extra things for supper?" she asked, hoping he would understand it was a ruse for them to have the chance to speak alone.

He nodded tightly, and she wasn't sure that it was so much because he understood or just because he was so bothered he wasn't thinking straight. She turned to lead them inside but he paused in the doorway, jerking a head back in Julia's direction, where she sat playing with the oddly thoughtful toy from Edward.

May knew what he was asking. "Willa?"

Willa looked up and nodded, moving to sit next to Julia.

May and Harry went inside. She led him to the far edge of the kitchen, away from the hustle and bustle of the dinner preparation, into a quiet nook by a door that led to the outer yard. It was a small space, and this close, she could smell the lemonade on his breath, could see how surprisingly soft his hair looked, and almost automatically, her hand reached out, as if to touch it.

She snapped out of it, pulling her hand back and focusing on him.

"What happened?" she asked, her voice low. "Are you all right?"

He grimaced, and she could see a number of expressions pass across his face as he thought about how to answer her.

He looked at her, and for just a moment, she thought he was going to tell her what he was thinking, open up and let her in.

Behind them, a heavy-bottomed pot was dropped, and his eyes snapped away. When they met hers once more, he was closed up again.

"Nothing," he said. "Sorry. It's just a lot today." He shrugged and gestured outside. "All the people, and the memories and all that. I'll be glad once this dinner is over and Edward leaves."

Steeling herself against the possible rejection, she reached out and took his hand in hers. He looked at her in surprise, but then, to her relief, he relaxed.

His hand was warm, the knuckles thick, calluses ridging them. As his hand circled hers, she marveled at how much smaller hers looked there.

She cleared her throat, internally scolding herself for so many flights of fancy in one afternoon, and when she was hosting a party, no less.

"Wait a little longer," she said soothingly. "The sun will set soon, and everyone will leave. Today has gone perfectly. We have shown the whole town how united we are as a family, and Edward will see that, too, and he will finally leave us alone."

No matter how much calmness she tried to convey, no matter how many times she scolded herself, she could not fight the feelings rising in her at this moment.

May had never been the type to get flustered, but right now, standing this close to Harry, her heart was hammering in a way she wasn't used to. It wasn't fear, nor was it uncertainty. It was something warmer, something that pulled at her, something that made her lean in before she even realized she was moving.

But it was clear Harry was feeling it, too.

He didn't respond, but as his finger began to slowly stroke her hand within his, a surge of lightning bolted so strongly between them that she knew it was impossible that he hadn't felt it, too. It was so strong she wondered if the food in the kitchen behind them, a world away, wouldn't taste burnt.

Harry's eyes flickered to her lips, and just like that, the world outside the two of them ceased to exist. Then, he closed the space between them. His lips brushed against hers, hesitant at first, as if waiting for her to pull away. But she didn't. Instead, she melted into it, pressing forward until the kiss deepened, until the heat between them felt like it could ignite the very air around them.

It felt right. More right than anything had in a long time.

A shiver raced down her spine. Her other hand, which had been curled at her side, lifted without her thinking, fingers brushing the front of his shirt as if to anchor herself. The fabric was warm, and beneath it, she could feel the solid strength of him. This was new, unfamiliar, and yet, it felt like something she had been waiting for without realizing it.

The kiss stole her breath, sent a wave of warmth through her that left her dizzy. There was no hesitation in the way Harry kissed her now, no holding back. It was firm, sure, as if he had made a decision and wasn't turning back. And God help her, but she didn't want him to.

She should have been thinking about what this meant. About the consequences. About why he was here in the first place. But all she could focus on was the way her pulse roared in her ears, the way her body ached to press closer.

May had never been kissed before. There had never been time, never been any men she felt any sort of attraction to, and so much of her life had been focused on running the ranch, on proving herself and never letting anything slip. And yet, here she was, standing in the quiet glow of the fading sunlight, her breath caught in her throat at his nearness and the energy sparking palpably between them.

Then, the door behind them swung open, and a sharp whistle cut through the moment, and they jerked apart as if burned.

May turned quickly, cheeks flushed, only to see Willa standing a few feet away, arms crossed and a smirk playing on her lips. "Well, now," Willa drawled, "if I didn't know any better, I'd say this marriage was real."

May's heart sank, knowing full well that Willa's teasing could easily be misinterpreted. She opened her mouth to respond, to say something—anything—to brush it off, but before she could, Edward appeared behind her.

Edward leaned back against the bottom step, slow and deliberate, the look on his face one of smug satisfaction. "I knew it," he said, his voice dripping with triumph. "I knew all along that you were lying to me. Silly, silly little May."

May glanced at Harry, who had already straightened, his expression unreadable. She could feel the shift in the air, the way something delicate had suddenly turned into something dangerous.

"Willa was only joking," May said quickly, stepping forward. "You're reading too much into what she said; that's just the way she is. Always playing for the next laugh." She shot a look at Willa, whose face had turned white and panicked, and she nodded so quickly her cheeks shook.

"Of course I was joking!" she said, her voice reedy thin and squeaking.

Edward tilted his head, amusement dancing in his eyes. "Am I reading too much into it? Because from where I'm standing, it sure seems like I just walked in on a happy little newlywed moment." He laughed. "And yet! Isn't our Willa just a hoot? She made sure instead of seeing that, I saw the truth."

Harry exhaled through his nose, clearly working to keep his temper in check. "Believe what you want, Edward. What you think doesn't change a thing."

Edward chuckled easily, as if he had just won some unseen battle. "Oh, I'll believe what I want, all right. And I think I'll be paying my lawyer a visit. Seems like I ought to stick around town a bit longer." He went down the stairs and made to go before turning again to face them, still smiling. "You know, you really almost had me." He wagged a finger at May like she were a naughty child caught red-handed. "You just about had me." He shook his head, laughing to himself, and with that, he rounded the corner and left, leaving May standing there with her stomach in knots.

"My God, May. Harry," Willa gasped. "I'm so...I'm so sorry." Her voice was trembling, and she wrung her hands at the bottom step. "I can't believe I did that," she stammered, but May interrupted her by walking down the stairs and pulling her into a tight hug.

"It's all right," she said, rubbing Willa's back. "It's not your fault that Edward is the way he is."

She wasn't lying; it wasn't Willa's fault, but why had she made a joke like that, in this place, on this day? Of all days? She could have cursed, but she swallowed the anger and the what-ifs plaguing her mind and forced herself to remember what was important. Willa had been there with her through everything. She could be forgiven this mistake.

"Our problem is with Edward," Harry said, his voice hard. "Not with you. It was an honest mistake."

Willa took a deep, shuddering breath, and she and May pulled apart. May made herself smile as warmly as she could manage at her, knowing Willa would be searching her face for any sign of distress.

"I am sorry," she said, looking anxiously from May to Harry.

"It was a long shot today would have really sent him running, anyhow," Harry said. "It didn't feel right, having him here as a guest. I had a bad feeling about today and how it was going to go." He shot a quick smile at Willa, and May saw her friend relax a touch.

Willa let out a low whistle, her laugh a bit watery. "Well, that went about as bad as it could've."

May swallowed hard, looking up at Harry. Their kiss was forgotten now, replaced by something heavier. She didn't know what Edward's next move would be, but she knew one thing for certain.

Whatever game Edward thought he was playing, they had just stepped right into the middle of it.

Chapter Twenty-Two

The morning air had a weight to it, thick with the remnants of yesterday's events and something else, something invisible but no less oppressive. Harry felt it the moment he stepped downstairs, and he knew May did, too. She was already at the dining room table, sitting stiff-backed at the table, fingers curled around a cup of coffee she hadn't touched.

She looked up when he entered, and though she didn't say anything at first, her eyes told him enough. She was worried. The truth was that he was, too. Edward knew too much, and it had become very clear to them both that he wasn't going to walk away from them or the ranch.

Harry poured himself a cup and leaned against the bar on the wall opposite her. "You're thinking too hard about this," he said, keeping his voice steady. "There's nothing illegal about a marriage of convenience. We don't owe anyone an explanation, least of all your no-good cousin."

May exhaled sharply, shaking her head. "You think Edward's going to let it be that simple? He looked like a cat that had just caught a mouse last night."

She bit her lip, glancing behind her and then lowering her voice. "I just can't believe Willa saying that. I feel I owe you an apology, for the behavior of my friend." She straightened, the stiff grace returning once more along with her normal tone of voice. "I apologize."

Harry fought the urge to laugh. He had thought of a number of words to describe May since meeting her: strong, elegant, formidable, beautiful. But for the first time, he found himself assigning a description he wouldn't have thought possible:

adorable. It was a thought he would like to come back to another day.

He took a slow sip of his coffee, choosing his words carefully. "Edward likes to play games. He likes to see people squirm. But at the end of the day, he's got no leg to stand on. If he thought he could use this against us, he would have done it already."

May wasn't convinced, and truth be told, neither was he. Edward wasn't stupid, and he didn't seem like a bluffing man, either. He had something in mind; Harry just didn't know what it was yet.

He had stayed up much of the previous night considering different ways Edward might try and steal what was not rightfully his. What could a lawyer do if there was no law they were breaking? His thinking had amounted to little, and he had decided they needed to see a lawyer of their own, to figure out what could and could not happen.

Before either of them could say more, a firm knock sounded at the front door.

Harry exchanged a look with May. Her fingers tightened around her coffee cup. He set his down, straightening as he moved toward the door.

It was too early to be a normal social call.

The moment he opened it, his stomach twisted.

Sheriff Mitchell stood on the porch, hat in hand, his expression unreadable. Harry still didn't know very much about the man, but he did not imagine he was the type to do much of the dirty work of the job himself. If this were a regular sort of call, or something simple or tedious, he would have sent one of his men here to deal with it.

The fact that he had come himself did not bode well.

"Sheriff," Harry said, keeping his voice even. "What brings you by?"

Mitchell nodded in greeting but didn't smile. "Morning, Harry. I've got some questions for you and your wife." He looked around Harry's shoulder, his sharp eyes sweeping the entryway. He smiled then, revealing a mouthful of sharp teeth, one gold tooth winking from the right side. "I'll want you to remember that it's important that you answer truthfully," he paused, as if speaking about something delicate. "In case you've forgotten that since your time in law enforcement."

Harry didn't let his face betray anything, but that twisting in his gut tightened. He didn't like this. Not one bit. But refusing to let the sheriff in would only make them look worse. And Mitchell didn't seem to be the sort of man who took well to any type of refusal.

He stepped aside. "Come on in."

Mitchell stepped inside and followed Harry down the hall to the dining room, nodding toward May as she rose from the table. "Ms. May."

"Sheriff," she returned, her voice steady despite the way she gripped the back of her chair.

Harry moved to stand beside her in a quiet show of solidarity. "What's this about?"

Mitchell took his time answering, removing his hat and dusting it off as if he were still deciding how to go about this. Then, he looked up. "Edward Allen came to see me last night. He told me he had a few concerns about the nature of your marriage." He scanned the table, eyebrows rising dramatically at the spread of fruit, breads, and coffee. "Maybe you'd allow me to take a seat? Perhaps a cup of coffee for an old friend of your father's?" This he directed at May, who went rigid beside Harry.

Harry's fists clenched at his sides, fury burning a path through his veins, but he forced himself to stay silent. It was clear the man was purposely insulting May, trying to rile them both up at once. He wouldn't fall into that trap.

"Of course," May said stiffly, stepping forward and gesturing to a seat. "How do you take your coffee?"

Mitchell walked past the seat she indicated, sitting instead at the head of the table, where Harry's own cup of coffee already sat, still steaming and hardly touched.

May lifted the cup of coffee and passed it to Harry, her motions managing to communicate disapproval for his lack of manners even as she stayed silent. She prepared him a cup, and Mitchell took it, breathing it in with a gusty sigh before taking a drink.

"My, that's a good cup," he said, smacking his lips.

May's nose wrinkled, but by the time she was seated and wrapping her hands around her own cup of coffee, her face was impassive.

Harry spoke, eager to get to the point and have this over and done with. "And what concerns would those be?"

Mitchell studied him. "He claims your marriage isn't legitimate. That it was done under false pretenses." He looked over at May. "Or that perhaps his dear, sweet cousin was coerced into something she didn't want."

May's face tightened, and her lips thinned into a straight line. "Allow me to ease your mind, Sheriff. I went into this marriage willingly and of my own free will. There is no reason for him to be concerned about that." The extra heat that smoked from her final word had Harry turning quickly to look at her. What did that mean?

Mitchell smiled at her. "Now, I can't take that for the truth while you sit here across from the man accused of the coercing, can I?"

"I'll ride in tomorrow and tell you one-on-one at your office," she said, and her tone turned sugar-sweet as she continued. "Unless you're not sure about your ability to protect me if that were to be the case?"

Harry bit back a smile. May was always able to say the right thing at the right moment, the kind of thing that would come to someone hours later, when they were alone in the dark, cursing that they hadn't thought of it to say in the moment.

Mitchell nodded, his tone turning short. "You do that." He turned back to Harry. "But that's not the only concern."

Harry scoffed. "It's a legal marriage. Signed and witnessed. There's nothing false about it."

"He says it was arranged strictly for financial gain." The sheriff's voice remained level, but Harry caught the careful way he watched them. "And that's where things get tricky. See, the law doesn't much care why two people marry, so long as they do it lawfully. But if one party can prove fraud—if a person were to be misled, deceived, or coerced—well, then it becomes a matter for the courts to handle."

May's knuckles were white where they gripped the chair. "That's ridiculous. No one was coerced. We both agreed to this marriage."

"And there's no deception?" Mitchell asked, arching a brow. "Nothing either of you might've omitted?"

Harry didn't like the way he said that. Like he was giving them an opportunity to slip up. He knew a trap when he saw one, and Mitchell had just put out just enough rope for him to hang himself if he wasn't careful.

He forced a casual shrug. "We're newly married, Sheriff. We're figuring things out like any couple would. If Edward's got sour grapes over it, that's his problem. Anything that comes up now is between man and wife, as it should be."

Mitchell watched him for a long moment, then nodded slowly. "I figured you'd say that. Let me give you one more chance to answer me straight. If there's anything you're not telling me, best to clear it up now."

Silence hung heavy between them. May's breathing was steady, but Harry could feel the tension rolling off her.

"Anything like what?" Harry asked, his anger finally getting the better of him. "What we had for supper yesterday? What my bedclothes look like? That's a mighty large circle you're drawing there, Sheriff."

Mitchell laughed. "I think I'll be asking the questions from here on out, Mr. Danvers."

Harry clenched his fists under the table, forcing himself to stay calm as Sheriff Mitchell leaned back in his chair, a smug grin stretching across his face. The man had the air of someone who knew he had the upper hand and was enjoying it far too much.

"So tell me again," Mitchell drawled, tapping his fingers against his belt. "When exactly did the two of you tie the knot? Was it before or after her parents passed?"

In a town this size, there's no way Mitchell didn't know the answer to that question. Harry would have bet he had even attended their funerals. But if this was how he wanted to play it, then fine. Harry would play, and though it had been a long time, he had not forgotten the rules.

Harry kept his voice even. "After."

Mitchell raised an eyebrow. "Convenient timing."

"What are you getting at?" Harry asked.

Mitchell let out a short laugh. "Oh, just that a grieving woman suddenly getting hitched right after her parents die seems like a strange coincidence. Must've been a whirlwind romance."

May leaned forward, her cheeks blazing. "It's not a crime to get married when we did."

Mitchell turned his sharp gaze on her. "That depends. If a person misrepresents themselves to gain property, well, some might call that fraud. And fraud is very much a crime." He looked back at Harry. "It's also a crime to arrange for an accident to occur so that one can marry into a large, high-earning ranch."

Harry felt like a freight train had smashed into him. Was that where this was heading? Something cold settled in his stomach.

He had prided himself, in his time as sheriff, on doing everything he could to make sure the only men he put into jail were guilty. But he had heard tell of many other sheriffs who weren't so careful, of men who lost decades of their lives to crimes they hadn't committed. He couldn't imagine a worse fate than wasting away without being able to touch his little girl. With May being saddled with a branded criminal.

He was shaken, but he did his best not to show it.

"That's not what happened," he said.

Mitchell leaned forward, lowering his voice as if they were conspiring together. "Then you won't mind clearing things up, will you? Let's see, you two got married after her parents died, right? But how long did you know each other before that?"

Harry and May exchanged a glance. The sheriff was digging, hoping to trip them up.

"A few months," May said quickly.

Harry tried not to flinch. He realized now they would likely be better off just being honest. They could show the sheriff the advertisement she had put in the paper, show him the letters they had written back and forth to one another. They had evidence to back up the truth, though he could try and skew it to mean what he wanted it to.

But it was too late now. If he didn't back May up, it would only make them look more suspicious. He nodded.

Mitchell made a face like he was unimpressed. "Only a few months, huh? And yet you knew you wanted to get married? Seems like a rush. Most folks take their time with that sort of thing."

"Not always," Harry said flatly. "Sometimes, a man knows what he wants."

Mitchell chuckled, shaking his head. "Sure, sure. So tell me this, Harry. Where exactly did you propose? I'm sure a man like you did something real special for a lady like May."

May sucked in a quiet breath. They hadn't discussed anything like this. Harry shot her a quick glance before saying, "By the creek. Near the cottonwoods."

Mitchell hummed. "Romantic spot. Funny, though. I asked around town, and no one remembers you two spending much time together before the wedding. Mighty strange, don't you think?"

May crossed her arms. "We weren't parading around town, if that's what you mean. Not everyone flaunts their business."

The sheriff smirked. "Mhm. And yet, Edward seems to think otherwise. He claims you deceived him and the rest of the town. That he had a right to this ranch, and you schemed to keep it from him." He folded his hands atop his belly, looking as easy a man enjoying a drink on a summer evening. "He thinks your parents wanted him to have the ranch and you to be his wife, and for it to pass down through that bloodline the two of you would then create." His eyes glimmered, and Harry knew before he spoke that whatever came out of the man's mouth next was going to be the lowest blow he could muster. "That little girl you've got up there is sweet and all, but what if you two don't make a natural-born child? It passes on to some girl child that has not a drop of blood in the Allen line?" Mitchell tsked. "Doesn't sound to me like what your father would have wanted, little May."

The blow was even lower than Harry had imagined, but he was grateful he had prepared himself for it. His mind reeled as his thoughts looked for a place to land. What had he brought his daughter into by taking her to this place?

May's face flushed with anger. "Edward is a liar," she snapped.

Mitchell held up a hand. "Maybe. But he's a known quantity. I know Edward. I know the Allen family, and I know you. Harry and his child are strangers to us. I believe it is worth investigating what he's doing here. I intend to see this through until I can be sure that our town is protected from any sort of criminal." He smiled at Harry and then turned back to May.

"And you, Miss May, are just a woman trying to hold on to land that some folks think shouldn't belong to you." He smiled, slow and condescending. "Now, I'm not saying I believe Edward, but I do have a duty to look into things. So, here's what's going to happen. You two have twenty-four hours to come down to my office and make a statement. Set things straight. Or...." He let the word hang in the air with a genteel little shrug, the implication clear.

May swallowed hard, her hands trembling at her sides. Harry stood then. They had had enough.

From upstairs came the sound of Julia's feet. He wanted this man gone before she came down for her breakfast.

He moved forward, stepping between May and Mitchell. "We'll be there." His voice was firm and brooked no argument.

Mitchell tipped his hat with a smirk. "Good. I sure would hate for this to get messy." He turned and walked out, leaving behind the scent of tobacco and something oily, leaving behind a silence so thick Harry could hear the ticking of the clock on the wall.

May let out a slow, measured breath, then turned to him. "He's not going to let this go. Neither of them are. I don't know what's in all this for Sheriff Mitchell, but there's something he wants, and he's out to get it."

Harry raked a hand through his hair. "No. They aren't going to let it go. But we knew that already."

She crossed her arms, pacing a few steps before stopping, looking out the window as Mitchell climbed atop his horse. "What do we do?" He wasn't sure if she was asking him or asking herself.

Harry looked toward the door, jaw tightening. "We stay ahead of him. If Edward's looking for a fight, we make sure we're ready."

Chapter Twenty-Three

May had always prided herself on her strength in difficult situations. It was the way she had been raised. Her father had always told her, no matter the circumstance, to keep your back straight and your chin up.

The closest she had come to failing was after losing both of her parents that terrible day. She had gotten through it.

And then she had thought managing the day-to-day operations of the ranch had been the hardest thing she would have to deal with.

Now she was looking at a chance of losing the ranch her parents had given their lives to working on, had meticulously set up for her to inherit, that had been passed down from her father's grandfather.

To Edward, who would squander it. He would strip it down and sell it in pieces or run it into the ground. What would happen to Adam, to the staff that felt like family and had lived and worked here for decades? The thoughts and questions made her feel as if she might collapse beneath the weight of them, and she could not bear a moment longer in the house, surrounded by the things that her parents had so dearly loved.

As Harry turned to help Julia get her breakfast, she moved as quickly and unobtrusively as she could down the hall and, once through the front door, began to run, her heart pounding so hard it nearly drowned out the sound of her own ragged breath. The rising sun cast long shadows across the ranch, painting everything in gold and deep purple, but she barely noticed. Her feet carried her straight to the corral, to one place that had always been her refuge.

Storm, her favorite horse, lifted his head as she approached, ears twitching forward. She barely managed to unhook the gate before she was at his side, pressing her face into his strong, warm neck. The scent of hay and sweat filled her nose, grounding her even as the world around her spun wildly out of control.

Tears spilled hot down her cheeks. "They can't take it, Storm," she whispered into his shining coat. "This ranch is mine. My parents built it with their hands. I won't let them take it from me."

She felt the horse shift, his large, muscular body steady and sure beneath her touch. For a moment, she imagined he understood, that he knew the weight pressing on her chest.

But he was a horse, and she was a woman with no family, her only ally a man she hardly knew from Adam. Kissing Storm's velvety nose, she stepped back, sinking down against the fence post and dropping her head into her hands.

A scuff of boots scraping the dirt outside of the corral made her tense. She didn't need to turn around to know who it was.

"May." Harry's voice was softer than usual, stripped of the iron she had come to expect. "I won't let any of that happen."

She sniffed, straightening, but didn't turn to face him. "How? How do you stop something like this? Edward's got Mitchell wrapped around his finger. He's already turning the law against us." She shook her head. "We have no idea the lengths they will go to, or the connections they have to make things happen. We're alone, Harry."

Harry stepped through the gate and moved to crouch beside her, resting a hand on her shoulder. "We fight. We prove them wrong. I won't let them take what's yours." He put a finger beneath her chin and lifted it so that her eyes had to meet his. The surety in his blue eyes took her breath away. "I promise you, May. I'm going to take care of you. Of this. If you believe anything, please believe that."

May swallowed hard, finally turning to look at him. He was so steady, so sure. She wanted to believe him, wanted to let some of his certainty seep into her bones. But fear still gnawed at her. And she had seen his face, back during their conversation with Mitchell.

He had looked afraid.

Before she could respond, hoofbeats pounded down the drive, a rider coming in quickly. They exchanged glances, and May rose, moving to the gate and stepping through, shielding her eyes against the sun to try and see who was approaching the ranch with so much urgency.

"You don't think—" she started, but before she could complete the thought, she recognized the rider from their stance. "It's Willa," she said, and she was running now, through the gate, down the dirt path, to the place where the front drive leading into the ranch would meet the fence line.

Her heart was in her throat as she ran. Willa was many things, but she was not one for speed. Everything she did, she did slowly, more focused on making the people around her laugh than accomplishing anything in a timely manner. Besides that, May knew her to be afraid of galloping.

If she were galloping in now, something was badly wrong.

Harry's boots sounded behind her, and she had a flash of gratitude that he was here with her, that whatever they were about to face, they would face together.

Willa shouted something, but they couldn't hear it over the sound of her horse's hooves. She slowed the horse as she approached them, turning so that she was moving right toward them instead of the front door as she spotted them waiting for her.

She was dismounting before the horse came to a full stop, her foot slipping out of the stirrups so that she half fell out of the saddle. May rushed forward and caught her as she fell, stopping her from landing flat on the ground, but stumbled herself under the weight of her friend.

At once, strong arms circled behind her, lifting both her and Willa up with ease. Harry reached around, steadying them both, and May was in his arms, pressed back against his chest, with the weight of Willa in front of her.

For just a second, she leaned back against him, enjoying the feeling of his strength at her back, the feeling of being nearly weightless.

And then Willa scrambled to stand, her chest heaving, and May reached for her friend's hands, moving away from Harry.

"What is it?" she demanded. "What's happened?"

"Joseph—" she gasped. "Joseph—"

"My God, Willa, spit it out!" May half-shouted, wild with fear now.

Harry put a calming hand on her arm as he stepped past her, then put a hand on Willa's shoulder, crouching a little so that he could look into her eyes.

"All right," he said, as if he were soothing a wild horse. "Everything is all right. You're here now. We will help you with whatever it is. Take a deep breath."

She stared at him, sucking in air, and then another.

"There you go. Once more. Go on."

Willa released a loud, shuddering sigh and then straightened, pressing a hand to her chest. "Joseph sent me here," she said, her voice still gasping, but steadier now. "We were robbed last night." She looked at May. "They tore apart his office; all of his records and books are in pieces. And the gold—all of the gold." She swallowed hard. "It's gone."

May could feel Harry stiffen, and she knew his mind would be the one at a full gallop now. She asked the question she knew he would want to ask. "What about your horses?" she said. "Did they take them?"

Willa did a double-take. "The...horses? I-I hadn't checked the barn fully. Puff is right up in the first stall. Joseph sent me here for Harry, so I just came as quickly as I could."

"Me?" Harry asked. "Why not the sheriff?"

Willa scoffed. "I don't trust that man, and neither does Joseph. Joseph has long said something stunk in regards to Mitchell and his cadre."

This was news to May. She hadn't had the chance to tell Willa about their visit with Mitchell that morning. But they didn't have time to dig into that now.

Harry was wasting no more time. "You two get inside." He looked at May. "Stay inside today. Don't let Julia go wandering or get out of your sight. I'm going to get Adam and have him sit up in front of the house with his gun and keep watch." He turned back to Willa. "Stay here. I'll go to Joseph as soon as I get Adam."

Willa nodded, and May could feel the relief rolling off of her in waves. She wrapped a tight arm around her and turned her toward the house. "Come, I'll get you some coffee and something to eat." Before they made it a few steps, she turned to say one last thing to Harry.

"Please," she said, surprising herself with the depth of emotion in her voice. "Be safe."

He locked eyes with her, and she could sense the things still unsaid between them. For a moment, she wondered about how they might have proceeded without all of the things that had plagued them since the start of their union. If they had had the time to get to know one another, to court, or even just take a walk on a cool evening, where would they be now?

But what surprised her was that even though they had missed out on sharing those types of sweet, simple moments, if she had the choice, she wouldn't want to change it.

Harry put his hat on and nodded at her, his jaw set. "Watch out for Julia."

She turned back to the house, and he turned to the barn, and they separated, each with their own missions to accomplish.

Chapter Twenty-Four

Harry rode hard to the Carter farm. From studying town maps, he knew exactly where it was. He had marked it after meeting them, and had meant to ride out, get to know Joseph better, and take a look at their own farm's borders and boundaries, to do what he could to help them protect their farm as well.

But he had been too wrapped up in his own life, and look what had happened.

Before, he had been the type of man who always knew what came next and what type of work would be required of him to get it done. He hadn't let anything slip. Until he had. And those consequences lasted still to this day.

He gritted his teeth, letting the weight of that settle as he rode.

It still wasn't full daylight as he approached their farm, a fact that struck him. For how early it was, this had been a remarkably eventful day. He hoped it didn't continue to be that way.

The Carter farm was large and sprawling, with hundreds of heads of cattle grazing in their fields and three barns that he could spot just from the drive, but the house itself was small and relatively modest.

The morning light cast long shadows over the land, making the broken window at the front of the house stand out starkly against the white frame. He swung down from his horse, tightening his jaw as he took in the damage. Whoever had broken in hadn't been subtle.

Joseph met him at the steps, his face set in a hard frown. They had only met twice, but even so, Harry could pick out the lines of worry creasing his forehead.

They greeted one another, shaking hands.

"I'm sorry," Harry said directly. "I hope I can help."

"Thank you for coming," Joseph said, his grip tight. "I'd hate to be doing this alone."

"Show me what happened," Harry said, keeping his voice even.

Joseph nodded and led him inside. The office was in shambles—drawers yanked out, papers scattered, furniture overturned. The window on the far wall had been shattered inward, leaving glass shards on the floor. Harry crouched down, running his fingers over the splinters of wood where the frame had been forced open.

"They knew exactly where to look," Joseph said, his voice tight with anger. "They didn't waste time on any other parts of the house." He pointed out of the doorway. "Our bedroom is across the house, about as far as you can get from here. We didn't even wake up. What a fool I am, to have slept through being robbed blind." He gave a harsh laugh. "But they didn't leave this room, far as I can tell. All they wanted was the gold."

"You and Willa are safe, and that's all that matters." Harry tried not to let his own history color his words, but it was difficult, even these years later. What he would have given if those men that night had just taken his horses and left his family behind, safe in their beds.

Harry stood, surveying the wreckage. He could practically see the scene play out in his mind. Someone slipping in under the cover of darkness, moving with certainty, knowing exactly what they were after. This wasn't a random burglary. It was planned. And that made it all the more troubling.

"Have you seen anyone suspicious around the farm lately?" He was thinking of the horse salesman who May had run off from their ranch.

Joseph hesitated, then exhaled sharply. "Sheriff Mitchell came by," he said in surprise, as if the thought had just occurred to him. "Just a few days ago, actually."

Harry could see the gears turning in Joseph's head. He had just heard Willa say that both of them distrusted Mitchell, but he still wanted to proceed with caution. He was just two steps from being a complete stranger to them, and Mitchell had been a foundational part of the town for decades. He let Joseph think for a minute, and then asked the question as casually as he could manage.

"What did he want?"

Joseph's voice was trembling when he answered, whether out of fear or anger or something else, Harry wasn't sure. "He...he said there had been trouble in the area of late. He said crime was up in Chambers, alluded to some reasons that might be the case, like strangers come to town." Harry filed that tidbit of information away to consider for later, but he didn't like the sound of any of this. Joseph went on. "He said he was doing his due diligence. Blast it, Harry. He asked me what kind of assets we had."

"He what?" Harry's pulse sped up. He had known something fishy was going on, could smell it in the air like a storm headed down the pass, but this—this was beyond the pale.

Joseph started pacing the room now, raking his hands through his thin blonde hair. His eyes took on a wild look. "He asked what we had here in the house of value. And I answered him! Told him plain we kept some gold here, probably made it clear somehow, though I don't know how I did, that it was here in my office. I'm a fool, by God. I'm a stupid, stupid fool." He dropped into a hunch, pressing his hands to his face, and his shoulders heaved with dry, tearless sobs.

Harry kneeled beside him, gripping the man's forearm until he looked up, panic streaking his face. "That's enough of that now, Joseph." He kept his tone firm but lacking judgment. "I can only imagine what you're feeling, but blaming yourself gets us nowhere. Let's look at the facts, and we will figure this out. I'm in this with you now, and I won't stop until we've found the men responsible for this." The moment the words left his mouth, he regretted them.

They had come back to haunt him before.

He shook it off and continued, "Besides, if this went down the way I'm beginning to think, I don't know that you could have avoided it. Say you didn't tell him what you had. Say he wasn't able to pick up that it was here in the office. Then what? You think old Mitchell would have just rode on to the next farm and asked them until someone told him what was what? No, he came here because he knew you had gold already, and he wanted it. So he comes back without knowing where it's at but knowing it's here. So now, he's searching the house. You hear something, or maybe Willa does, and come to investigate. Someone takes a bullet."

Joseph's face went white.

"So be glad. You lost some gold, but you have your safety. Willa's. Everything else can be replaced. Or found."

Then, he remembered his plan to play it careful and quickly added, "If it was Mitchell who did this, I mean."

Joseph barked a laugh. "I don't have a doubt in my mind that it was that no-good, crooked backstabber of a lawman who went and did it. So, let's dispense with the niceties and get down to brass tacks."

Harry decided right then and there that he liked Joseph. He liked him a lot.

Mitchell was dirty; he was sure of it, but knowing it and proving it were two different things. He needed evidence, something solid enough to expose him and anyone working with him.

It irked him, deep inside, like a splinter digging into his gut, to see a fellow sheriff so blatantly abuse his power. For a sharp, surprising moment, Harry found himself missing his time wearing the badge, a thought he hadn't thought he would ever have again.

He clapped Joseph on the shoulder and stood, reaching down and pulling him up to stand, as well. "Now, let's continue. We've got a lot of work to do, and it's just me and you, so there's not a minute to waste. Did anyone see anything? You or your men?" Harry asked. "Tracks? Strange horses nearby?"

Joseph shook his head. "It rained hard last night. Any tracks there might have been were washed away by morning."

Harry clenched his jaw. That made things harder. He walked back toward the broken window, scanning the ground outside. The mud had dried some since the storm, but it was still soft enough that a careful boot print might remain if he looked hard enough.

Avoiding the glass, he climbed into the sill and dropped down on the other side of the window so that he was outside in the dirt, taking care to land in a thick patch of grass where any prints would be impossible to spot anyway.

His eyes swept the area, searching for anything out of place. A few feet from the window, he spotted a faint impression in the mud—a half-worn boot print. It wasn't much, but it told him one thing: Whoever had done this wasn't careful enough to cover their tracks completely. He crouched down, studying it. The boot had a distinctive worn heel, a mark that could help him if he found a match.

"What are you thinking?" Joseph asked, watching him closely. He was leaning out of the window.

"I'm thinking Mitchell has been running a scheme for a while," Harry said. "I just don't know how deep it runs yet."

Joseph exhaled heavily. "We have no proof, though."

"Not yet," Harry agreed. He turned back to the other man. "I need a list of the trustworthy men in town. Anybody who isn't under Mitchell's thumb."

Joseph frowned but nodded. "I can put something together. You'd be surprised; there are more of us than you might think. A lot of people in town have been done bad by him at one time or another. Although, maybe that won't surprise you to hear at all."

Harry gave him a firm look. "Be careful who you talk to. If Mitchell's got men working for him, they'll be listening, and they'll know to be watching you."

Joseph crossed his arms. "What are you planning to do?"

"A lot. Right now, I don't know anything. I don't know why he's doing all this or how he's gotten away with it for so long. I don't know what kind of connections he has outside of Chambers. But we've got a little bit to go on now. And I'm thinking something has changed; he's desperate, or he's just grown greedier. Why rob a man from his town, and so brazenly? A child could have put the pieces of this puzzle together. Does he feel so untouchable, or is he just being stupid?" Harry shrugged. "And then, when I've got enough to bring him down, I will."

Joseph's expression darkened. "That's dangerous talk."

"I know," Harry said. "But if someone doesn't do something, he's just going to keep taking from people. And next time, it might be more than gold alone."

A heavy silence stretched between them. Joseph finally gave a small nod. "I'll get you those names."

Harry tipped his hat and headed back to his horse. He was anxious to get back to the ranch, back to Julia. And May. He trusted Adam, but now he wished he had set more of the ranch hands to guard the house.

There were too many questions, too many concerning pieces here. Whatever was going on, he and his were right in the middle of it.

As he swung into the saddle, he glanced once more at the broken window. He had asked Joseph why now, but to him, the answer seemed clear. Mitchell thought he was untouchable. It was time someone proved him wrong.

His thoughts churned. If Mitchell was behind this, then it meant he had men working with him. Men willing to break into the houses of their neighbors and fellow townsmen, willing to steal from hardworking families and intimidate people into silence. That kind of corruption didn't start overnight. How long had it been going on? And how deep did it run?

Harry thought of May, back at the ranch, worrying over their own troubles. If Mitchell was desperate enough to steal, he was desperate enough to do worse. The threat to her and Julia loomed in the back of his mind like a storm cloud. He clicked at his horse and leaned forward, preparing to set a quick pace back to the ranch.

He hadn't made it very far down the drive when another rider appeared, coming toward him. With the day he had had, it was a surprise to see another man on his horse riding at such a relaxed, easy pace. The man waved, smiling broadly as their horses approached. Harry recognized him from the birthday party; it was the butcher. But he had forgotten his name.

"Ah, how nice to run into you here!" he called. "Harry, right?" He pulled his horse to a stop, and Harry responded in kind. "Getting to know Joseph, are you? You can't go wrong with a friend like that. He's as fine a man as they come." He leaned in close, as if he were going to share a secret and faux-whispered, "Although, even if he wasn't a good man, I'd be friends with him anyway, just for access to Willa's pies! Best in the state, probably best in the West!" He laughed, a big, booming laugh that nearly made Harry flinch, his nerves still so on edge, and patted his large stomach. "I could stand to eat less of them, though. But not today! I'm here to pick up a few she made for me special."

Joseph's voice came from behind them. "William," he said. "You heard?" He strode toward them quickly.

"Heard what?" William looked between the two men, and then back at Joseph. He did a double-take, and the easy smile disappeared from his face. "You look terrible. What's happened?"

Joseph looked down the road. "Come in, and I'll tell you everything. I'm glad you're here." He looked at Harry. "I'm sure you're eager to be off back to the ranch, but can you stay? I made up that list already, and I can send one of my ranch hands into town to collect them. Here's one now." He nodded at William. "The rest won't take long to come, I'm sure. You can meet everyone, and we can talk about a plan."

Harry looked down the road. He itched to lay eyes on Julia and May, but that was his past talking. Mitchell had been there just that morning; the odds were low that he would come back again so soon. He had said they had 24 hours to come in and give their statements. He would be in town now, preparing for them.

He needed to be careful. He needed to be smart. This couldn't wait.

He nodded at Joseph in agreement and turned his horse back around. He couldn't drop everything just to set his anxious mind at ease. It was important to get all of this done, to do it all right.

Because if he made the wrong move, they could all lose everything.

Chapter Twenty-Five

May's eyes kept sliding back to the lock on the front door. She had locked it, had checked it, and after checking it again, had forced herself to leave it and go into the parlor with Julia, where she sat now.

They were on the floor together, crouched over a pile of dried-out corn cobs and silky husks, twine, buttons, and strips of cloth. May was teaching Julia how to make corn cob dolls. This had served three purposes: one, to distract herself; two, to keep Julia from sensing something amiss; and three, to lure Willa to stay.

She had been horrified when Willa had begun to insist on riding back home.

"I need to see Joseph," Willa had said, shoving her hair back from her face. May's fingers twitched, a quick, untimely longing to tidy her friend's hair back to at least its usual state of disarray. "He needs me."

"He needs you to be safe. Not go riding off on your own on a day like today."

They both glanced outside. The day was stunning: a brilliantly blue sky and gentle wisps of clouds. Willa raised a brow.

"I'm not talking about the weather, Willa," May snapped, irritation rising in reaction to her fear. It was not a habit of hers that she liked, but she couldn't tamp it down. Not today.

Willa had leveled a look at her. "I love you, May, and I appreciate your looking out for me, but you are not my keeper. I'm leaving now to check on my husband."

The two women looked at one another. Their friendship was not one that often dealt with seriousness. May chewed her lip, but backed down. Willa was right.

Willa dropped a kiss on Julia's head and strode out, nodding to Adam as she went. May stared from the window until she could see her no longer, and wished there existed a way to communicate instantaneously, that she might know when her friend made it safely into the arms of her husband.

Adam retook his place on the stairs, May locked the door, and she and Julia got to work.

"The buttons are for eyes?" Julia looked up at her, the tip of her tongue peeking out from between her lips as she concentrated on making the hair for her doll.

"Yes, choose whatever color you like." She reached up, rubbing at the tension in her neck. "What do you think, sweetheart?" she asked, forcing her voice to stay gentle. "Should we put another flower here?"

Julia hesitated, then nodded, carefully pressing the delicate petals onto the strands of twine. May ran a soothing hand over the little girl's hair, trying to ignore the way her own fingers trembled.

Later, May would think about that moment of peace, there on the floor, little dolls being made, Julia's eyes sparkling with the pleasure of discovering something new, the satisfaction of creating something out of her own preferences.

But she didn't get to enjoy it for long.

A series of things happened at once. From outside, she could hear Adam. "Away from the windows, please, missus," he called, rapping on the glass. "Take the child to the kitchen. Make sure the back door is locked."

Her heart jumped into her throat, and she did as he said without a second thought. She scooped Julia into her arms and carried the protesting child into the kitchen. There were windows in the kitchen, but they were small and pointed to the back of the property. Every other room on this level had windows that faced the front. The fact that Adam had sent them here told her enough to take him seriously, but she wished desperately to be able to try and see or hear what was happening.

It was a Sunday, the staff's day off, so there was no bustling in the kitchen, nothing being baked or kneaded or stirred. There was nothing but the sound of Julia asking why they couldn't finish the dolls, could she have a snack, and then sobs of fury and indignation. Finally, May had had enough.

"Hush," she said. "Enough now." The harshness of her voice made Julia jump, and May was awash with guilt. She knelt in front of her, taking her hands and looking her in the eye. "I'm sorry to be firm with you, but this is serious. I need you to listen to me and do as I say. Okay? Do that, and everything will be fine."

Julia's eyes searched hers, and May wished she could ease the fear in them, but it was all she could do to keep from unraveling herself.

Then, there came a wild, furious pounding on the front door. Julia shrieked, and May stood quickly, whirling around to face the doorway to the hall.

Her mind raced. Adam wouldn't be doing that. Would he? It must be someone else. But who? What did they want?

The pounding continued. She considered just ignoring it. They were locked inside. Maybe Adam had ridden for help.

"I know you're in there, May!" Edward shouted, so loudly he could be heard clearly even from her place in the kitchen.

"Come out here and be quick about it!" The pounding did not let up, even as he yelled.

Fury gripped her. She was finished with this foolishness. She crouched back to Julia once more. "You stay right here, okay? I'll be back in a few minutes."

Julia nodded solemnly.

May stood, back straight and chin up, and strode to the door. She waited until the opportune moment and then swung it open, saying as she did, "You need to leave, Edward."

She could have laughed, seeing the way Edward stumbled through and nearly fell flat on his face. She had timed it perfectly.

But he was followed by Sheriff Mitchell and another man she had never seen before, the two of them bursting through as if they had any right to be there.

"What on earth?" she barely had time to get the words out when Mitchell grabbed one of her arms, yanking her up and forward so that she stumbled. She tried to snatch her arm back, but the other man surged and grabbed her other arm.

May gasped, twisting, struggling against them, but they were too strong. Panic surged hot and sharp in her veins as they yanked her forward. "Let go of me!" she cried, kicking out, fighting, but Mitchell only tightened his hold.

"You need to come with us," he said, his voice as calm as it had been that morning when he had asked her for a cup of coffee. "You're wanted for questioning."

"Questioning?" May's breath came fast, her vision swimming. "You gave me twenty-four hours! My time's not up!"

Mitchell chuckled darkly. "The timeline's changed."

She twisted in their grip, eyes darting desperately toward the porch. Adam lay sprawled on the ground, his rifle discarded in the dirt, his chest rising and falling in shallow breaths. He wasn't dead, but he wasn't waking up either.

She whipped back to Edward, fury burning through her fear. "You did this."

Edward only smiled. "You always were a smart one."

Julia's wail shattered the air, high and piercing. "May!"

The sight of the little girl standing in the doorway, eyes wide with terror, sent a fresh wave of rage through May. She thrashed harder, mind racing in desperation. She couldn't leave her here alone. The girl could get into anything, could hurt herself.... Her mind filled in the blanks with endless terrifying possibilities.

An idea came to her. It wasn't ideal, but it was all she had.

"Julia, listen to me," she gasped. "Run! Find your father! He's at Willa's house—go, now!" She and Julia had taken rides together often, and she always pointed out the fence line that divided her ranch from Willa's farm. They bordered one another, and if Julia crossed in the spot where May pointed it out, it was a straight shot to Willa's house.

Julia hesitated, trembling, but May fixed her with a fierce look. "Go, Julia! Now!"

The little girl let out a sob but turned and bolted, her small figure disappearing into the open land beyond the house.

Edward cursed. "Go after her!" he barked at the second man, but Mitchell stopped him with a firm hand on his chest.

"Let her go," the sheriff said lazily. "Harry will find out sooner or later. Might as well get this started."

May's blood ran cold as the implications of his words hit her.

Mitchell hauled her down the steps, his grip like iron. "Now, May, let's not make this any harder than it needs to be."

May dug her heels into the dirt, her breath coming in ragged gasps. "You won't get away with this," she spat. "Harry won't let you."

Mitchell only chuckled, dragging her toward the waiting horses. "Let's see if he's got the guts to stop me."

As they forced her onto the back of a horse, her last thought was of Julia running, her tiny legs carrying her across the open fields.

She screwed her eyes shut and begged whatever higher power was out there that she would make it safely to her father.

Chapter Twenty-Six

William had insisted they slice up his pie and talk plans over a piece alongside a cup of coffee. The other men had trickled in, more quickly than he might have expected, which spoke highly to both their character and Joseph's, that he could inspire that kind of response. Harry knew what he was doing was important, that he was where he needed to be, but he was irritable and short-tempered, eager to get this over with, his mind back at the ranch.

He hated that Julia and May were on their own. Felt even worse when Willa appeared, knowing not only that she was a great comfort to May, but that she also was a strong woman not to be trifled with herself.

But he was glad to hear from her that all was well back at the ranch, that May was teaching Julia how to make dolls, and Adam was ready for trouble. He was able to relax some after that, not by much, but enough to keep him from jumping out of his skin as the other men made cups of coffee and talked about inane things like the blasted pie.

Although, it was a very good pie.

When William stood for a second slice, he had had enough. "All right," he said, his voice sharper than he had intended. "Let's get to work."

The others all looked up at him, and at once, the room was quiet. Forks were placed down, and conversations halted abruptly. He cleared his throat, and felt the mantle of the man he once was slide easily onto his shoulders.

"I'm about to cover a pretty sensitive topic," he said. "It's understandable if you decide not to be a part of what's about to happen; no one has to stay here against their will, but if that's how you feel, speak up now, because the man we're about to discuss is the sheriff, and I can't have word of any of this getting back to him or any of his men."

The men stared at him, serious, as he scanned them one by one. "Last chance," he said. "After this, if you don't want to be a part of this, we can't let you leave until it's all through."

William spoke up. "Mitchell is as shady as they come. It's about time we did something about him."

The men around him nodded, and Harry wondered what actions the sheriff had taken to turn so many men against him. As Joseph had introduced each of the men upon their arrival, he had noticed that they were all hard workers, integral parts of the running of the town and its community. The butcher, the innkeeper, the blacksmith, the cattle drivers. A town needed men like these to keep afloat. What did it say that they were the first ones to turn on the sheriff?

Nothing good.

When Harry had been sheriff, these were the type of men he had gone out of his way to partner with and support. It was the way things were done, the way his former sheriff had taught him as he was showing him the ropes. The fact that Mitchell didn't think he needed these men on his side showed how untouchable he thought he was, but it might also just be his downfall.

He took a seat at Joseph's kitchen table, his hands clasped together as he studied the faces of the men seated around the room. These trusted friends of Joseph were men who had known hardship, men who had seen enough of Sheriff Mitchell's dealings to suspect he wasn't the upstanding lawman he claimed to be. Still, he needed to tread carefully.

"I don't like saying it," Harry began, voice low, "but I don't believe we can trust Mitchell. He's got a way of twisting things, and now, after what happened at your place, Joseph, I think he might be more than just crooked. He's dangerous."

The men exchanged glances, nodding in quiet agreement. One of them, an older rancher named Earl, let out a heavy sigh. "I've had my suspicions for a while now. Mitchell has too much interest in things that ain't his business. Folks who get on his bad side tend to have a run of bad luck soon after."

"He came asking about my assets just a few days before the gold was stolen," Joseph said, jaw tight. "And now my house is in shambles."

Before he could say another word, however, a voice came from outside that made Harry's blood turn to ice.

"Papa!"

It was like a physical blow, the fear. He staggered from it, righted himself, and shoved through the pack of men until he was through the front door.

Julia was running from the far field that bordered the Allen ranch, her face tear-streaked and panic-stricken. She was alone, barefoot.

He sprinted to her, catching her in three long strides, and swept her into his arms, checking her from head to toe for injuries. Aside from the condition of her bare feet from running across open fields, she appeared unhurt.

But May would never have allowed her to come here alone, particularly not today.

He pulled back, holding her upper arms, and looked at her urgently. "What happened?" He knelt, gripping her shoulders, pushing back her hair as his breath came in short, sharp bursts.

The men gathered behind them as she attempted to speak, little shoulders shaking.

She could barely speak through her tears, hiccupping between words. "They...they took her! They took May!"

Harry's fingers tightened around her arms, his stomach bottoming out. "Who? Who took her?"

Julia's wide, terrified eyes met his. "Uncle Edward and...and the tall, angry man in the hat! He hurt Adam! He—" She broke into another sob, her tiny hands clutching at his shirt as if he might disappear too.

For a moment, Harry couldn't breathe. A cold, vicious rage surged through him, gripping his spine like a vice. Beneath it, deep but so very close to the surface, was another feeling. A hopeless, aching voice telling him he had failed his family once more. He slammed the thought down as hard as he could, attempted to control his brain. There was no time for that. Not now.

Behind him, he heard a sharp intake of breath. He turned just as Willa appeared at the front of the group. Her wide eyes darted between him and Julia, confusion giving way to panic. "Where's May?"

Julia only cried harder.

Willa shook her head, taking an unsteady step forward. "No. No, she was supposed to stay in the house. She was supposed to be safe." She looked back at the fields, as if May would appear there. "I would never have left if I hadn't thought she would be safe!"

Joseph was at her side in an instant, his steady hands gripping her arms. "Easy, Willa."

She pushed back against him, nearly hysterical. "They can't take her. They can't just—" She turned to Harry, desperation thick in her voice. "We have to get her back."

"We will," Harry vowed. His voice was hard, steady, but inside, he was barely holding himself together.

Joseph pulled Willa into his chest as she pressed a hand to her mouth, trying to stifle her sobs.

William was the first to speak. "The sheriff's got no right to treat May like a common criminal." He looked at Julia, face buried in her father's neck. "To cause a child pain like this. We can't stand for this."

A younger man, Samuel, the blacksmith, nodded sharply. "This is wrong. We've all seen what Mitchell does to people who don't fall in line. If we don't stop him now, it won't just be May. He'll keep taking what he wants."

Joseph looked at Harry over Willa's head. "What's the plan?"

"Willa," Harry said, and something in his voice cut through her tears. She raised her head and looked at him. "I need you to watch over her," he said, gesturing to Julia.

Willa nodded, and she stepped forward. Harry shifted Julia into Willa's waiting arms, and she pulled Julia close.

The little girl fought against her hold at first, fresh tears springing to her eyes. "No! I want to stay with you, Papa!"

Harry leaned close to her, cupping her face in his hands. "I need you to stay with Miss Willa, sweetheart. She's going to keep you safe. And I need you to be brave. Can you do that for me?"

Julia sniffled, searching his face, before finally nodding, though fresh tears slipped down her cheeks. Willa gathered her close, murmuring soft reassurances, even as her own shoulders shook with fear.

Then, Harry turned to the men. His voice was steel. "We ride for the jail. We get May back." He pointed to one of the younger men. "All but you. I need you to fetch the doctor and get him to Adam as quickly as you can. Make sure he gets the help he needs."

No one hesitated. They grabbed their coats, their hats, their weapons. There was no more talk. Only action.

And as Harry strode out the door, the fury inside him turned to something sharper, something unshakable. Sheriff Mitchell had made a mistake. And Harry was going to make sure he never got the chance to make another.

Chapter Twenty-Seven

May sat in the hard wooden chair, refusing to allow her fear to show on her face. The man with the hat had lashed rope tightly around both arms, securing them to the table. When he had leaned in close, he had rubbed his face on her neck with a leer, and she had spat right into it.

He had made to slap her, but Mitchell had ordered him from the room. Now, he smiled at her, his face kindly but condescending, like he was speaking to a naughty child. She kept her back ramrod straight, her ankles crossed, and her face as expressionless as she could imagine.

Her wrists burned where the rope bit into her skin, her arms stretched taut across the rough wooden table. The chair beneath her creaked as she shifted, trying in vain to loosen her bonds. The air in the cramped room was thick with sweat, dust, and the sharp scent of her own fear.

She had never been in the sheriff's office before, had never seen a room like this. It looked like it was part of a horse stable. One ugly, scarred table in its center with two hard chairs on either side. The windows were covered with heavy curtains, making the room almost entirely black, and various horse training and other mysterious instruments hanging on the wall.

Inside, her heart beat a tattoo against her chest, aching with the thought of Julia running off to Willa's on her own. She prayed that the girl had made it safe. She glanced at the window, though heavy curtains covered it. She would know soon enough. If Julia made it to Harry, May knew that her husband would not stand for the way the sheriff had put his daughter in danger.

She hoped he would forgive her for not protecting Julia herself.

She hoped he would come for her.

She swallowed hard as Edward reentered the room and began walking in long, lazy circles around her. Mitchell settled heavily in the seat across from her, taking out a cigar, though he did not light it.

"Miss May, I've known you since you were a little girl," Mitchell drawled. "Why don't we dispense with all this nonsense, and you just tell me the truth."

"What truth is that, Sheriff?" she asked coolly, laying just a touch of sarcasm into the title.

"We know you're lying!" Edward exploded from behind her. He circled back around to the front of the table and slammed his two hands, palms flat, on top of it.

She raised her eyes from his hands to his face slowly. "I have no idea what you're talking about."

Edward's face went blood red, and he moved quickly forward as if to grab her, but Mitchell cleared his throat.

"Now, now, Edward," he said, his voice as smooth and rich as molasses. "Let's not be hasty."

Edward whirled and strode quickly back around the room in a large circle, his breath coming fast and heavy like a bull dying to charge.

Mitchell's lips curled in amusement as he spread his short, thick fingers wide on the surface of the table. "Let's lay all of our cards on the table, shall we? No sense in dancing around together." He raised brushy brows. "Although I'm sure you make a mighty fine dance partner."

She raised one brow and remained silent, waiting for whatever he had to say.

"Edward here has been speaking with his lawyer," Mitchell said smoothly, his voice thick with false concern. "You might know Mr. Laramont. Fine man, fine lawyer. Sharp as a tack. Now, Mr. Laramont says if Edward can prove that you weren't legally married before your parents passed, well, now, that changes things. The land, the house, the horses, the business itself, that will all go to your cousin here."

May's heart came to a stuttering stop in her chest, and for a moment, she felt she could not drag in even a sip of air. So it was even worse than she had dared think.

"That is absurd," she said. It was all she could think to say. Her mind raced, wondering if this was true. She had never heard of this lawyer before, but that didn't mean anything necessarily.

"Is it?" Mitchell asked easily, leaning back and steepling his fingers together. "To me, it seems only sensible, actually. Think about it. You're a woman, alone, with no siblings to speak of. Why shouldn't the business go to the closest male relative?" He pointed his chin in Edward's direction. "You know as well as anybody that it would be considered mighty strange to leave such a large, profitable business in the hands of a single woman. A young single woman at that! I knew your father; he was an intelligent man. He would have wanted the safest bet to protect what he had worked so hard for."

Her temper flared. How dare he speak about her father like he knew better than her what he would have wanted. Rage made her heart race, made her blood boil in her veins.

She flexed against the ropes. "He wanted it to go to me. He raised me to run it." She bit the words out as she looked at

Edward in disgust. "He didn't even like you. You never made it a full month on our property because of it."

Edward slammed one fist into his open palm. "That isn't true. You know as well as I do that it should have been mine!" he shouted, his voice taking on a whining edge that made her skin crawl. She imagined what her father would say about all this, and her lips twitched up into a smile. Edward roared. "Are you laughing? I'll show you—"

But Mitchell lifted a hand, and Edward turned to the wall again, breathing in and out loudly. She rolled her eyes.

"Really, this is terribly unseemly," she said. "Are we through? If this is a matter for lawyers, then let us move forward that way."

She tried to sound calm, but it was the last thing she wanted. She imagined years of back and forth, of a judge telling her that everything she had worked for, every piece of her family left, was gone. For the first time, she wondered if it might have been better, less risky, to have married Edward after all. To end this claim once and for all by leaning into it.

But watching him, leaning into the wall, shoulders rising and falling with the struggle to maintain his temper, she knew it would not have been the better choice. She could not be sure she might even have survived a marriage with a man such as this.

"That's one way to go about it," Mitchell conceded. "But it's slow, and costly. And really, why bother with all that when it's clear what is right and needs to happen? What they'll tell you at the end of all this is what I'll tell you now."

He leaned in, and she could see the shade of tobacco stain on his teeth as he smiled. "You're lying, and none of this belongs to you any longer. The rightful owner is Edward." He leaned back once more, cocked his head at her. "So let's go on and get this done with here and now, shall we? Go on and tell us the truth, little May. Tell us you were not legally married—and I tell you what, you can choose the reason; whether it be because it wasn't by the time your parents died or because the marriage isn't legal at all, I leave that up to you—and all of this nastiness can come to an end. And who knows, if you ask very nicely, Edward might just give you that little farm up the road to have to yourself. That is, if he doesn't still want to marry you."

Edward had grown very still, still facing the wall. May looked from him to Mitchell. She could no longer feel the sting of the rope burn on her arms or the itch in her throat from the dust; all there was was this moment.

It didn't matter what she and Harry had told Mitchell back at the ranch. She had to stick to this new story.

She lifted her chin, swallowing hard against the dryness in her throat. "I was married before they died, and my marriage is fully legal," she said, her voice steadier than she felt.

Edward stiffened.

Mitchell sighed dramatically, shaking his head. "Lying won't do you any favors."

She said it again, this time feeling stronger. "I was married before they died, and my marriage is fully legal."

Mitchell stared at her, and for the first time, she saw a flash of something besides the genteel lawman that he was pretending to be cross his face. Something hard, something angry. Something frightening.

Then, he shrugged, and the mask fell over his face once more. "She's stubborn," he mused. "I suppose you were right, after all, Edward."

Edward turned around then, and her stomach went ice cold at the look on his face. Gone was the fury, the loss of control, the childish petulance. In its place was a look of hard, malicious glee. He crossed to the wall with the horse tools and lifted a switch, turning it over once, twice, in his fingers with a sort of reverence before passing it to Mitchell.

"Thank you, Edward," Mitchell said, and she didn't even have a moment to wonder about this, to wonder how they had had this planned, what they were going to do, why the switch—before he whirled to face her, snapping the switch down hard across her arms.

The pain was instant and searing. A strangled cry tore from her lips, and she jerked against the ropes, but they held firm. Tears blurred her vision. Mixed with the pain was the humiliation of being strapped down and at their mercy, and beneath it all, fury as cold and hard as a rock at the audacity of these two men.

"Shall we try again?" Mitchell said. He and Edward exchanged a laugh. "Maybe our little lady here didn't understand the question. All these legal things can get mighty tricky; I know that." He leaned in, switch at the ready. "What's the truth?"

May squeezed her eyes shut, her body trembling from head to toe. She wouldn't give them what they wanted. If she admitted to anything, if they forced a false confession out of her, she would lose everything.

"Say it," Edward urged, his voice nearly coaxing. "Say you weren't married before their deaths. Just say the words, and this will all be over."

May swallowed back a sob. "No."

Another lash, this time across the back of her hands. She screamed, the pain so sharp it nearly stole her breath. Her shoulders shook as she bit down on her lip, tasting blood.

"I'm losing patience now," Edward hissed. "Don't make me keep hurting you. I dislike this as much as you do."

The lie rang clearly through his words. He was enjoying this; he wanted to hurt her, and he wanted to get what he wanted from her. She didn't know how long she could last this, but would not give in yet.

"I'm legally married, and it happened before my parents died," she said, and she steeled herself against the switch.

It whistled through the air as Mitchell lifted it, and she squeezed her eyes shut tightly. But before it could fall, a violent pounding sound made them all jump.

A shout came from the front of the building, and she recognized Harry's voice at once. "May!"

Her head shot up at the sound of his voice. Relief, raw and desperate, surged through her. "Harry!" she cried, her voice hoarse. "Harry, I'm in here!"

A chorus of shouts echoed through the building, followed by a heavy slam against the door. The wood groaned under the force. Mitchell and Edward exchanged quick glances before stepping back, straightening their coats. Edward took the switch and mounted it back in its place on the wall, and they relaxed, as if nothing at all could be amiss.

She watched them in disbelief as there was another slam. She could hear the man at the front desk yelling as boots pounded the length of the building.

"This one!" shouted someone, rattling the door so that the hinges rattled. Then, with a final, deafening crash, the door burst open.

Harry was the first through, his face flushed with fury, his gun drawn and ready. Behind him, Joseph, William, Earl, and Samuel followed, their expressions thunderous. Edward barely had time to step back before Joseph grabbed him by the collar and shoved him against the wall.

Harry's eyes landed on May, taking in the ropes, the bruises already forming on her arms. In his eyes, she could see as something in him snapped. He rushed forward, shoving Mitchell out of his way so hard the sheriff stumbled back. His hands found the knots at her wrists, fingers working quickly despite his shaking fury.

"May," he breathed, his voice raw. "Are you hurt?"

She let out a shuddering sob, relief overwhelming her as he freed her hands and lifted her out of the chair. The moment she was loose, she collapsed against him. His arms came around her, holding her so tightly she could barely breathe, but she didn't care.

"Julia..." she muttered, scarcely able to get the word out.

Despite her lack of clarification, Harry understood her. "She's safe. She's with Willa." She clung to him, trembling, as he whispered against her hair, "I've got you. You're safe now, too."

Behind them, Edward was sputtering. "This—this is a misunderstanding!" he stammered. "She was free to go at any time!"

Mitchell straightened his hat, lifting his hands in mock innocence. "No harm done. We were just having a conversation. What's all this fuss about?"

Harry turned, his grip still firm around May, his eyes burning with barely restrained rage. "You don't lay a hand on my wife and call it a conversation."

Earl stepped forward, his hand resting threateningly on the gun at his hip. "If you think for a second the town's gonna look the other way after this, you're dumber than I thought, Mitchell."

Mitchell's jaw clenched, but he didn't argue. He knew they were outnumbered. He shrugged. "We have everything we need from her for now." He shot a warning smile at May. "We can finish this conversation later."

Her blood ran cold, and she pressed harder against Harry, his grip tightening in response.

Joseph shoved Edward toward the door. "Move out of the way. We're leaving."

Edward hesitated, then sneered. "This isn't over."

"No," Harry agreed, and his voice was a promise. "It's not."

Mitchell and Edward had no choice but to move out of the way under the watchful glares of the men standing against them. As soon as they were through the door, Harry turned back to May, brushing a trembling hand over her cheek. "Let's get you home."

May nodded weakly, still shaken, but as Harry guided her out of that dreadful room and into the searing sunlight, she knew one thing for certain.

She was safe now.

And she wasn't going to let Edward take anything else from her.

Chapter Twenty-Eight

It took every part of Harry not to shoot Mitchell and Edward then and there. Joseph was clearly operating under the same pull, hissing at Harry as they left, "Aren't we going to do something? Look at her arms!"

Harry couldn't bear to look again at the bright red marks on May, the skin beneath already mottling into bruises. If he did, he would lose control for certain.

"They're lying about it all," Earl agreed. "That was no conversation. That wasn't legal."

Harry knew Mitchell and Edward were lying. The moment he'd burst through that door, he had seen May tied to that chair, her arms strapped down, and the red welts rising where Mitchell's switch had struck her. Now, as she trembled beside him, he felt he might explode from rage, but he had to play this correctly. First—get her to safety. The rest would follow.

"Stand down," he ordered the men behind him, his voice like steel. "We got what we came for."

He slid his arm around May's waist, steadying her as he pulled her toward the door. She clung to him, her breath ragged, and he knew she was barely holding herself together. Outside, in the cool night air, he turned to her, brushing a hand over her cheek.

"Are you all right?" he asked, his voice low, laced with guilt. "I should've been here. I should've stopped this."

May shook her head, swallowing hard. "You came," she whispered. "That's what matters."

Before he could say more, the door behind them slammed open, and Edward stormed out, his face twisted with rage. The man was a fool of the highest order; he never knew when he was beaten. Harry gritted his teeth.

"You think this is over?" Edward spat. "You think you can steal from me and just walk away?"

Harry pushed May protectively behind him, his muscles coiling with tension. "You don't have a claim to May's ranch, Edward. You never did."

Edward let out a humorless laugh. "Oh, I will. My lawyer's working on it, and I promise you, when this is all said and done, I'll have the land that's rightfully mine."

Harry held his ground. "You'll never get your hands on that ranch. I won't let May's legacy be tainted by the likes of you."

Edward's face darkened, his lips curling into a sneer. "You think you're some kind of hero, don't you?" He stepped closer, lowering his voice. "You should watch yourself, Harry. You've got a little girl to think about."

Harry's blood turned to ice. "What did you just say?"

Edward smirked, leaning in. "I said, you had better watch yourself. You wouldn't want your daughter meeting the same fate as her mother, would you?"

A roaring filled Harry's ears. The world narrowed to Edward's smug face, to the terrible weight of his words sinking in. His hands clenched into fists, and his body coiled like a loaded gun. It would be so easy to put an end to Edward right here, right now.

But May's trembling hand on his arm brought him back. He couldn't lose himself to rage. Not yet.

Edward chuckled at Harry's silence. "Yeah. That's what I thought." He turned on his heel and walked off into the night, leaving Harry standing there, his fury barely leashed, his mind racing with a thousand dark possibilities.

He had known Edward was ruthless. He had known the man was willing to cheat and lie to get what he wanted. But this— this was something else entirely.

There was no way that Edward could know about his wife unless he had had a hand in her death. The horse he had given Julia, an exact replica, the smugness. He still couldn't connect how Edward knew about Beth's horse, whether he had been a part of that gang on that long ago night or something else, but the pieces fit together too well to deny the truth of them.

This man had had a hand in the worst day of his life. He had laid a hand on May. He had threatened Julia.

He had been wrong about Edward. He wasn't just a fool; he was a fool with a death wish.

A death wish Harry would be happy to oblige if it came to it.

Chapter Twenty-Nine

May sat on the edge of the bed, her hands still trembling as she wrapped the woolen blanket tighter around her shoulders. The room was dim, lit only by the glow of the oil lamp on the nightstand, its flickering light casting restless shadows along the walls. She could still feel the bite of the ropes on her wrists, the sting of the switch against her arms. Every time she closed her eyes, she saw Edward's sneering face, felt the sharp snap of fear in her chest.

She was still shaking as she lay back against the headboard, even as she pulled the warm weight of Julia against her. Julia was sleeping, but fitfully. She only relaxed once Harry and May were with her, and had spent the entire afternoon touching the both of them as much as she could, as if afraid that they would disappear if she didn't.

Harry was sitting in the window, one hip perched in its wide, low sill, facing out across the grounds with his gun at his side. He had insisted that they all stay in the same room that night, himself also unwilling to let the two of them out of his sight since returning to the ranch.

May stayed as still as she could, ordering her body to listen to her, to remember that she was the boss, not it. It refused to comply, and as much as that infuriated her, it seemed that there was nothing she could do but lie in her bed and shake and fight the cold pit growing inside of her.

Julia shifted in her sleep, brow wrinkling, and pressed her face into May.

May put an arm around her and drew her closer, so that her head rested against her chest. Minutes ticked by, and as they did, she could feel the heartbeat of the little girl, quick as a hummingbird, grow slower and steadier, and hers, as if guided by it, began to do the same. Finally, she could feel the shaking begin to ease. She stretched her fingers, toes, wrists, and ankles as slowly as she could so as not to disturb Julia. Her whole body ached as it relaxed, exhausted from the day and the adrenaline crash.

The weight of Julia on her chest helped. Watching Harry helped as well. He was vigilant at her window, and she found herself idly thinking about all of the years she had spent sleeping in this room, wondering about the man who would one day join her in it.

She had never pictured anyone quite like Harry.

Her eyes traced his broad shoulders, his thick hair, his long legs. An unfamiliar heat began to glow in her chest, and she wondered at it, wondered at what they might be doing in this room together if they weren't being hunted like wild game, and if his daughter wasn't asleep beside her.

Julia twitched in her sleep, nose wrinkling, and then settled once more. It had taken them almost the entire rest of the day to get her to calm down. She had been nearly overcome with panic after watching May dragged away and then making a barefoot, desperate run to Harry.

It infuriated her. The pain these men had inflicted on a little girl, and to what end? Their own selfish interests. Now Edward had threatened Julia, clear as day; she had heard him, as had the other men. Joseph and the others had been ready to kill him, then and there, she was sure of it, but she could only imagine the repercussions if they had laid even a hand on him in broad daylight outside of crooked Sheriff Mitchell's office.

She shivered at the thought, and not wanting the shaking to start back up again now that it had finally stopped, turned her mind with effort to something positive. Adam was in one of the guest bedrooms, resting comfortably, though she knew that he would be beating himself up at his perceived failure. He had a nasty bump and bruise on his head and had been ordered to do nothing but rest for a week at least. She and Harry both had gone to great pains to assure him that it was not his fault that May had been taken, that he could not have been expected to withstand an attack by a lawman and his henchman with no backup, but she knew Adam and knew he would not be happy about any of it.

At least he was all right, however. Seeing him crumpled on the ground had shaken her.

Harry couldn't seem to sit still. Every few moments, he stood from the sill, pacing the far length of the wall, eyes so fixed outside the window she could not be sure he was even blinking. She felt a surge of regret that she had dragged him and his daughter into all of this. He could have married another woman, one without a scheming, malicious cousin in a town that did have an untrustworthy sheriff.

The next time he paced past the head of the bed, she reached out and laid a careful hand on his arm, halting him in his tracks. He looked at her, but only for the briefest moment before turning back to the window.

"You should take a break," she murmured, hoping not to wake Julia. "Get a little rest. You have all the ranch hands patrolling the borders. Joseph and his men are taking turns at the gate and front door. You can afford a few hours of sleep."

He didn't reply, just continued to stare fixedly out the window.

"Harry," she tried again, her voice barely above a breath. "You need to rest. You won't be able to fight without it."

Still no reply.

She sighed. "All right, think of it this way. It is unlikely that Mitchell and Edward will ride out again tonight. Not after everything today. They know we will be ready and waiting for them, expecting an attack."

His jaw tightened, but he didn't stop his pacing. "I can't rest," he admitted, his voice low and taut. "Not when I know they're still out there."

May shifted carefully, not wanting to disturb Julia, and stood, settling the girl onto the pillow and covering her with the blanket. She stretched briefly and then reached out, brushing her fingers over his knuckles, where they gripped the handle of his gun like a lifeline.

"They won't come back tonight," she repeated, though she wasn't sure she believed it herself. "Not after everything that happened."

Harry let out a humorless laugh. "Men like Edward and Mitchell don't tend to take losses lightly." He hesitated, his dark eyes flicking toward her, hesitation warring with something heavier. "There's something you should know."

She waited, something her father had taught her. "The truth can't come out if you're talking too much to hear it," he had said. He had been right.

Harry looked out the window, back at her. His grip tightened around the handle of his gun. "I think they were part of the same gang that killed my wife."

May sucked in a sharp breath. How could that be? Her mind struggled to put the pieces together, but exhaustion was rolling over her like waves; it was too much, and none of it made sense.

"They knew too much. Edward—he as much as admitted it." Harry's grip tightened on his gun. "I've spent years wondering who was responsible. If I'd just—"

May placed a hand over his. "Don't go down that road," she said firmly. "You can't know how things might have been different."

He exhaled, long and slow, the tension still thrumming in his muscles. He didn't believe her. Not yet. But at least he let himself be still for a moment, his fingers lacing with hers.

Julia stirred, turning one way and the other, and made a small whining sound.

"I had better stay close to her," May said, regretful to end the moment, but knowing she had to.

Harry nodded, his face softening as he looked at his daughter. "Get some rest," he said. "You need it, too, after today."

She slid into the bed, pulling Julia back into her lap as she sat back against the headboard, leaning her head against it and closing her eyes. She could hear Harry begin to pace once more, his boots scuffing softly against the wooden floorboards.

When he passed their side again, his hand brushed hers, then returned. He squeezed her hand in his, held it, and then let go and started his path again.

"Rest easy," he whispered, so softly she was not sure if she was meant to hear it. "I'll be watching over you."

She held onto that small moment, the warmth of his touch, the affection in his voice, before exhaustion finally pulled her under.

***

A sharp jolt startled May awake. Her eyes snapped open, taking in the first tendrils of dawn creeping through the curtains. The spot where Julia had once been was now vacant, the sheets cold. She scanned the room, but Harry was not in the window, either, not pacing, nowhere to be seen. A panic she could not explain clawed up her throat.

She shoved back the blanket and hurried downstairs, her heart pounding. The house was silent, the air thick with something unspoken. The wooden floor was cool beneath her bare feet as she stepped toward the door, wondering if he was speaking with the ranch hands, or checking on the horses. The embers in the fireplace smoldered, casting an eerie glow across the room.

Pushing the front door open, she stepped outside, wrapping her arms around herself against the chill of the early morning air. Mist rose over the green fields, the first rays of sunlight beginning to shine over the horizon. It was a beautiful, still morning.

So why was every hair on her body standing on end?

She took a hesitant step forward. "Harry?" she called quietly across the space. Where were the ranch hands? Shouldn't someone be at the front door?

The barn door swung open with a bang, smacking against the far wall, and she relaxed a bit. He was in the barn, tending to the animals. She was being foolish.

She went to the stairs and watched, hoping to see him come out. They could sit down over coffee, talk about their plans for the day.

But the man who stepped out of the barn was not Harry. It was not one of their ranch hands, not a man she had ever seen before. When he saw her, he grinned, and it was not a kind grin.

The first creak of the porch floorboards behind her sent ice through her veins.

A rough hand clamped over her mouth before she could scream. She knew it was Edward by the smell of his sweat, the softness of the large palm.

May thrashed, her muffled cry swallowed by the pressure of Edward's palm. He yanked her backward, his grip an iron vice around her waist. She kicked wildly, her breath coming in frantic gasps. The scent of sweat and leather filled her nostrils, turning her stomach.

"Well, now," Edward sneered in her ear. "Look what we have here."

Sheriff Mitchell loomed in front of her, his eyes glinting with cruel amusement. "We warned you we'd be back," he said. "Didn't we?"

May struggled, but Edward threw her over the back of a waiting horse. The world tilted as she was hoisted up, her stomach slamming against the saddle. She gasped, twisting to try and fight back, but rough hands secured her wrists.

The cold morning air bit at her skin as the horse shifted beneath her. She strained to see beyond the pounding of her own heartbeat. Through the haze of panic, she caught movement from above. Harry. He stood in the upstairs window, his eyes locking onto hers just as Edward spurred the horse forward.

"No!" she screamed, her voice raw and desperate.

Harry disappeared from view as they galloped into the pale morning light, and May realized with a sickening twist of her gut—he had been there the whole time, just one room away. And now, she was being ripped away from him once more.

The thundering hooves pounded against the dirt road as Mitchell and Edward rode hard, dragging her away from the only safety she had left. Dust kicked up around them, stinging her eyes, the scent of damp earth and sweat filling her lungs. She writhed, her wrists burning against the rope that bound them.

Mitchell glanced back at her with a smirk. "You ought to settle in, darlin'. You're in for a long ride."

Terror twisted in her gut, but May forced herself to breathe. She had to think, had to fight. Because no matter how far they took her, she knew one thing for certain—Harry would come for her. And this time, she wouldn't let them take her without a fight.

Chapter Thirty

Harry's world tilted the second he saw May thrown onto that horse. His pulse pounded in his ears, his breath coming in ragged gasps as he tore through the house, taking the stairs two at a time. By the time he reached the front door, they were already halfway down the road, dust rising in thick clouds beneath their horses' hooves.

"May!" he bellowed, shoving the door open so hard it slammed against the wall. He bolted toward the stables, barely aware of his own movements. He yanked the reins from the hook, his fingers fumbling with the leather as he mounted his horse in one swift motion.

Julia.

The thought slammed into him like a hammer. He couldn't leave her alone. He swiveled back toward the house, his mind racing. Adam was still weak from the blow he took, and Julia—God, she had already seen too much. He couldn't risk her getting caught in the crossfire.

He needed Willa and Joseph.

There was no time to think, no time to worry about scaring Julia. He pounded back up the stairs, lifting her into his arms and holding her tightly to his chest as he ran back to his horse.

"Papa!" she screamed, and the fear in her voice shook something loose inside him, made him want to issue a guttural roar out across the plains. There was too much to do, too little time. He was scaring her, but every moment he wasn't chasing after May could mean losing her forever.

"I'm sorry," he said. "My girl. Hang on."

She clung to him, blanket falling into the dirt as she wrapped her arms around his neck and her legs around his waist, and he hopped into the saddle, settling them both.

Kicking his horse hard, he tore down the road, the morning mist curling like ghostly fingers around the trees. The chill in the air bit through his shirt, but he barely felt it. All he saw was May's face as she'd been yanked away, her wide, desperate eyes locked onto his.

The memory of it burned, seared into his mind. He had been right there, just one room away. Julia had awoken early and, wanting to let May sleep, he had brought her into the next room to change and play. If he'd been faster—if he hadn't let exhaustion lull him into false security—he could have stopped them.

Where had all of the men been? The men who were supposed to be watching over them, making sure that precisely this did not happen?

There was no time to find out.

His grip on the reins tightened as his horse galloped over the uneven path, hooves clattering against the hard dirt. The sky was still gray with the last traces of night, but already, a storm was brewing. He could feel it in the air, in the charged stillness that settled over the land. Fall in Nebraska was always unpredictable, and this storm, rolling in heavy and fast, threatened to wash away any tracks Edward and Mitchell had left behind.

Within minutes, Willa and Joseph's house came into view. The warm glow of an oil lamp flickered behind a lace-curtained window. Harry leaped off his horse before it had even stopped moving, barely remembering to tie it off before he pounded his fist against the door, Julia still in his arms.

"Willa! Joseph!"

The door flew open, Willa standing there, her dressing gown clutched tightly around her. The moment she saw Harry's face, her eyes widened. "What happened?"

"They took her," he said, his voice raw. "Edward and Mitchell. They came back. They took May."

A sharp gasp escaped Willa's lips. She pressed a hand to her chest, her fingers trembling. "No," she whispered, shaking her head. "Not again. Not again."

Joseph appeared behind her, already reaching for his gun. "Where?"

"Headed east. I saw the tracks before I left, but the rain's coming in. We don't have much time."

A small cry made Harry's chest constrict, and he looked down at Julia, her dark curls tangled around her tear-streaked face. "Papa?" she whimpered.

He set her on the porch, knowing he needed to take this moment to comfort her, even though his heart was aching to be back on his horse, racing across the plains.

Harry bent down, opening his arms, and she ran straight into them. He crushed her against his chest, pressing a kiss to the top of her head. She smelled like lavender soap and woodsmoke, so small, so fragile in his grasp.

"Papa, please don't go," she sobbed. "Don't leave me."

His heart clenched so hard he could barely breathe. He pulled back just enough to cup her face in his hands, brushing his thumbs over her damp cheeks. "I have to go, sweetheart. I have to bring May home."

Her little fingers fisted into his shirt, her entire body trembling. "But what if you don't come back?"

He swallowed hard. "I will." He forced steel into his voice, into the promise he was making her. "I always come back for you."

Willa stepped forward, placing a gentle hand on Julia's shoulder. "Come here, honey," she murmured. "You're safe with me."

Julia clung to him a moment longer before finally, reluctantly, letting go. She stepped back into Willa's arms, though her wide eyes never left his face.

Willa wrapped Julia in a quilt she had quickly procured and looked at Harry with fierce determination. "Go," she said. "I'll keep her safe."

Harry stood, his jaw tight, his muscles coiled with restless energy. He turned to Joseph, who was already shrugging on his coat, his rifle slung over one shoulder.

"We ride now," Joseph said grimly.

Harry gave Julia one last look before he strode out the door, his heart a drumbeat of urgency in his chest.

Outside, the wind had picked up, rustling through the dry grass and sending a sharp chill through the air. Harry mounted his horse in one fluid motion, Joseph right beside him.

"What about the ranch?" Joseph asked, adjusting his hat against the rising wind. "They could be leading you away from it, setting you up."

"It doesn't matter." Harry's voice was low, firm. "The ranch is just land. May is my wife." He met Joseph's gaze, unwavering. "She's what matters."

Joseph gave a single nod, then kicked his horse into motion.

The rain started as a light drizzle, cool and misty against Harry's skin, but he knew it wouldn't stay that way for long. They rode fast, following the tracks that cut through the muddy road, winding toward the trees.

Harry's breath was steady, controlled, but his hands ached from how hard he gripped the reins. The memories clawed at him—another night, another woman stolen from him. His late wife had been ripped from his life without warning, and for years, he had lived with the weight of that loss, the rage of knowing her killers had never been brought to justice.

Now, it was happening again. But this time, he had a name. A face. And he wouldn't let them take May without a fight.

Joseph pointed ahead, toward a dark smudge nestled in the trees. "There."

Harry narrowed his eyes. A small house sat in a clearing, its roof bowed from years of weather. A single lantern glowed through the cracked front window.

They slowed their horses, slipping into the cover of the trees. The wind howled through the branches, carrying the scent of wet earth and smoke.

Through the window, Harry saw her.

May.

She was tied to a chair, her wrists bound in front of her. Her hair hung loose around her shoulders, and even from here, he could see the tension in her body, the way her chest rose and fell in quick, shallow breaths.

A man sat in a chair beside her, facing away.

Harry turned to Joseph, pressing a finger to his lips. Joseph nodded.

Harry moved quickly, stepping onto the porch without making a sound. His heart slammed against his ribs as he reached for the door handle.

A deep breath.

Then, he kicked the door in.

It splintered off its hinges, crashing into the room with a deafening crack. May gasped, jerking in her chair as the guard remained sitting opposite her, unmoving.

Harry didn't hesitate. He raised his gun and aimed.

"Let. Her. Go."

Chapter Thirty-One

The gag in her mouth tasted sour. She held on to that fact, hoping if she remained focused on the taste of the gag, the smell of the old, dusty room, and the feel of the rope biting into her wrists, she would not collapse under the weight of the fear weighing down on her.

She was quite sure that whatever Mitchell and Edward had planned would involve either her death or a fate that she might consider to be worse than death.

Their brazen disregard for the rules of society, for the laws that Mitchell himself was supposed to uphold, shocked her. Yes, Mitchell had power as sheriff, and all right, Chambers was a small enough, out-of-the-way town that it was unlikely any other lawmen would take notice of it, but was he afraid of no repercussions at all?

A man only acted with such disregard if he felt so powerful it caused him to lose all his good sense, or if he stood to lose all that he had and so had come to the table facing a choice of all or nothing.

Either choice made fear streak ice cold through the veins of her body, the kind of fear that made a person want to shut down completely, to lose themselves just so that they did not have to feel that any longer. The longing to give in was strong, but she would not give them the satisfaction. She kept her back as straight as she could, bit down on the sour-tasting gag, and glared with every bit of strength she could muster.

They could kill her, but they would not take her pride or her dignity. If she were scheduled to meet her Maker today, she would do so with her head held high.

"You're looking mighty comfortable, considering you're a woman alone in a shack with two not-so-friendly men," Edward leered, leaning in close to her. The sheriff had left shortly after delivering her to this Godforsaken place, and she tried not to worry about where he had gone or what he was doing.

She only wished she could spit in Edward's round, pudgy face, but she was denied that satisfaction due to the gag.

He laughed as if he could read her thoughts, then stroked her cheek with the back of his finger. "I have somewhere to be, so I'll leave you to your thoughts. Maybe you can think about how this all might have been avoided if you had just done as I said?" He chucked her on the bottom of her chin, and she jerked her head away from him, making him laugh again. "Maybe a bit of time to think will make sure you don't forget that in the future."

He patted the shoulder of the man sitting in a chair, his back to the only window in the small space. "My man here is going to keep a close eye on you, so don't try anything funny, now."

She looked at the man, eyebrows rising skeptically. He was slumped forward, hat pulled down low over his face.

"Don't worry about him. He'll do what needs doing." Edward tipped his hat at her in a mock show of gentility and left. She listened as his horse pounded off into the distance, and when those sounds faded, there was nothing left behind.

The darkness of the small cabin pressed in around her, the air thick with the scent of damp wood and the lingering smoke from a long-dead fire. Her heart pounded like a war drum against her ribs, every nerve in her body on edge as she waited for the next blow, the next cruel word, the next moment when her fate would be decided.

She peered at the man left behind, but he didn't move a muscle. She called out a muffled cry, hoping to get his attention, but he stayed still as a stone, not responding at all. It was hard to make out any of his features in the gloom. Finally, she settled back against her chair and struggled to find a position that did not make her arms ache.

Time passed, but nothing changed in the cabin. The man stayed still and silent, her arms continued to protest their positioning, and the gag continued to taste awful. She could not use it to keep her panic at bay any longer. The taste was so overpowering it was all she could do not to retch.

"Please," she attempted to call to the man through the gag. "Please, just at least remove this gag."

He made no move in response, and suspicion began to grow inside of her. Before she could think on that, however, a sound outside, a crunch of footsteps against the wet leaves, sent a fresh wave of panic through her. Had they come back? Had Edward and Mitchell returned to finish what they started?

She jerked at the restraints, her muffled cry of terror smothered by the gag. Tears stung her eyes as she thrashed, her muscles screaming in protest. She didn't want to die here, bound and helpless in some forgotten shack in the woods.

She couldn't lose herself to panic. If she did, all would be lost. She forced herself to pay attention to her surroundings, to hook her attention into something to quell the rising tide of fear inside of her.

The lantern flickered beside her, its glow casting long shadows on the rough plank walls. Closing her eyes, she explored the room with her other senses. The faint scent of lamp oil and pine sap stirred something in her, something old. For a moment, she wasn't in a cabin in the woods, tied to a chair. She was ten years old, curled up on the wide windowsill of her father's study.

She used to sneak in there when the house quieted in the evenings, still dressed in her riding clothes, boots kicked off in the hallway. Her father never sent her away. He'd look up from his books, smile in that quiet, steady way of his, and pat the armchair beside him.

Her mother would come in with a plate of biscuits, and May would sit cross-legged on the rug, listening as they spoke in low, thoughtful tones about the ranch, about rainfall and herd counts, about what they would plant come spring. It wasn't just numbers and work to them. It was *theirs*. Horses and land they loved. The things they taught her to love as well.

She remembered the crackle of the fireplace, the warm amber glow that lit the room, and the smell of oil and wood polish that clung to her father's hands when he tousled her hair. He had taught her how to read ledgers before she was twelve. Her mother had pushed for her to lead the men during branding week by fourteen. They gave her everything, not just comfort and softness, but confidence, expectation. Trust.

She'd grown up believing she would live forever in that house. That she would marry someone strong and kind, someone she had chosen for herself and for the ranch, and that her children would run through those same halls.

Her throat tightened.

Instead, here she was. Tied to a splintered chair in a stranger's shack, gagged like an animal. Her jaw ached, and her wrists burned. The wood floor was cold beneath her feet.

What would her father say, if he could see her now? What would her mother do?

She knew the answer.

They would come for her. No matter how far, no matter the risk, they would come.

The tears slipped down her cheeks before she could stop them. She bowed her head, shoulders shaking once, quietly. Then she lifted her chin.

Harry would come. He had to.

And if he didn't.... Well, May Allen had not survived finishing school, herd drives, and Edward by being delicate. She would find a way.

She *would.*

Resolve hardened inside of her, sweeping out the last of the lingering panic, the desire to give in and be afraid.

May shifted her weight, slow and careful, testing the ropes around her wrists again. The chair creaked faintly beneath her, the sound far too loud in the quiet of the shack. She froze, her eyes flicking toward the man in the corner.

He hadn't moved. He just sat there, broad-shouldered and still, the brim of his hat casting his face in shadow. She couldn't tell if he was asleep, or just biding his time. Waiting. Watching.

Her earlier suspicion arose once more.

Something was not right here.

She counted to ten under her breath, the way her mother had taught her when facing down a room full of cowhands who didn't yet believe a girl could run a ranch. Then she did it again.

She needed a plan.

The chair legs were uneven, and if she could rock just right, just enough, maybe she could get the back leg to splinter. Then the ropes might slip. Or loosen. Or at least allow her to have one hand free.

She gritted her teeth, then remembered there was cloth there and stopped, wincing. She knew this plan wasn't much of a plan at all—it was a hare-brained mess of possibilities—but she couldn't just sit here and be afraid.

She curled her fingers as much as she could, feeling for a knot, a frayed edge, anything to work with. The rope scraped her skin raw. Still, she moved her fingers slowly, flexing and stretching, biting down against the pain.

She kept one eye on the man in the corner.

No movement. Not even a twitch.

Maybe he was asleep. Or drunk. Or cocky enough not to worry about a woman in skirts tied to a chair.

If that were the case, then that would be his mistake.

She shifted again, slower this time, rolling her shoulder just enough to test the give in the ropes. Nothing. They remained as stubbornly tight as ever.

The gag in her mouth muffled her breath, but she tried to stay quiet. She could feel sweat gathering at the back of her neck despite the chill. She blinked it away from her lashes and kept working.

Another glance at the man, still unmoving.

Something about him didn't feel right. She squinted at the outline of his chest, the way the light caught on the folds of his coat. It looked stiff. Lumpy, almost.

Her brow furrowed. Was he—

The door creaked faintly in the wind, and her heart jumped. Her gaze snapped to it. No one entered.

When she looked back at the man, she noticed that his sleeve had shifted slightly in the lantern light. It wasn't filled out; it was just...hanging there.

Her breath caught.

That wasn't a man.

It was clothes. Stuffed. Propped up on a chair. Like some sort of scarecrow, only who was it supposed to scare? She didn't think it would have been left there purely for her sake.

Her blood ran cold with realization.

This wasn't a guard. It was a trap, a delay. She suddenly felt sure it was there to greet Harry when he arrived to save her. They had left her here for Harry to find, and they had not even left a real man along with her to guard her. Why would they do that?

And if they'd gone to the trouble of luring Harry away, of making her believe she was being watched, then what was happening back at the ranch?

She pulled against the ropes harder now, heedless of the noise, heedless of the pain.

"Harry," she tried to say around the gag, but it came out muffled and broken.

Panic surged in her chest and, along with it, questions she had been forcing herself not to ask bubbled up to the surface. Would Harry come for her first, or would he go straight to the ranch? Would he be more focused on hunting down the men who had taken so much from him and wanted to take more?

Then, as if he had heard her call, through the dim light creeping through the cracks in the walls, she saw movement. It was a shadow. Broad shoulders, a familiar gait, a presence she knew down to her bones.

It was Harry.

Relief crashed over her so powerfully that for a moment, she felt weightless, as if she might simply dissolve into the air. She tried to call out, but the gag turned her cry into a muffled sob.

The door to the shack flew open with a bang, smashing so hard against the opposite wall that she wondered that it hadn't separated clean from its hinges. Joseph and Harry burst in together, guns drawn.

"Let. Her. Go." Harry's voice boomed through the small space, echoing off the walls.

Joseph and Harry had their guns trained on the man, who still had not moved. She made to warn them that he wasn't real, calling out through the gag, but they could not understand her.

"Put your hands where I can see them."

Neither man moved for a breath, their eyes locked on the figure in the chair.

But the figure still did not stir.

Joseph took a step forward. "You deaf, there? The man said, 'Drop your weapon.'"

Silence. May tried to speak again, irritation a wave crashing over her. They were here, and she was finally going to get this gag out of her mouth, but they were wasting time on a scarecrow. She wanted to scream in frustration.

Harry's brow furrowed as he looked at the body-shaped figure. He took a step forward, then another, gun aimed steady.

Joseph moved to the side, flanking the man, his boots whispering against the floor. He extended a hand and, in one swift motion, knocked the figure's hat from his head.

Straw spilled onto the floor, and Joseph cursed.

Harry lunged forward, grabbing the figure by the front of the shirt and yanking it from the chair. The whole thing collapsed in a heap of old clothing and dried grass, the crude stuffing spilling across the ground. She saw them both process that the "man" who had been guarding May was nothing more than a scarecrow, a trick meant to fool them from a distance, and it had worked.

"They played us," Joseph muttered, his voice thick with anger.

Harry wasted no time. He spun toward May, shoving his gun back into his holster as he reached her side. "May," he breathed, his hands working quickly to untie the knots binding her to the chair. His fingers trembled against hers as he freed her wrists, then tore the gag from her mouth.

May gasped, sucking in air, and before she could say a word, Harry crushed her against him. She leaned into him, savoring even the taste of the stale air of the old cabin now that the gag was finally out of her mouth, and sweeter still, the smell of him, and closed her eyes.

"I was so afraid," he murmured, his voice rough with emotion.

Tears blurred her vision as she clung to him, her fingers twisting in the fabric of his coat. "I-I thought—" She choked on the words, her throat raw from fear, from screaming against the gag. She had stayed strong, but now that he was here, she did not feel that she had to stay strong on her own any longer. He was here. He had come.

A fear struck her. "Julia?" she asked quickly. "She's all right?"

"She's safe, with Willa."

May relaxed back against him, awash in gratitude.

"I've got you," Harry whispered, pulling back just enough to cup her face in his hands. His eyes, dark and filled with an agony she'd never seen before, searched hers. "I swear to you, I'll never let them take you again."

She believed him.

But the moment of relief was short-lived.

May's mind snapped back to reality, the pieces falling into place with horrifying clarity. She looked up at Harry, panic flaring in her chest with what she needed to tell him, and she explained quickly the fact that they had left a strawman guarding her, that Edward had ridden east. That he had alluded to her being under his thumb in the future.

"They tricked you," she finished, gripping his arms. "They wanted you to come for me and leave the ranch unprotected."

Harry's expression darkened, realization dawning across his own features.

Joseph turned to face them and swore under his breath. "Edward's there now, isn't he? He'll be staking a claim to your ranch with no one there to stop him."

May nodded. "If they can hold it long enough, they'll try to make it legal. You know Edward. He'll have some document drawn up by morning, some excuse, some twisted law to take it from us." She bit her lip. "Even if he doesn't, it won't matter. He'll be there, and we'll be left out of it all."

Harry set his jaw, his hands tightening into fists. "Over my dead body."

Joseph moved restlessly nearby, his rifle slung over his shoulder, scanning the trees through the cabin window. "We should go after the trail," he said. "It should still be fresh. We can make out for sure which direction they went if we move fast."

Harry didn't look away from May. "You go. I'll stay with her."

Joseph hesitated, just for a moment, then nodded. "I won't be long."

The door creaked shut behind him, and just like that, they were alone.

Harry still had not let go of her. Even now, with the ropes off, even after she'd coughed the gag from her mouth and gasped in a full breath, he stayed there, in front of her, one hand still around hers, the other steadying her shoulder like he needed the contact just as badly as she did, his body angled between her and the door.

"I'm fine," she whispered, though her voice was hoarse, and her wrists were raw and red. The skin had split in two places. "I just—"

Harry looked down and caught sight of the abrasions.

He inhaled sharply through his teeth. "My God, May."

She started to pull her hand away, embarrassed by the blood, but he held it gently in his own.

"I should've been here sooner."

"You came," she said, her voice firmer now. "That's all that matters."

Harry leaned back on his heels, studying her face like he didn't quite believe she was real. "I was so afraid I wouldn't make it to you in time. I didn't know what they were planning. I didn't know if I would get to you before it was too late."

AVA WINTERS

May reached up and touched his jaw, just a light brush with her fingers. "You did."

He glanced down again, at her wrists, at the angry red rings where the ropes had cut. His hands curled into fists. "I'll kill him," he said quietly. "I swear it. Whatever Edward thought he could take, if he thought before I was going to stop him, I'm even more determined now."

May leaned forward slightly, enough that her knees brushed his. "Harry."

He met her eyes.

"There will be time to fight. And I know that you will do what needs doing." She paused. "But what matters most to me right now is that you stayed."

He looked at her like she'd knocked the wind out of him.

"I know what that cost you," she said. "Sending Joseph instead to track them. You're a man who goes first. You're the man who leads, who does the work himself to be sure it's done right." Her voice softened. "But you stayed. With me."

His throat worked. "You were hurt."

"You chose me."

"I'll keep choosing you," he said. "As long as I've got breath in my body."

It was so quiet in the cabin she could hear the clicking of the heat in the lantern, the slow settling of the logs in the stove. He was close, so close. His eyes searched hers, and for a long, breathless moment, nothing moved.

She leaned forward. He did, too.

Their foreheads nearly touched.

246

May let out the faintest breath, and he caught it like it meant something.

Then the door burst open.

"Hoof prints," Joseph said, wiping rain from his coat. "Fresh and deep. Headed east. It's just as we thought."

Harry stood slowly, his body tightening again like a man ready for war.

Joseph met his gaze. "They're going to your place. They're headed to the ranch."

May closed her eyes.

Of course, they were.

Joseph slung his rifle back over his shoulder, swiping his wet hair from his eyes. "We need to get moving before these crooks can carry out whatever they're planning to do."

May's legs were weak, shaking beneath her, but she pushed forward. She wouldn't be left behind, not now.

Harry turned to her, his eyes conflicted. "May—"

"I'm coming," she said, cutting him off. "That's my home they're trying to lay claim to."

He hesitated for only a breath before nodding, reaching for her hand. "Let's go."

The three of them burst from the cabin and into the rain-drenched woods, moving swiftly through the trees. Lightning flashed in the distance, illuminating the path ahead, the muddy ground sucking at their boots with every hurricd step.

She ached to go home, to stretch in her bed and wash the stench of this terrible place off of her, but there would be no time for that. If they didn't win this battle, she would never be able to do those things again.

She squared her shoulders and thought of her parents, of what they would do. She knew they were watching, marching alongside them, and glanced, just once, up into the dark sky, nodding.

"Joseph," she said, turning to him. His face was taut, his lips pulled tight. She knew she could count on him. He had always been there for her and her family, just as her parents had looked out for him, once upon a time. "Are there others who can help us? Can you ride ahead and gather anyone who is willing to stand up against the sheriff?" She chewed her lip. "I know it's a big ask."

He set his jaw. "I'm sure I can find a few."

He and Harry clasped hands, and before he jumped into his saddle, he turned to May and pressed a kiss to her cheek. "Be safe. I can't be going home and telling Willa that something else has happened to you. She'd have my head." A quick, mischievous smile overtook his face, and then, he was gone, kicking his horse's sides and riding out into the deepening dark.

Harry took her hand in his as they walked to his horse, his grip strong and sure. There were many obstacles ahead of them, obstacles that could perhaps be insurmountable, but she was not afraid. Not anymore.

Harry was beside her, good friends were on their way to help them, and together, they were going to protect the Allen land together.

And God help anyone who stood in their way.

Chapter Thirty-Two

Harry had no idea how they were going to win this fight. He could feel May's grip around his waist, and from her touch, from the look on her face, all he could see and sense was a surety from her. She was not afraid. She trusted him. But all he could think was that he could be bringing her smack dab into the center of a fight it was impossible to win.

Edward and Mitchell had the upper hand. They had the power of the local lawmen on their side, they had weapons, and they had already made a move on the ranch. If Harry had been thinking clearly, he might have stopped for more help, might have come up with a plan before charging back here. But there hadn't been time for caution, not with May in danger, not with everything on the line.

So, he had left everything that mattered to May open for the taking. He had failed her, allowing her to be kidnapped by them at all, and now again, by allowing these men to make a move on her land and her family's legacy.

He wondered how many men Joseph would be able to gather in this short period of time. He was sure they could count on William, on Earl. Maybe a few of the others who had sat around the table at Joseph's. But May was right; it was an awful lot to ask of people to stand against the law in their town. It was more than risky; it was downright foolish.

And yet, as he and May rode through the trees headed into town, the sound of doors opening and hushed voices made him slow.

At first, his heart leaped to his throat. Was it more of Edward's men? Had they been ambushed before they even reached the ranch? He tensed, putting a hand to the holster at his hip. The moonlight filtered weakly through the thinning canopy, casting shadows that flickered like ghosts across the damp earth.

As he rode closer, the figures emerged from the dark more clearly.

The figures were not enemies. They were neighbors.

"We're with you," came one voice, clear and strong across the road.

Harry's head snapped toward the sound. It was coming from Miss Carter's boarding house. The widow stood on the porch, a lantern in her hand, her sharp eyes assessing them in the dim glow.

Before he could answer, another voice called out. And then another.

Mr. Walsh, the blacksmith, stepped out of his shop, wiping soot-stained hands on his apron. Mrs. Moreno, still in her nightclothes, stood on her stoop with a rifle in her arms. Young Tommy Higgins appeared in the doorway of the general store, holding his father's old shotgun like it was the only thing keeping him standing.

More and more of them emerged onto the street, lanterns bobbing in the darkness, voices calling out together. These were people who had lived under Mitchell's corrupt rule for too long, saw him take what he wanted and hurt anyone who stood in his way. They were tired of it. And tonight, they saw their chance.

Joseph sat tall in his saddle at the fork at the end of the road leading out of town, toward the Allen ranch. He nodded once at Harry, and Harry knew what he had to do.

Dust swirled in the air as Harry guided his horse to the front, saddle leather creaking as he turned to face the crowd. Men with weathered hands and women with steady eyes looked back at him, some clutching hunting rifles, others holding only pitchforks or lanterns.

Harry addressed the growing group. "Sheriff Mitchell and Edward have taken the Allen ranch," he told them, voice rough with exhaustion and fury. "They took May and tried to force her hand. They mean to keep her land as their own. But we're taking it back."

He pulled off his hat, holding it low against his leg. "I never thought I'd be the one standing here, asking you to fight," he began, his voice quiet but strong. "I came to this town looking for peace. I found a home, a family, and a place where law was supposed to mean something."

A murmur of agreement rippled through the crowd.

He went on, voice gaining strength. "But what kind of law lets a man like Sheriff Mitchell walk free? What kind of justice lets him turn on his own people? On you?" He looked out at the faces he'd come to know: shopkeepers, ranch hands, mothers and sons.

"He took bribes from the gang that's been bleeding this land dry. He turned his back when your barns were burned and your cattle stolen. He looked away when Edward Allen"—his voice caught briefly on the name—"laid claim to something that never belonged to him. And in the process, he harmed the woman I love to get it."

Someone near the front, who he recognized as Miss Carter, lifted her chin. "He told me my boy's thievin' was his own fault. But Mitchell knew who'd done it. Didn't lift a finger."

A young man in suspenders stepped forward. "He took ten dollars from my pa, said it'd keep our property safe. Next week, our fence was burned and our well poisoned."

Murmurs turned to muttering.

The tension swelled.

Harry held his hand up, steady. "I won't pretend this will be easy. They've got guns and numbers. But they don't have what we do." He gestured to the crowd. "We have each other. We have a community that's tired of being bullied. We have a reason to fight."

He let that hang in the air for a moment before adding, "You don't have to come with me. I'll go, even if it's alone. But if you ride beside me, if we go together, we show them this town won't kneel for crooks in badges or men with stolen deeds."

A beat of silence passed. Then, a voice rang out from the back. It was Mr. Walsh, the blacksmith, towering and soot-smudged. "I got a daughter asleep in my house. I'll be darned if I let men like that decide her future."

A silence settled over the gathered crowd.

He swallowed. "It's a risk to join us. We both know that. But anyone who does will have our undying gratitude."

May cleared her throat. "Please," she called out, and he knew what it must cost her, a woman who had for so long stood strong on her dignity and ability to get things done on her own. But she didn't hesitate; she did not shy away from asking for help. "Please help us."

There was a long moment of silence.

Then, Earl wiped his hands on his apron and let out a long breath. "Well," he said, "guess we'd better get going."

More voices followed.

"We're with you."

"Enough is enough."

"Let's finish this."

Harry nodded, swallowing the tightness in his throat. "Then saddle up," he said. "We ride for justice."

One by one, they moved. Some grabbed their weapons from inside, while others joined with nothing but determination in their eyes. Yet, all followed as Harry and Joseph turned their horses toward the ranch.

What started as a handful of people became a dozen, then two dozen. More still joined as they made their way down the road, forming a growing train of bodies, a force moving through the night with quiet resolve.

Harry's throat felt tight. For so long, he had believed himself an outsider, someone who would always have to fight alone. He had spent years hunting for answers, never feeling like his house was his home after his wife died. He had come here with one goal: to raise Julia somewhere safe, somewhere he wouldn't have to look over his shoulder. But safety had always seemed just out of reach.

Even after coming here, he had kept his distance, never expecting anyone to stand with him when the time came.

But they were standing with him now.

Now, staring at these people—these farmers, smiths, merchants, all standing beside him, ready to fight for what was right, he realized something that nearly stole his breath.

He wasn't alone anymore.

Joseph clapped a hand on his shoulder as he rode up to his side, grinning at the look on his face. "Told you people 'round here wouldn't stand for this."

Harry exhaled sharply, shaking his head as he turned back toward the ranch.

They slowed their pace to accommodate those on foot. Now that they had more people with them, he felt less pressed to get to the ranch in a hurry, like he had more time to think things through.

As they approached the bend in the road that would lead to the drive, Harry called the group to a stop. They dismounted their horses, and he, Joseph, and a few other men slipped around the side of the property, moving silently through the tree line so that they could take a look at the ranch without revealing themselves.

The house loomed in the near distance as they cut through the darkness, warm light spilling from the windows. The woods were thick with breath and boots, the underbrush quieting only as the group huddled together beneath a grove of pin oaks that bordered the Allen ranch's northern fence line.

Edward paced on the porch, hands clasped behind his back, his usual smirk replaced with something more calculating. Mitchell stood beside him, the lazy slouch of his shoulders betraying just how comfortable he was playing the role of lawman while protecting a band of criminals.

Around the property, figures moved in the darkness, men neither he nor Joseph recognized, patrolling the perimeter with rifles slung over their shoulders. They walked like they owned the place. Like they had already won.

The ranch hands had reported to Joseph that the men had ousted them, sending Adam and all of the ranch staff on their way with guns at their backs. Adam had, of course, fought back. He'd been knocked unconscious once more, and was now under the care of the town doctor at his home.

Not having Adam at their sides was a loss, but Harry was glad he was getting the care he needed, and the ranch hands and household staff had joined their cause eagerly.

Harry clenched his fists.

These men were wrong to think they had won by simply moving in to a home that was not theirs. He would not let them get away with it.

Joseph crouched beside him. "They got more guns, but we got more people."

"We need a plan," Harry said, his voice low but firm. "Let's go back and think this through."

They made their way back as silently as they came, and as they walked up to their ragtag group, he surveyed the gathered townsfolk as he and Joseph talked through what they had seen. These were good people, but they weren't soldiers. He couldn't lead them into a bloodbath. He had to be smart. "We need to draw them out, separate them—"

"We can't match them in firepower," said Henry Mott, the aging owner of the dry goods store. "If we rush in, we'll get slaughtered."

There was a ripple of quiet agreement, along with the anxious sounds of boots shifting and throats clearing.

"We have more people," someone else muttered.

"Sure, but not more guns." It was the same thought on repeat, the same wall they were running into again and again.

"I have an idea."

Harry turned at the sound of May's voice.

She had come to stand beside him, the moonlight illuminating the sharp determination in her eyes. Her face was still pale from her ordeal, but there was steel in her spine, a fire that no amount of fear could extinguish. She stood straight and composed, looking like she'd slipped into something familiar.

"They think they're clever," she said. "They baited Harry with a false guard; they knew how to draw him out. They swooped in and took the ranch while he was gone, coming after me." She gestured toward the house. "They think they've won."

Harry watched her. He could see something settle over her as she looked at the land, her land. She wasn't afraid any longer. In her face, all he could see was resolve.

"What if we used their own trick against them?" she said.

Some heads turned toward her.

"What do you mean?" Harry asked.

"They lured you away from the house by using me as bait." Her gaze flickered toward the ranch, then back to him. "I say we do the same to them."

Harry frowned, not understanding.

"Give them something to chase," she said. "Lure them out of the house, split them up, and leave the rest of you to take it back."

Joseph let out a low whistle. "That's awfully risky."

"I know it is," May admitted. "But we don't have the numbers to take them head-on, not with them dug in like you say. If we can shake them up, split them up, cause chaos and confusion, then we will have a better chance of retaking it."

There was a long pause.

Then Joseph grinned. "They'll be out in the open. And we'll have the high ground."

"Exactly," May said.

Someone chuckled quietly.

"Reckon that's what they deserve," muttered a voice from the back.

Harry glanced around at the group. Faces that had been tight with fear now carried something different: belief. They looked at May like they could already see the plan working.

Henry Mott shook his head slowly. "You're your father's daughter, all right," he said, his voice warm.

May dipped her head. "He taught me how to protect this land. I don't intend to lose it."

Harry stepped closer to her. "Neither do I."

Their eyes met for just a second longer than they had to.

Then, he turned to the others. "You heard her. Let's get to work."

As everyone began to move, whispered details passing from person to person, he bit his lip. He hated the plan. Every part of him recoiled at the thought of May putting herself in danger again. He had barely gotten her back, and he wasn't about to lose her now. But he also knew she was right.

Mitchell was arrogant. He thought himself untouchable. If they gave him a reason to leave the house, he would take it, never stopping to question whether he might be beat.

Harry looked around at the group, at the neighbors who had come together for this fight.

He wasn't alone anymore. And as much as he hated the idea, this might be their best shot.

His jaw tightened. "All right," he said quietly to himself, looking out across the ragtag army they were building, his voice steady. "All right, then. Let's give them a taste of their own medicine."

Joseph took three men and slipped off toward the barn to assess the fencing and guards. Others spread through the trees, rifles checked and loaded, boots muffled against the damp earth.

Harry stayed near May. She moved quietly through the trees, murmuring about a fence line she wanted to check. The night settled deeper. A low mist crawled over the field, and far off, a barn owl called once and fell silent.

He followed her, keeping one eye on the house. He could just make out Edward pacing in front of the porch. Another man sat on the fence rail, his rifle across his knees.

It was strange, looking at the manor this way. When he had first arrived, he had thought only of how it was too fine a house for the likes of him, how he hadn't earned the right to live in it. He shook his head.

"Do you think they'll take the bait?" May asked.

"If they're arrogant enough to try this in the first place," Harry said, "they're arrogant enough to fall for that."

She stepped up beside him, wrapping her coat more tightly around her shoulders. He saw her fingers tremble just once before she stilled them.

He reached for her hand and held it between both of his.

Her skin was cold.

"You still have time to go back to Willa's," he said softly. "This doesn't have to be your fight."

"It's my ranch," she said. "It's my family's name on it. It's my parents' hard work, my hard work, that went into it." Her eyes met his again. "This fight belongs to me as much as it does to you."

He nodded.

They stood like that for a long moment. Not touching now, but close enough that he could feel her resolve like heat off a flame.

"Harry," she said, quieter now. "If something happens—"

"Don't," he said. "Nothing is going to happen."

"But if it does."

He looked at her. Really looked. The way her jaw stayed firm even with fear flickering behind her eyes. The way she wasn't asking for comfort, only for honesty.

"I'll protect you," he said. "With everything I've got."

A crack of wood sounded nearby, and they both looked around sharply, but it was just Joseph returning from the barn.

"Just one guard on the barn. He's sitting around front. Not a single man around the paddock side."

Harry gave a single nod.

Then, he looked at the house one last time and exhaled.

"Let's finish this."

Chapter Thirty-Three

After Joseph and Harry had circled the property a few more times, the plan she had started had begun to take shape.

"There's only one man on the back east side of the property," Joseph had explained. "That's our entry point. That's where they aren't paying attention."

"There's a weak spot in the fences here, where the east fields open up into the horse paddock." May quickly drew a line in the dirt with her finger to indicate fencing and then marked an X in one spot.

"Good," Joseph said. "That's very good."

Harry and Joseph had been ready to strike right away, but May convinced them to wait until morning.

"They'll be expecting a nighttime attack. They know we're worked up and desperate; they know we are panicking. They'll be ready and waiting for us. If we wait them out, hit at first light, we might catch them tired and more unaware."

They both reluctantly saw the sense in that, and Joseph spread through the group of townspeople, asking them all to meet back in the minutes before dawn the next morning, telling them what they needed to bring to make May's plan come to life.

Joseph had returned eagerly to Willa and had sworn to keep a close eye on Julia. Harry didn't like being separated from her but knew it was likely safer that way. The rest of the townspeople returned to their own homes, and May and Harry watched them go, struck anew by their own inability to do the same.

The Wellingtons had offered to take them in, and they were grateful, but May tried not to let the fear gnaw at her as they followed them into their small, sturdy cabin, thinking that if all did not go to plan tomorrow, this could be how she spent the rest of her life: dependent on the kindness and generosity of friends and neighbors with nowhere of her own to lay her head.

The Wellington house was quiet, tucked back from the main road in town behind a windbreak of cottonwoods that rustled softly in the cool night breeze. May sat near the hearth, her hands folded in her lap, though they wouldn't stop trembling. She stared into the fire, watching the flames lick the logs, throwing soft amber light across the parlor walls. The warmth couldn't quite reach the tight knot in her chest.

Harry sat across from her, polishing his revolver with a rag, the motion slow and methodical. He hadn't said much since supper, and neither had she. Every sound outside made her flinch, every gust of wind, every creak of the shutters.

Mrs. Wellington had fed them cornbread, dried venison, and apples stewed with cinnamon, served on mismatched porcelain dishes that had clearly survived the journey west in a covered wagon. May had eaten out of politeness, though her stomach twisted with nerves.

Now, the house settled into the quiet of a tense, sleepless night. Mr. and Mrs. Wellington had bid them good night and retired for the evening, but May and Harry were too full of nervous energy to do the same.

She looked at Harry now, his profile limned in firelight, his brows furrowed in that way he got when he was working through something heavy. The lines around his eyes seemed deeper tonight. He wore a loose shirt, collar unbuttoned, sleeves rolled to his forearms. His suspenders hung down, and his boots were beside the hearth. He looked tired. Older than he had when they had first met, though that was not so long ago. But solid and steady, like he always did when she needed him to.

"I can't sit still," she said suddenly, her voice barely above a whisper.

Harry looked up. "Would it help to walk a little?"

She shook her head. "I have already walked the length of this room a dozen times." Her hands twisted in her lap. "I just keep thinking...what if it doesn't work? What if they hurt someone? What if we lose everything?"

Harry finished his work, then carefully placed the revolver down and stood, crossing the room in two strides. He crouched in front of her, taking her hands into his. His fingers were warm and calloused, and their roughness grounded her.

"I've seen you face worse than this, May. You didn't back down when they took you. You didn't give up when they hurt you. And tonight? You outsmarted them. You got us here, and I know together, we'll beat them."

His belief in her should have made her feel better, but instead, she could not stop wondering if she was right after all. She bit her lip and rocked forward, putting her hands on her knees. "It's just a plan," she said softly, twisting her fingers together. "A good one, maybe. But we don't know if—"

"Hey." He gently tipped her chin up so she'd meet his gaze. "We're not alone any more. We've got half the town behind us. People who are tired of looking the other way. You lit that fire, May."

She blinked fast. "I was just scared. And angry, I suppose."

"And you did something about it." He smiled, small and tired, but warm. "You gave them a reason to stand up."

Silence stretched between them, easy for a moment. The fire popped. Somewhere upstairs, a floorboard creaked.

Harry stood and offered her his hand. "Come sit with me a while. Over here."

She let him pull her up and guide her to the small bench by the window. They sat together in the moonlight, the prairie stretching silver and endless beyond the glass. The wind blew gently through the cottonwoods outside. Harry rested his arm across the back of the bench, and May leaned into him without thinking, her head against his shoulder.

"You remember that chestnut colt you helped me with last month?" he asked after a while.

She gave a soft laugh. "The one that kept bucking every time you tried to put the saddle on? I thought you were going to swear off horses altogether."

"I nearly did," he said, chuckling. "Until you walked right into that corral like you had nothing to prove. You spoke to him so calmly I thought he'd fall asleep standing up."

"I just knew he was scared," she said. "He'd been tied up too long, handled too rough. It wasn't me that fixed it; all it took was patience."

Harry looked down at her, his voice quieter. "Still. I watched you that whole afternoon. You didn't yell, didn't flinch when he reared. You just stood your ground. You made him trust you. I remember thinking—"

He paused, uncertain.

"What?" she asked.

"I remember thinking I'd never seen anyone braver."

A flush rose in her cheeks. She glanced down at their hands, still twined together in her lap. "I didn't feel brave. I just didn't want to see him broken."

"Exactly," he murmured. "That's who you are."

She laughed suddenly, a quiet, surprised sound. "You were so gruff back then. I didn't think you liked me at all."

"I was gruff because I liked you too much," he admitted.

The admission sank into the quiet, slow and tender. The room settled into stillness. The fire was down to glowing embers, and upstairs, the house was silent, as if holding its breath for morning.

She turned to look at him. "What happens after tomorrow?"

He reached for her hand again, threading their fingers together. "We take care of each other. However we can. One day at a time."

Outside, the wind shifted. The house groaned with age, but it felt safe here. For now.

They sat like that for a long time, listening to the wind, the fire dying down to glowing coals. The future pressed close and uncertain, but May found herself clinging to the peace of this moment. She didn't know what the next sunrise would bring. But Harry was here. And that, for now, was enough.

They finally said a quiet good night and retreated to their separate rooms. Harry would be staying out in the main living area on a cot, blocking the only door into the house. May was in a small side room, what looked to have once belonged to the Wellingtons' children, all of whom were now long grown. She had assumed she would not be able to sleep a wink, that she would toss and turn in the small, narrow bed all night long, but with Harry's whispers in her ears and the knowledge that no matter what, they would stay strong together, she found herself falling into a deep, dreamless sleep.

She slept so deeply, in fact, that Harry had to wake her the next morning, the room still black. She felt his hand touch her shoulder in the dark, and instead of being afraid, even in her sleep, she knew his touch.

She leaned into him for one brief moment and then stood. He returned back downstairs while she dressed, splashed cold water on her face, and followed.

The Wellingtons had made coffee, strong and bitter, no cream or sugar like she had back at the ranch, but no matter. It suited the day. They ate a quick, simple breakfast and then made their way back to the meeting point they had set the day before.

Though the sun had not yet begun to rise, the meeting spot already teemed with townsfolk. Harry had worried that if they lost the momentum of the prior evening, if people returned home, that they would not come back again. In the night, their rational minds would take over, and they would talk themselves out of taking action against the town's only lawman.

"Not here," May had assured him. "Not these people. When someone here says something, they mean it."

And she had been right.

They all stood now, faces shadowed in the dark, but here, ready.

People passed strips of dried beef, whispered plans, gripped shoulders, and shared strength as the sky deepened and the moon began to decline, and finally, the sun started its rise.

The woods were quiet except for the occasional shifting of boots on pine needles, the soft clink of a rifle being checked one more time. Everyone was waiting, watching the Allen ranch from the cover of the trees as the sky turned the color of bruised ash.

"Do you really think this will work?"

Harry and May turned to the sound of the voice. It was Thomas Cobb, the young blacksmith's apprentice with broad shoulders and nervous eyes. He held his rifle wrong, like it felt foreign in his hands. May's father had taught her enough about guns to know her way around them, and even she could tell by the angle that he was uncomfortable with the lightness of it, likely more used to the heavy tools he used in his day-to-day trade. The boy's voice was quiet but edged with tension.

"If we're wrong," Thomas continued, "if we go in there and they're ready for us, what happens then? What happens if we lose?"

Heads nearby turned. Not all the way, not enough to admit they were listening, but May knew they were.

She watched as Harry stepped closer to the young man and lowered his voice.

"If we lose," Harry said, "they won't stop with the ranch. Edward will be a ranch owner; he will have the money and power to run this town in whatever way he wants to. Mitchell will jail anyone who speaks against him. And the rest of us, those of us who stood up, might not live long enough to regret it."

Thomas swallowed hard. "That's what I'm afraid of."

Harry nodded. "Me, too."

266

The frank admission quieted the others more than any false bravado ever could.

"But here's the truth," Harry continued. "Every one of us standing here has already made a decision. We came out here tonight because we knew something had to change. Because we knew we couldn't let a man like Edward Allen win by force. Because we're tired of watching men like Mitchell carry a badge they don't deserve."

He turned to look around the group as a whole now, not just at Thomas.

"I can't promise you this will be easy. And I can't promise you we'll all walk away without a scratch. But I can promise you this: I will not leave anyone behind. I will fight beside you until the last of them is gone or the sun comes up, whichever comes first."

A few heads nodded. More than a few now.

Harry turned back to Thomas.

"Fear doesn't make you weak," he said. "It makes you careful. It keeps you sharp. Just don't let it stop you."

Thomas straightened slightly and gave a small, tight nod. His hands still trembled, but his grip on the rifle steadied.

"Thank you," he said.

Harry gave him a brief pat on the shoulder. "We'll get through this."

From the edge of the woods, May met his eyes. She didn't speak, but she hoped that he could see the pride there, unmistakable. She believed in him. And whether he felt ready or not, she hoped it would be enough to know that.

Behind them, the wind stirred the leaves. Somewhere in the near distance, a dog barked.

It was almost time.

Harry leaned in close to Thomas and gently corrected his hold on the rifle, shifting his hands so that they were far enough apart to handle the weight of the gun more easily. He spoke instructions in a low voice, and as he did, a few other young men gathered in close, listening and adjusting as well. It was enough to bide the time, until the sky began to lighten.

Until it was time to make their move.

The chill of early morning clung to the ground, the prairie grass wet with dew, the sun still no more than a golden smudge behind a low bank of clouds.

And the group had begun to split.

Those with rifles and grit in their teeth followed Harry deeper into the tree line, crouched low and moving quiet as ghosts. The rest, the women, older men, the few injured or green enough to hold back, gathered behind May, heading toward the edge of the eastern pasture. The horses would be there, penned up in the dark, waiting, though they didn't know that yet.

She turned toward the pasture, heart pounding beneath her coat. The horses would be restless by now. They would smell the tension in the air.

Harry caught May's arm before she could follow them.

"You sure about this?" he asked, his voice low and rough.

May looked up at him. His eyes searched hers like he might find a way to stop her, like part of him still didn't want her to go.

"I'm sure," she said. "The horses will follow me. I know where to lead them, and I know the land better than anyone else here."

"You don't have to—"

"Yes, I do." She kept her voice calm, steady. "They're counting on me. You are, too."

He opened his mouth, then closed it. His jaw worked, and it looked to her as if it was tense with the things he wanted to say but couldn't.

"If something goes wrong—"

"It won't," she said quickly. Then she added, more softly, "But if it does, you find Julia. You protect her."

His eyes left hers, looking out to the side, toward the ranch, and he nodded once. "Always."

There was a beat of silence, heavy with everything they hadn't had the time to say to each other. They had had so little time together, and yet, the connection she felt between them was as strong as steel.

She reached up then, almost without thinking, and straightened the edge of his collar. His coat was worn, frayed in one spot near the seam, and for some reason, that small imperfection made her throat tighten.

"You're a good man, Harry," she said. "Whatever happens tonight, whatever's already happened, you should know that."

His hand came up and covered hers where it rested against his chest. "I never wanted to bring danger to you."

"You didn't." She gave him a faint smile. "This is all my cousin's doing. Without you, I'd be under his thumb. In that house but powerless."

He exhaled sharply, like that had hit him somewhere deep. He leaned in, forehead brushing hers for just a moment. His breath was warm and steady. She wanted to stay there, just like that, until the world stilled.

But time wouldn't slow for them. It was time to go.

May stepped back before the ache of the moment could swallow her whole. She joined the group moving ahead of her, pulling on her gloves, and gave a small nod. "Let's go."

The dogs shifted forward, barely restrained, and the women tightened their reins, ready. May didn't look back as she led them toward the pasture. There was no room for doubt now. Only the path forward.

She could feel Harry watching her until the trees swallowed her.

They made their way together, quiet, grips tight on the dogs, until they stood at the far edge of the ranch, just past the barn, where the fence dipped and bowed beneath the weight of late-season wind and wear. She remembered fixing that section herself, hammering in a few bent nails, muttering under her breath while Julia stacked pebbles nearby. She remembered grumbling to herself about the rot, the way the wire sagged between the beams. Now, that weakness was their advantage. Her quick fix hadn't been perfect. But it had been enough. Enough to hold. Enough, now, to break.

A fine mist hung in the air, catching in her throat and curling her hair with damp. Around her, the group assembled, the women with their shawls drawn tight, eyes steeled with purpose, the men hanging back for now. Some clutched pitchforks or old rifles. Others had nothing more than the steel in their gaze. The women who made up the front line all held tight to herding dogs.

May stepped forward, close to the fence, her gloved fingers finding the same spot where the wood had warped. Her stomach fluttered, not with fear, though that lingered, but with anticipation, the feeling of standing on a wire between courage and collapse. The herding dogs shifted at their heels, ears alert, waiting for the signal.

She whistled, sharp and sure. The same call she'd used since childhood.

From the open pasture, several horses lifted their heads. Sweetpea whinnied, her dappled coat pale in the mist. Grit stamped and turned. Old Bandit ambled forward like he knew something was afoot.

"That's it," May whispered. "Come on now."

She gave another whistle. Her voice cracked as she called out. "Come on. It's me."

May reached out and tugged on the loosened wire, careful not to rattle it too loudly. It gave easily. With practiced hands, she peeled back the fence just enough to create a gap wide enough for the horses to pass. "This way," she whispered.

Two boys crept forward with feed sacks in hand, the rustling drawing the attention of the ranch's horses beyond the fence. May cupped her hands around her mouth and gave one more sharp, clear whistle.

A pause, and then a snort. The creak of hooves shifting. Then a low whinny in the fog.

They came slowly at first, ears forward, nostrils flaring at the scent of people. Then, one of the lead mares, May's favorite, a cinnamon-colored mare named June, recognized her. She let out a high call and began trotting forward. The rest followed, their hooves thudding softly over the cold, damp earth. The fence groaned, then cracked, splintering beneath their weight as they pushed past the rotted wood. The herd poured through.

May stepped aside as they surged through the broken fence, her heart pounding. "Go on," she said, voice thick. "Go."

The dogs took the lead then, barking and circling as they'd been trained. Townsfolk followed, waving arms and calling out, guiding the herd down the dirt lane. The sound grew louder as hooves struck packed earth, as the group moved toward the ranch house and, just beyond, the open road into town.

And then, just as planned, they crossed in front of the manor.

May had drawn the line carefully, because it was imperative that they be seen as quickly as possible, before they left the drive. The dogs and people moved just like they should, rounding the barn, crossing in front of the house, and running down the road, making their way for town.

May ran, too, skirts hiked in one fist, boots slick with mud, her heart pounding with each thud of the hooves pounding the air around her. She glanced back just once, toward the ranch house half-hidden by mist and distance.

"Keep to the road," she called. "Remember where we circle back."

One by one, as they moved past the outer farms and into town, doors opened. Sleepy eyes widened. People stepped out, some barefoot, some clutching their coats. The sight of the herd moving fast and purposeful pulled them from porches and shops. A few grabbed tools. Others, just their resolve. One by one, more joined their line, becoming part of the strange parade.

The group became a train: women, men, horses, and children trailing behind on tired legs. A growing line of resistance. They gathered them all and joined those who had been waiting at the meeting point, making a long, wide loop that turned back and headed toward the Allen ranch.

As the sun climbed, they crested the last bend before the ranch house came into full view. There it stood: May's home.

Mitchell stood on the porch, rifle in hand, brow furrowed. He called something to Edward.

Edward stepped out, eyes narrowing. He took one look at the oncoming herd and cursed, raising his arm to signal.

"What the—stop them!" he bellowed. "They're stealing the herd!"

A gang of men erupted into movement. There were shouts as weapons were grabbed, and Mitchell called orders from the porch. Men ran from the sides of the house and out the front door, tripping over each other in their haste.

But then came the second wave.

From the trees, where Harry and his group had waited, came a thunder of footsteps. Harry led them with his jaw set and revolver drawn. Joseph ran beside him, his rifle already raised. Townspeople poured from the woods, those who had circled behind, hidden by trees and fog.

"Now!" Harry shouted.

Gunfire cracked. The gang spun around, caught between two fronts. A few dropped their weapons. Others stood and fought. But it was clear to anyone that they had been caught on the back foot, unawares and unprepared.

Mitchell tried to rally them, shouting something lost in the din. Edward ran toward the corral, trying to cut off the herd, but May was already there, herding June and the others back around.

The horses added to the confusion of the men holding the ranch. None of them knew which way to look, who to listen to.

"The trees!" Mitchell shouted, but the sound disappeared beneath the pounding hooves.

One of the men May did not recognize leaped for one of the horses, trying to stop it, only to fall and have to roll to the side to avoid being crushed by its hooves.

The man who had stood in the doorway to the barn the morning Edward and Mitchell had taken her came running out of the barn once more. She wondered if he had been put in charge of watching over the horses. The thought made her smile grimly at how deeply he had failed at that role. The smile disappeared, however, when he caught her eye, and his brow furrowed, then cleared as his mouth stretched into a tobacco-stained, menacing grin.

She held tight to June as she continued to run, angling so that the horse would be between herself and the man, but he had begun to run.

He ran around the perimeter of the herd, bobbing and weaving to avoid the shouting townsfolk, the barking dogs, and the absolute chaos that had become the front of the stately manor in which she had grown up. That's when she realized.

He wasn't after the house.

He was after her.

Her breath hitched. She made a snap decision, pulling June so that she nearly came to a full stop and then climbing on top of the fence so that she could drop, bareback, onto her horse. She turned June with her knees, urging the mare into motion, but not quickly enough. The man raised his rifle and fired.

The bullet missed by a foot, slamming into the fencepost behind her with a sharp *crack*. Splinters flew. May ducked low against June's neck, gripping her mane, as the mare surged forward, hooves tearing up the damp earth.

"Come on, girl," she whispered. "As fast as you can."

The man broke into a run, cutting across the field to intercept her. Another shot rang out, closer this time. She twisted on June's back and saw him reloading, jaw clenched in frustration.

She heard Harry's voice through the noise, hoarse and furious. "May!"

He was in the tree line, fighting to break through a cluster of men. His rifle was lost, thrown down or taken, and he was ducking the fists of someone, throwing out hits of his own.

No—not just someone.

Edward.

The two of them crashed to the ground, fists flying, mud spraying up around them. But May couldn't watch. The gunman was almost on her.

She yanked June hard to the right, just as the man lunged. He missed the horse by inches but managed to grab May's boot. She kicked down hard, boot heel catching his shoulder, but it wasn't enough to shake him.

"Get off of me!" she shouted, leaning down, scrambling for anything to use to push him back and break his grip.

He pulled her leg again, nearly yanking her from her precarious seat atop the horse. But June reared, whinnying high and shrill. May scrambled for purchase, twisting both hands deep into June's mane, her knees pressed in against the horse's flanks for dear life, barely managing to keep her hold and stay upright. June's hooves struck out, and one caught the man square in the chest. He staggered back, eyes wide.

As June came back down to the earth, May twisted and kicked the man with everything she had.

This time, he went down.

Hard.

He didn't move again.

Chest heaving, May turned back to the trees and saw Edward crumpling beneath Harry's fists, collapsing to his knees in the mud. His lip was split wide, blood dribbling down his chin. Harry stood over him, shoulders heaving, one hand clenched so tight it shook.

She kicked June forward, closing the distance in seconds.

Harry turned at the sound of hooves and looked up at her, eyes wild and shining.

"Are you all right?" he asked, voice rough.

"I'm fine." She dismounted in a single motion, running the last few steps. "You?"

He nodded, just once, but it was enough.

She threw her arms around him without hesitation.

His arms came around her just as fiercely.

They didn't say anything for a moment. They didn't need to.

When they broke apart, the air between them was warm and charged.

Harry looked toward the chaos still raging near the house. "This isn't over."

"No," May said, as he put out his hands, boosting her so that she was back atop her horse. "But we're winning."

They raced back into the fight together.

Gunfire still cracked across the field, but the rhythm of it had changed. Slower now. More purposeful. The townsfolk had the upper hand.

May rode, Harry sprinting alongside her as they cut toward the barn. A woman's voice shouted from the rooftop: Cora, with her twin boys crouched low beside her, both firing down with steady precision.

"East side!" someone bellowed. "They're trying to flank the shed!"

Harry turned at once, waving Joseph and two others with him. May urged June into a gallop, cutting across the field where a handful of townspeople had surrounded one of the gang's wagons, smoke curling from its busted wheel. One of the hired guns made a break for it, but caught a boot in the face from Earl, who stood tall with a pitchfork in his hands and fury in his eyes.

Another shot rang out, this one too close. May ducked instinctively. She turned and saw the sheriff.

He was stalking around the side of the porch, rifle in hand, eyes fixed on something straight ahead. May's blood ran cold as she followed his gaze to see Harry tying up one of the gunmen with his back to Mitchell.

She stuck her heels sharply into June's side, and the horse surged forward. Mitchell didn't even hear her coming until she was nearly on him, so focused was he on his target, his rifle so carefully aimed directly into the center of Harry's broad back.

"Mitchell!" she roared, pouring every bit of strength and fury into her voice.

He turned at the sound of her, rifle raised, now pointing at her, but May didn't hesitate. She was coming at him and quickly, and he had to dive to avoid being trampled, howling as he landed in a ball in the mud, dropping his weapon.

Before he could recover, Joseph was there, slamming the man to the ground with the butt of his rifle and pinning him with a knee to the back. "Got him!" he yelled. "He's done!"

May didn't stay to watch. She turned her horse back toward the house, eyes scanning, heart pounding.

Harry was near the stables again, tangled up in another fight, oblivious to how close he had come to death. Mud splattered his shirt, his knuckles raw. He was everywhere, in a constant state of movement, dragging one of the gang's shooters behind a trough, then yelling orders to two teenagers guarding the animals.

More townsfolk poured in from the tree line. Eliza, the schoolteacher, stood on a crate, shouting for the remaining gang members to lay down their arms. One by one, they did, confused, outnumbered, and disoriented by the coordinated counterattack.

The women had driven the herd straight down the hill in a thunder of hooves and barking dogs. Horses, cattle, and sheep had scattered the gang's formation, and in the chaos, the townsfolk had moved like clockwork: flanking, overwhelming, capturing.

May dismounted again, running to the back of the house where a trio of teenagers had cornered a gang member in the smokehouse. He came out with his hands up, eyes wide with disbelief.

Just beyond the main barn, Harry wrestled the last gun from a man twice his size and planted a fist square in his jaw. The man dropped like a felled tree.

And then, like someone had turned the volume down on the world, the noise faded.

No more shots.

No more shouts.

Just the low hum of voices—orders, questions, reassurances—and the shuffle of boots in the churned-up mud.

Harry emerged from the haze, wiping his brow. May met him halfway, both of them breathless, muddy, and marked. Their eyes met, no words exchanged, just the look of two people who had survived. Two people who had won.

Around them, the town moved quickly to restrain the last of the gang.

The last of the chaos dissipated in only minutes. The gang, caught off guard, never stood a chance. By the time the dust settled, all of them were tied and gagged. Mitchell was held under the barrel of a hunting rifle. Edward was on his knees, bloody lip curling in a snarl.

May slowed her pace, walking June toward the ranch gate. The herd followed behind her, now calm. The dogs panted at her heels. Mud streaked her skirts, and her arms ached, but her chin was high.

Harry stood beside Edward, revolver steady. His chest heaved. Sweat ran down his temples. May dismounted and went to stand in front of him, looking down her nose at this pathetic man who had tried so hard to steal something that had never belonged to him.

"Well, cousin," she said. "What do you have to say now?"

"She yours?" Edward sneered, not even looking at her, his eyes on Harry. "You just going to stand there and let a woman do your talking?"

Harry ignored him.

May stepped closer. "I've done more than talk," she said coolly. "You lost, Edward. And you don't even know how badly."

He looked up at her then, hate and confusion mingling in his eyes. "This isn't even close to being over."

Harry pressed the gun closer. "Oh, it's over."

Behind them, the townspeople had started to gather near the front steps. Some checked the wounded. Many exclaimed and shook hands. They had shown up. And they had won.

May turned to the porch. The house loomed ahead. She didn't know what awaited her inside, what damage they might have done in their evening alone in her home, but it was hers once more, and anything else could be handled.

Harry moved to her side as someone else took charge of Edward, brushing mud from her cheek.

"I was so worried I would lose you," he said, voice thick.

"You didn't lose me," she whispered. "And I thought you'd chase vengeance. But you stayed. You did the right thing."

Harry looked at the men around them. "Justice is vengeance enough."

Her breath hitched as she looked back at the house, the land, the people standing with them.

"No one's taking anything from us again," she said.

And with that, she led the herd back into the yard, past Edward, past Mitchell, past every man who thought they could break her.

The land was hers. The fight was theirs. And the future was just beginning.

Chapter Thirty-Four

The jailhouse door creaked as Harry leaned against the frame, arms crossed, eyes fixed on the gang members being loaded into the prison wagon. Dust swirled at their boots as Edward was shoved forward, his hands bound and his face bruised from the scuffle during the arrest. Sheriff Tom Landry stood beside Harry, his tall frame stoic under his worn brown duster. His mustache twitched as he glanced sideways.

Harry had known Tom for years. He had been one of the men who had trained Harry to become a sheriff, way back when, and it just so happened that he was sheriff of the nearest larger city to Chambers. The moment they had gotten all of the men rounded up and tucked safely, if not comfortably, into the few small cells that the town had, Harry had sent for Tom, who had pulled together a team and ridden hard, arriving first thing that morning. He hadn't wanted to chance them breaking out or causing more trouble and had brought back up as quickly as he could.

"I'd heard tell about Mitchell. Stories trickled out my a'way every now and then. I met him a few times, too, but he was always puffed up, proud, like he never had to answer to nobody. I'm sure he never thought this day would come," Tom said, voice as low and dry as the wind. "That man always figured he was too slick for the law to catch him."

Harry didn't respond at first. His gaze followed Sheriff Mitchell, who was pale and tight-jawed, refusing to look Harry's way as he climbed hang-dog into the wagon behind the others.

"They thought they owned us," Harry said finally. "The land, the people, even justice. They thought that they were above it all."

Tom nodded, then tilted his head toward the wagon. "Thanks to you, they're not."

The gang would be transferred to Tom's jailhouse in Cotton Ridge, a larger town with sturdier walls and more space. It was a few days' ride away, and the steel-reinforced wagon looked more like a mobile vault than a transport. A pair of deputies flanked it on horseback, hands lingering at their holsters, eyes never leaving the prisoners.

The sound of wagon wheels groaning under the weight of shackled prisoners filled the yard, mingling with the sharp clang of iron and the low murmur of townsfolk who'd come to see justice served. Tom leaned back against the split-rail fence, watching his deputies at work.

"Mitchell's glaring like he still thinks he's got a badge somewhere in his coat pocket," Landry said, nodding toward the disgraced sheriff, now being secured with extra chains. "Not that it ever meant much."

Harry's gaze stayed fixed on the group, but he replied, voice low. "He never cared about the law. He only used it to get close to money and power."

Landry spat into the dirt. "That he did."

They stood there for a while, silent, until the last prisoner was tied down. Landry adjusted his hat and gave Harry a sideways glance. "You want to talk it through? All the pieces?"

Harry hesitated, then nodded. "Yeah. I do."

Landry crossed his arms and leaned on the fence post, waiting a beat before speaking. "We started digging once you sent that first letter. Mitchell's file was thin, but there was a pattern. He had his men out, moving from town to town like a dust storm. Every time, crime picked up. Not always the same sort—sometimes cattle rustling, sometimes robberies—but always something. Then, those men of his would vanish just before things caught up to any of them. It turns out he kept company with the same handful of men each time. Most of 'em were in that barn of yours."

Harry nodded slowly. "He played some part in the crew who came for us years ago. That's clear now."

"That's what it looks like," Landry agreed. "We think that first attack, the one on your ranch back when Beth...." He trailed off. "Well. We think they were after a herd of prize horses stabled two properties over."

Harry's expression darkened as he worked through what that meant. "They came to the wrong place."

"Exactly. You might remember that a storm rolled in the night before. Muddy roads. No lanterns to guide them. They got turned around. Instead of the Hargrove place, they ended up on your land. Just a crew of crooks at the wrong time, going after the wrong target."

Harry exhaled hard through his nose. "They killed her over a mistake."

Landry didn't argue. He just said, "Mitchell kept quiet about that job, but one of the men we picked up in the barn finally talked. Said the horses were worth a fortune, purebred stallions, some kind of new bloodline coming from Kentucky. Edward knew about them. He'd been working to buy them off Hargrove, but the man wouldn't sell. So Edward found another way."

Harry looked over sharply. "You mean—"

"Yeah. Edward helped plan the raid. He wanted the horses and figured if they couldn't be bought, they'd be stolen. He wasn't there that night, but he hired the men who were."

Harry's fists clenched. "And Mitchell?"

"Just another greedy man along for the ride. He helped cover up the botched job. He hid those men of his in some other town, helped them lay low. Then, once the dust cleared, they hit the next spot."

They were quiet for a long moment. The sun was rising higher, warming the dirt yard, the scent of hay and horses drifting through the air.

Landry broke the silence. "I'm sorry, Harry. About Beth. About how long it took for the truth to come to light." He shifted from boot to boot. "I know how long you searched for answers."

Harry didn't respond right away. He was watching Mitchell, who now sat slumped in the wagon, defeated. "It's not just about Beth anymore," he said. "They came back. They came for my family again. For May. They impacted Julia, our life here." He shook his head. "I'm just glad to see them all coming to face justice at last."

Landry nodded. "You stopped them this time."

Harry's voice was quiet. "Barely."

"You did what a good man does. You protected what's yours. With honor."

Harry looked at the older sheriff. "You think that's enough?"

Landry gave a slow nod. "For your girls, for May—for this town? Yeah. It's enough."

The driver called out, cracking the reins. The wagon rolled forward, and the clinking of chains grew fainter as the prisoners were hauled off the property, heading east toward justice.

Harry watched until they disappeared down the road, then turned to Landry. "Thanks for coming."

Landry clapped a hand on his shoulder. "You don't owe me a thing. Just glad to see you found something worth fighting for again."

"I did," Harry said softly. "I really did."

As the wagon disappeared into the distance, Tom turned to Harry again. "This town is going to need someone to take Mitchell's place. Someone the town can trust. The man who steps up now has a lot of responsibility. They're not just starting fresh; they'll be working against years of bad feelings about the law in Chambers. It'll be a tough job. The kind that takes just the right sort of man to do it."

Harry arched a brow.

Tom smiled. "What I'm saying is, we could use a good man wearing that badge."

Harry let the words hang there a moment, unsure of how to respond. A year ago, he never would have imagined agreeing to be a sheriff again. He couldn't have trusted himself to do the job right, to look out for the community the way it needed to be looked after.

But May was right. He'd had an opportunity for vengeance but had followed the law instead. And the town had stood beside him. Maybe it was time to stand for them, too.

"Just think about it," Tom said, clapping him on the back. "The town could use a fresh start. You already gave them the chance at one, but they could use someone to make sure it's done right."

He promised Tom he would think on it, and they shook hands, parting ways for now. Tom would fill the role for the next few days; he would oversee the transfer of the men and get them on their paths to justice. For now, Harry could relax. He began to make his way through town, eager to get to May and Julia. Eager to start a new day without the threat of looming specters lingering over them.

Shopkeepers were opening shutters, sweeping stoops, and hanging signs. The bakery already had the scent of rising dough drifting through the air.

The early sun was golden on the fields that stretched from the center of town, visible past the squat rooftops and puffing chimneys, warm on Harry's shoulders as he passed through the bustling streets.

"Morning, Harry!" one called. "Heard you got 'em all."

"We're safe, thanks to you," another added, tipping her bonnet.

Harry offered a nod and a small wave, his heart oddly full. Not from pride, but from something gentler. The town had stood with him, ordinary folks who had grabbed what tools or weapons they had and stepped into danger. That meant something. It meant everything.

He crossed past the chapel, where the minister was out covering the patch of flowers near the steps, readying them for winter. He straightened and crossed, extending one hand to Harry. "You brought justice back to this town."

It was strange, this feeling.

Harry had spent so long feeling ashamed of himself, feeling like a failure of a man, of a father, of a husband.

He had not been there on the night Beth had needed him most, and he had spent years after that continuing to fail his little girl as he hunted down the people who had taken her from

287

her husband and child. He had not even been able to continue the career that had for so long given him a sense of purpose and fulfillment.

But his mother-in-law had made him see sense. She had sent him away from her own home so that he would offer her granddaughter a better, happier life. He smiled to himself, thinking of all that had changed since she had last seen them. He decided then that he would write to her and ask her to come visit. May and Evangeline would get along just fine, and it would do the older woman good to be around Julia once more.

His steps lightened as he continued down the road, buoyed by a feeling that was so new, so unfamiliar, it took him a minute to place it.

Excitement.

He was excited for the future and all of the many things it held for him, and for his family.

By the time Harry reached Joseph and Willa's house, his legs ached in the best possible way. The smell of bacon frying drifted through the open kitchen window, and the front door creaked open before he could knock.

Julia barreled out onto the porch. "Papa!"

He caught her just in time, lifting her high in the air and spinning her once.

"Hey there, sweetheart. Miss me?"

She grinned and threw her arms around his neck. "We made biscuits! Willa let me cut 'em!"

Harry laughed, heart swelling. "Well, then, I better get in there before they're all gone."

May stepped out onto the porch behind her, eyes shining. Her hair was tucked under a scarf, cheeks flushed from heat and activity.

"You're back early," she said softly.

"I couldn't wait a minute longer," he said, eyes never leaving hers.

They entered the warm kitchen, where the table fairly groaned beneath the weight of heaps and heaps of food. Biscuits, beans, whole rashers of bacon, johnny cakes dripping with golden honey, apples sliced and topped with cream and nuts. His mouth watered as he approached. Before he could take a seat, however, Willa caught sight of him and threw herself into his arms, collapsing against him in a wet, sobbing mass of tears.

Harry raised his eyebrows atop her head at Joseph and then May, who both shrugged at him in response one after another, nonplussed.

Willa wailed and smashed a fist against his chest. "Harold!" she cried, then stopped, sniffled, and looked up at him through watery eyes. "That's your full name, isn't it? Harold?"

"What else would it be?" May asked in wry amusement.

Willa considered this. "Harrington?"

Joseph piped in. "Harvey."

Julia looked up from the biscuit she had snuck into her mouth. "Harry!"

Before Harry could respond, Willa shook her head. "It doesn't matter. Harry, you did a good job." Her face fell into his chest again as she began to cry once more. "Thank you for bringing my most beloved people home safe to me." The last few words came out in a long, shaky cry.

289

Harry smiled uncertainly and gave her a careful pat on the top of her back. He had never been much of a touchy-feely sort of man and was eager to escape this display of emotion.

He cleared his throat. "Well, that's all right."

Willa stood and swiped at her eyes, glaring at Joseph and May. "I'll never forgive the two of you for running off into a battle without me."

Joseph gave an exasperated laugh. "Honey, we've been through this."

May came and wrapped an arm around Willa, guiding her to her seat at the table. Harry shot her a grateful look, and she winked at him, nodding for him to take a seat as well. "I just bet you will forgive us," she said soothingly, "especially considering I made your favorite dessert."

Willa perked up, scanning the table quickly. "You what? I didn't see—"

May reached beneath the table's surface and lifted a long, low-lipped bowl, whipping a cloth off the top with a dramatic flair. "Here it is!"

"Bird's nest pudding!" Willa shrieked. "That is my favorite!" She leaned forward, but May took a step back, smiling.

"You're welcome to a piece just as soon as you forgive me."

Willa's eyes narrowed. "Why, you wicked thing." She lifted her nose, sniffed. "I won't be blackmailed into forgiveness."

May shrugged and sat beside Julia, handing her a spoon. "More for us, then. Right, Jules?"

Julia grinned and dug her spoon into the side of the bowl, lifting out a mound of creamy, buttery pastry. "Yum!"

Willa's lips twitched.

May hovered her spoon over the pudding, looking at her friend with her eyebrows lifted.

Willa let out a gusty sigh, rolled her eyes mightily, and stuck out a hand. "God help me. Fine. I forgive you."

May grinned and passed her the spoon and dish. Willa tucked in at once, leaning back into her seat with a happy groan.

"Hey, now," Joseph protested. "What about me?"

May shot him a side smile. "Sorry, friend. You're on your own."

Willa took another few bites, and then, her eyes filled with tears once more.

"Oh, Willa, what now?" May asked, leaning over and putting a hand on her arm.

"It's just so...so good," Willa wailed, dropping her face into her hands and giving in to another cry.

Harry exchanged a startled glance with Joseph, whose own surprise seemed to indicate that this was not typical Willa behavior.

They both looked at the two women. Then, seeing that May had it handled, shrugged and turned to eat their meal.

As May and Willa sat and whispered, laughter breaking out, as Julia ate a third biscuit and argued with Joseph over whether baked apples counted as eating her vegetables, as the sun filtered through the clean glass and lit the whole room up in a buttery yellow, Harry felt a warmth and lift in his heart that he could not remember feeling for a very long time.

This place, this was what it meant to have a home and a family.

He looked out the window, at the dusty road that led in one direction to the ranch that was his family's home and in the other to the town full of people that had stood by him when he needed it most and decided then and there.

He knew what answer he was going to give to Tom.

As long as May agreed to it as well.

***

The walk home was slower this time. May held Julia's hand while Harry carried a small basket of biscuits wrapped in a cloth. They took the long way through the pasture, letting Julia skip ahead. The grass brushed at their boots, and the morning air was filled with the chirp of meadowlarks.

"Willa was...different than usual," Harry mused. "Is she all right?"

May smiled, and he could read a secret in her eyes. "I think she's more than all right, actually. In fact, I think that here soon, Willa and Joseph might be sharing a touch of very, very good news with us."

He thought that over and then felt a grin stretch wide across his face, taking her hand and giving it a quick squeeze as they walked. They hadn't made it far when they heard a loud, joyous whoop from Joseph and Willa's farm's direction. Harry and May exchanged knowing smiles.

"What was that?" Julia asked, looking back. "Should we turn around?"

Harry lifted her into his arms, enjoying the feel of her warm weight against him, right where it should be. "They've got some things to celebrate; that's all. We'll leave them be for now, and we can all celebrate together soon enough."

The ranch came into view over the last hill, unchanged and yet somehow appearing transformed. The barn stood tall, the fence mended strong and clean. The front porch was swept, and the smokehouse off to the side had fresh cords of wood stacked neatly against it. Julia squirmed in his arms, and he put her on the ground, letting her scamper ahead, knowing she was eager to be back home.

"I thought they might've destroyed it," May whispered. "I kept imagining fire, or windows shattered...."

"They didn't get the chance," Harry said. "We fought back. You did."

She glanced at him, her expression soft but wary. "I wasn't sure you'd come back. Those men." He could hear her swallow, saw her throat struggle, and knew she was holding back tears. "What they did to your wife."

Harry stopped. "May."

"I thought you might get caught up in revenge," she said, voice barely audible. "That it'd mean more to you than us."

He took her hand, pressing it gently. "Revenge would've eaten me whole. You saved me from that. You and Julia."

Julia ran ahead, chasing a butterfly near the porch.

"I never thought I'd have this again," he said. "A home, a family. A community where it felt like I belonged. Every time I thought I lost it all, I looked at you, and it pulled me back."

May's lip trembled, and Harry reached to brush a tear from her cheek. "We're safe now," he said. "Really safe."

She nodded, and they walked up the steps together, following the scent of home.

Inside, the house was cool and quiet. It was clear that some of the people from town had stayed behind to clean up any messes left behind. The house was nearly just as it should have been—better, even. Clean and ready for them.

They had only been gone two days, but it felt like much longer. Everything had moved so quickly, and now they were home at last.

The fire had died down but was easy enough to relight. May opened the windows to let the sun warm the space and chase out any last specters of the men who had been there two nights before. Harry stood in the parlor, running his hand along the mantle, where a few small items had been knocked aside during the gang's occupation. He carefully set each back into place: May's small porcelain horse, a drawing Julie had made, the Bible May's father had left behind.

May pulled off her scarf and apron, her hair tumbling down her back. She moved through the house with easy familiarity, checking the cupboard, the root cellar, the pantry.

"They didn't take much," she said, surprised.

"They thought they'd win, and all of this would be theirs for good," Harry replied. "They didn't think they'd have to steal anything."

Later, as Julia napped in her bed and May stirred a bowl of leftover beans, preparing to serve them both, Harry sat beside her at the kitchen table.

"Tom Landry offered me the sheriff's job. Here, in Chambers."

May turned, spoon paused mid-stir. "Did he?"

"He said the town could use someone decent. Someone they trust."

She laid the spoon carefully on a napkin and leaned closer. "Do you want it?"

He looked at her, searching her expression. "I think I do. But only if you don't take issue with it." He struggled to say what he wanted to say. He didn't want to leave anything unsaid, but also feared putting into words the things that haunted him the most. "Before, with Beth, I made mistakes. Part of it was because of the job, but part of it was rotten luck, I suppose. Our being in the wrong place at the wrong time. I won't let that happen again. But I can't promise that this sort of work doesn't bring its own trouble. I know that much."

May studied him, tilting her head. "This is a new town, with a new start. We've chased out the men who hurt Beth and the ones who would have done us harm. I think, if you're ready, we can move forward without fear."

He gave the unasked question the consideration it deserved. Finally, he nodded. "I can do that. With you by my side, I'm sure of it."

May smiled, that quiet kind of smile that settled all his nerves. "Then it sounds like the town just found itself a new sheriff."

That evening, as the sky painted itself in strokes of lavender and gold, they stood on the porch, watching the wind roll over the land. Julia had fallen asleep again after supper, curled up with a worn quilt in the corner of the sofa. She was tired from days of stress and adventures and more sweets than she had been allowed to eat in a lifetime. They closed the front door behind them softly as they went, careful not to wake her.

May leaned into Harry's side, her hand resting on his chest.

295

"You know," she said, "I always dreamed of this. Of standing right here, knowing the land was ours. Not just to survive, but to thrive."

Harry slipped his arm around her waist, holding her close. "It's not a dream anymore."

They watched the stars begin to wink into the sky, the last traces of dusk slipping away.

"I love you," he said, quietly. And he meant it. After Beth, he had never thought that he would feel this way again, and with May, it was something different, its own type of connection. It was a feeling that shook him to his bones, a feeling so overarching and powerful it made him feel like someone brand new. He turned his face into her hair, breathing in the sweet scent of her, and said it again, his voice soft. "I love you, May."

May turned to him, eyes luminous in the starlight. "And I love you."

He kissed her gently, reverently, and they stayed there for a long time, listening to the wind hum through the grass, the crickets singing in the distance, and the world at peace at last.

Epilogue

Two Years Later

The center of town was drenched in sunlight, the cloud a perfect, cloudless blue. It was the type of early summer day so sweet that May felt that she could taste the spun sugar of it on her tongue, even though all she had had so far that day was a cup of coffee, eagerly anticipating the treats the day would bring.

All around her, the air was filled with laughter, excitement, and anticipation. The carnival was in town, and it looked as if every resident of Chambers was out, ready to enjoy the day.

Julia skipped ahead of May, bright red ribbons bouncing at the end of her pigtails. A ribbon of the exact same color held up one poky little sprout on top of her baby sister's head, bobbing right at May's chin level as she balanced her on her hip.

Evelyn was two years old and the spitting image of her father and her older sister. Willa liked to jokingly ask if any of May had been used in the making of the baby, so exactly like Harry and Julia was she. May wouldn't admit it, but it thrilled her that her baby looked so much like her adopted older daughter. Though everyone in Chambers knew the backstory of their family, it still helped them slot together as one whole, like there was a physical reminder to keep Julia from ever feeling out of place or like she wasn't part of the family.

And aside from that concern, Evelyn was a beautiful child, just like her older sister.

As they grew closer, the scent of roasted peanuts and pipe smoke drifted through the warm summer air, settling thick over the dirt-packed main street of town. May adjusted her grip on her youngest daughter, shifting the two-year-old's weight against her hip. The girl's calico dress was already wrinkled, and the curls at the back of her neck clung to her skin in the heat. May smoothed them gently, the way her mother used to do for her.

Julia was ten paces ahead already, skipping in her leather boots, the hem of her dress catching the breeze. "Where's Papa?" Julia called back, shading her eyes from the sun as she scanned the crowds.

"He had to finish up at the sheriff's office," May replied, though she found herself also scanning the crowd for him. "He'll meet us here before long."

The noise of the carnival grew louder as they approached the town square. Fiddle music poured from a makeshift platform near the old general store. Bunting in red and white hung from every post and awning, fluttering in the hot wind that always seemed to sweep across the prairie this time of year. The click and whir of a hand-cranked shooting gallery echoed behind the line of booths where children tossed rings over milk bottles and women bartered over slices of gooseberry pie.

Adam walked quietly behind her, a steady, silent shadow. May didn't turn to make sure they didn't get separated in the crowds; she didn't have to. His presence was as familiar now as the creak of the barn gate or the scent of sun-warmed hay. He was never far, always watching. Though he'd always been a valued employee on the ranch, that had grown since the attempted takeover. May could no longer imagine their lives without him. He and his wife hadn't missed a Sunday supper in two years.

"Adam," she said, glancing back now. "I don't suppose you're thinking of trying your luck at the strongman's bell?"

He gave her a faint smirk. "I figure I'll let the traveling folk keep their pride intact. I wouldn't want to spoil the fun."

May smiled. The child on her hip gasped as she pointed a chubby finger at one thing and then another, too overcome to decide where to direct her attention. May bounced gently, humming a tune under her breath that her own mother had once sung in the parlor to her during long, drowsy afternoons.

The square was teeming now with neighbors greeting neighbors, children darting between wagons, and farmers laughing with mouths full of molasses-sweetened candy. A young girl was hawking lemonade from a wooden cart near the church steps, her apron streaked with sugar and pulp.

She slowed as they entered the heart of the square. Men wore their best Sunday vests, most with dust still clinging to their boots. The women's bonnets were pinned neatly, their dresses simple but pressed. Everyone had made an effort to look their best.

She looked around, half-expecting to find Harry leaning against a post or striding through the crowd in his uniform trousers. But there was no sign of him yet.

Julia came racing back. "Can I go see the pony rides? Please?"

"In a minute, darling. Let's wait for your father."

"But I want to go with him to see the goats!" Julia insisted.

May laughed softly. "Well, we'll be sure to find him. You can ask him about them then."

Adam nodded toward the booths. "Might not be a bad idea to settle somewhere in the shade for a bit."

"Agreed," May said, eyes sweeping the crowd again. "Let's wait near the bandstand."

She led them toward the edge of the wooden platform, where the fiddlers played a lively reel. For a moment, she let herself simply stand there with her youngest pressed close, Julia giggling as she tugged Adam toward the goat pen, the town filled with music and light and a kind of joy that didn't come often in this life.

The moment May spotted the familiar navy-blue trousers threading through the crowd, she felt her shoulders ease. Her hand rose instinctively, not to wave him over, but to settle the toddler's head against her collarbone, like a reflex to stillness.

Harry moved slowly through the bustle, not out of hesitation but with the quiet confidence of a man used to observing before acting. He tipped his hat at Mrs. Liddell as she passed with her hands full of plum preserves. He nodded to the Simmons boys, who stood arguing over a sack of boiled peanuts, and gave a brief wave to Earl, who was holding his new grandson like he was made of spun glass.

Harry was out of uniform save for the trousers. The badge had been left behind, along with his gun belt. There would be no calls to order today, no trouble to interrupt the music and laughter. And if trouble did arise, well, the blacksmith apprentice had taken a liking to doing deputy work when he had time, and he was on duty today.

She saw his eyes scan the crowd until they landed on her. His face softened, the way it always did, in that subtle way she never tired of seeing. He adjusted the brim of his hat and picked up his pace, weaving through the clusters of townsfolk.

Julia spotted him first. "Papa!" she squealed, barreling toward him with the fearlessness only a child could possess.

Harry stooped just in time to catch her, his arms wrapping around her in an easy scoop. Her bonnet slipped back off her head, and her dark curls caught the sunlight.

"There's my girl," he murmured, pressing a kiss to her temple. "You been winning prizes without me?"

"I saw a goat!" Julia shouted. "With a nose like a raisin. And there's a man who says he can guess your weight just by looking!"

"Sounds like a swindler," Harry said seriously, giving her a look of mock concern. "I hope you won't give him a cent."

"I'll give him Adam's cent," she replied, all innocence.

Harry laughed, the sound low and full in his chest. He looked up at May, still holding their littlest one, and crossed the final few steps to them.

"She's already a criminal," he said, reaching to tuck a flyaway strand of hair behind May's ear. His hand lingered a second longer than necessary.

May raised a brow. "And yet you look so proud."

"I wouldn't steal from Adam," Julia said, trying not to smile. "I would just wait until he's not looking."

Harry chided her gently and set her back down on the ground before he leaned in and kissed May's cheek, the pressure light but familiar, and for a moment, the noise of the carnival fell away. Just the two of them, with one child in her arms and another nestled against him.

"I missed you," he said, brushing his knuckles across the sleepy toddler's back. She stirred and let out a soft grunt, her fist curled beneath her chin.

"You were gone an hour," May replied, though her voice was quieter now.

"A long hour," he said.

She looked up at him, taking in the dust on his boots, the faint crease in his shirt where his badge usually rested. She could tell by the line of his jaw he hadn't eaten yet that day, and the dark beneath his eyes spoke of a sleep cut short.

"Did everything go smoothly?" she asked.

"No one arrested," he said. "Not yet."

May gave a small snort. "It's a carnival, Harry. Not a cattle drive."

"I've seen fewer arguments on cattle drives," he muttered, adjusting Julia as she clambered up onto his hip. "But it's quiet now. You ready to enjoy yourself?"

"I was trying," she said. "But Julia keeps attempting to adopt every barnyard animal in the square."

"Just wait until she sees the pig races," Harry said.

May groaned. "Lord, help us."

He shifted his weight and reached out with his free hand, lacing his fingers through hers. There wasn't ceremony in the gesture, nothing grand or performative. It was simply what he always did, this quiet tether between them.

They stood like that for a moment, hands clasped, children close, the carnival swirling around them in color and sound. Somewhere nearby, a fiddler hit a sour note, and someone else whooped with laughter.

"The town sure looks good," Harry said.

"It's a mess," May answered, watching a boy knock over a basket of apples in his haste to reach the lemonade stand.

He squeezed her hand. "It's a beautiful mess."

She looked up at him again, her heart pulling tight in her chest. "You still think this is paradise?"

Harry looked around at the familiar faces, the smiling neighbors, the freedom in Julia's laughter, and the weight of his daughter sleeping between them.

"I think it's better," he said.

And together, they turned toward the ring toss, their footsteps falling in time with the music.

Ahead, she spotted Willa and Joseph weaving through the crowd, their newborn son swaddled and tucked against Willa's chest. They waved as they saw her and stopped near the lemonade stand, and May picked up her pace to meet them.

Willa was fanning herself with her hat and looked, if May was being honest, only half alive in the summer heat.

"Well, look at you," May called as she approached. "You look like a woman who's been promised a nap and betrayed."

Willa grinned and swatted a fly away with her straw hat. "That's exactly what happened. My mother-in-law swore up and down she'd keep the baby this afternoon so I could rest. But I think she meant it in the spiritual sense."

May chuckled. "And now here you are. With a baby. At a carnival."

Joseph turned and gave May a one-armed hug, then passed her a tin cup of lemonade. "She said she was going to lose her mind if she sat in that house one more minute. I took that as a request for rescue."

Willa looked to Joseph with exaggerated sweetness. "He's very clever. He knows just when to drag me out into public so I don't start screaming into the laundry."

May laughed. "And how about Ella? Where's our favorite little whirlwind?"

Willa rolled her eyes, but her smile widened. "At home with Mama Porter. Napping, presumably. Though, if I know that child, she'll be up and rearranging furniture by the time we get back. She's reached the stage where she narrates everything she does. Everything. 'I'm climbing the chair, Mama. I'm jumping now, Mama. I spilled the milk, and now I'm sorry but not really sorry, Mama.' All day long."

"That sounds exhausting," May said, accepting a cup of lemonade from the vendor and watching Julia dart back and forth between booths.

"She calls Joseph 'Pa,' and she calls me 'No,'" Willa added, completely deadpan. "I think that says everything about how our days go."

Joseph chuckled, shaking his head. "She's not wrong."

May was laughing so hard she had to shift the baby on her hip. "I shouldn't laugh. It's just that I feel your pain so acutely." She looked down, faux-sneakily, at the curly head on her shoulder, beginning to droop as Evelyn grew ready for her own nap.

"Oh, Evelyn's a dream compared to mine," Willa said, waving a hand. "Evelyn asks before she throws dirt. Mine just throws it and then says, 'that was dirt, Mama.' Like she's filing a report after the crime."

"Maybe she's practicing for a career in law enforcement," Joseph offered with a wink.

"She'll have to take it up with Sheriff Harry," May said, smiling as her husband appeared in the crowd then, carrying a small sack of roasted peanuts.

Harry caught the end of the comment and raised a brow. "Who's taking over my post now?"

"Ella," May said. "Apparently, she's got the qualifications."

"Oh, absolutely," Willa agreed. "Strong opinions, a loud voice, and absolutely no regard for personal space."

"I'll be out of a job by spring," Harry said dryly, handing peanuts to May and tipping his hat toward Willa.

May took the bag and offered him a grateful look. "Thank you, love."

"I bribed the vendor," Harry said. "Turns out he likes the law after all."

Joseph snorted. "Or just doesn't want to be fined for short-changing children."

Willa leaned into May and lowered her voice. "Is it bad that I'm genuinely considering keeping Mama Porter at our house another week just so I can breathe in silence for half an hour a day?"

"Not bad at all," May said. "It's simply good sense. You grew a human being inside your body, and now you're expected to let her redecorate the kitchen with jam."

Willa raised her lemonade in a mock toast. "To mothering."

May clinked her tin cup gently against hers. "To daughters with strong wills, strong lungs, and excellent future leadership potential."

And together, they laughed, two mothers, elbow-deep in the messy beauty of it all, soaking in the warmth of the sun and the sound of the fair, for once letting the joy of the day outweigh the weariness of raising little legends in the making.

Their moment of peace didn't last very long.

Julia tugged insistently on her hand.

"Come on! I want to show Papa how good I am at the games! I've been practicing!"

Harry chuckled beside her, reaching down to ruffle Julia's sun-warmed curls. "I'm right behind you."

Julia didn't wait. She darted toward the ring toss booth with the gangly confidence of a girl who had practiced tossing everything from socks to corncobs into imaginary targets all year long.

"She takes after you," May said to Harry, watching her stand on her tiptoes to peer over the counter.

Harry grinned. "If she did, she'd be shy around strangers and terrible at throwing."

May handed Evelyn to Adam, who accepted her with practiced ease. The child was fast asleep, her chubby cheek pressed against his shoulder.

"You don't give yourself enough credit," May said. "You've become half the reason she believes she can do anything."

Harry looked away, the corner of his mouth twitching with emotion, but he said nothing.

Julia looked over her shoulder and waved frantically. "Papa! I need a coin!"

"I've got it," Harry said, stepping forward and fishing into his pocket. He passed one to the booth attendant, who nodded politely and handed Julia a set of three wooden rings.

Julia grasped the rings in her little hand and bit her lip in concentration.

"She's been practicing all morning," May said softly, standing close enough to feel the warmth of Harry's arm beside her. "Used up every washer I had in the house. Even asked Adam to build her a target from a barrel hoop."

"She's determined," Harry said. "Remind you of anyone?"

May didn't answer, just smiled.

Julia tossed the first ring. It clattered off the post and landed in the grass.

She huffed. "Too high."

The second ring hit the post and spun off. She groaned and stomped her little boot.

"She certainly gets *that* from you," Harry murmured.

May elbowed him gently. "That stubbornness is all you."

They watched as Julia stood perfectly still before her final throw. She squinted at the post, pulled her arm back slowly, and let the ring fly.

It landed perfectly around the wooden peg.

Julia gasped so loudly it made nearby carnival-goers turn and smile. "I *did it!*"

She spun around, face shining, and ran back to the two of them.

Harry knelt down and caught her mid-run. "That was the finest toss I've ever seen."

"I win a prize!" she said breathlessly.

The booth attendant held out a basket of small trinkets and toys. Julia's eyes roamed over them, then settled on a carved wooden horse, no bigger than her palm. She picked it up gently, holding it like it might break.

"Can I keep it?" she asked, already clutching it tightly.

"You earned it," May said.

Julia grinned and then turned to Harry. "I'm going to name him Sheriff. Because he's brave like you."

Harry blinked and cleared his throat. "That's a fine name, sweetheart."

May reached out and brushed his shoulder, a small gesture, but it steadied him. She knew what that meant to him, being seen that way, through Julia's eyes. Brave. Strong. Good.

Julia ran ahead again, wooden horse in hand, and Harry rose to his feet, his jaw tightening with emotion.

"She sees you clearly, Harry," May said.

He nodded once. "I hope so."

"You've given her a safe world to grow up in. That matters more than anything."

He reached for her hand then, curling his fingers around hers as they followed Julia through the crowd. The sound of fiddle music played from the other end of the fairgrounds, and children's laughter bubbled over the warm summer air.

"Did you ever think we'd end up here?" Harry asked.

"No," May admitted. "But I'm so glad we did."

Julia spun in a circle ahead of them, her dress flaring as she held up her new toy for another child to see.

Harry leaned close. "She's got you as an example of someone who built a life out of dust and courage. A mother who stepped in after she'd lost her own. I'd say that's her real prize."

May flushed at the compliment but didn't look away. "She's got a father who taught her that bravery doesn't always wear a badge."

And together, they walked forward, the past behind them, the fair ahead, watching the girl they both loved run headlong into a future they'd fought to protect.

***

They stayed at the fair until the sun began to set. May made her way to June, knowing she needed to prepare for the ride home before it became dark. It had been a long day, and she knew the girls would both be tuckered out and ready for bed once they returned home. She glanced over at them once more.

Julia was dancing with Evelyn to the tune of the fiddle, Adam and Joseph standing near them and clapping along to the bright, lively rhythm. She smiled at the sight.

May reached the livery, her skirts brushing against the dusty ground. She ran a hand along June's side, the mare's coat warm and familiar beneath her fingers. She hadn't ridden her much since a new baby had joined their household, but she'd brushed her down earlier in the week, feeling the pull of old habits and an ache for the comfort of her aging mare.

Harry approached from behind, leading his gelding, Boone, by the reins. He wore his coat unbuttoned and carried his hat tucked under his arm. His sleeves were rolled, and his collar open. He looked tired, but not the kind of tired she had once seen weigh so heavy on his face. This was a different sort of tired, satisfied, maybe.

"She looks good," he said, nodding at June.

"She's still strong as ever," May said. "She hates being left behind."

Harry smiled. "Funny. Boone's the same."

May turned to face him, resting a hand on her hip. "What do you say we take them out for a bit? Just around the ridge? The girls are with Adam and Willa, and I wouldn't mind a few minutes where nobody's hanging off my skirts."

Harry chuckled. "You always were the one to suggest the most reckless ideas."

"It's not reckless," she said, already putting a foot in the stirrup. "It's a quiet ride with my husband. Don't go making it sound more dramatic than it really is."

Harry mounted up and followed her out past the last few carnival tents, their horses falling into step beside each other. The town slowly faded behind them, replaced by the familiar sweep of tall grass and open sky. The sun sat just above the horizon, lighting the land in soft amber and shadow.

May let June pick her pace, letting the rhythm of hooves soothe her. They rode without speaking for a while, and it felt so easy, like the two of them had done this a hundred times together. In truth, they hadn't. They were only just learning how to settle into each other now that the fear had lifted, the fight was done, and the world had steadied beneath their feet.

Learning to parent together had been tricky as well, both of them struggling to balance all of the needs and responsibilities that weighed on them both inside the home and out. It had all left little time for riding for pleasure together.

"I think this is the first time in two years we've been alone like this," Harry said quietly.

May nodded. "It feels like it's been longer than that."

He looked over at her. "Are you happy, May?"

She didn't answer right away. She let the question settle, let the quiet wrap around her like a shawl. A soft wind rustled the grasses. Somewhere in the distance, a hawk cried out overhead.

"Yes," she said at last. "I'm happy. I didn't know it would feel like this."

"Like what?"

"Like peace."

Harry reached across and took her hand where it rested on the horn of her saddle. He held it tightly, his thumb brushing over the edge of her palm. "I spent so long thinking peace was something I'd never earn."

"You didn't have to earn it, Harry," she said softly. "You just had to stop running from it."

He looked at her then, and the expression in his eyes made her breath catch. There was no armor left in him, no hesitation. Just love. Honest, simple love.

She smiled.

June tossed her head, clearly growing impatient with the slowness of the ride. May laughed and gave the mare a nudge.

"Come on," she called to Harry. "Let's race. Last one back has to clean all the picnic plates tomorrow."

Harry's eyes narrowed, and he grinned. "You're on."

They took off in a blur of dust and laughter, the wind in their hair and the wide sky above them, riding not to escape, but to celebrate. Not to survive, but to live. They rode back to collect their daughters, and May felt her heart lift at the joy of moving so freely, of feeling light and like her old self, and made herself a promise that she would make time for this more often.

When they returned to the carnival, the fairgrounds were beginning to empty as the sun dipped low over the prairie, casting a golden hue across the town. Children with sticky fingers clutched leftover sweets, and lanterns began to glow softly along the boardwalk. The sound of fiddle music had slowed to an easy tune, no longer calling people to dance, but lingering like a memory in the warm air.

They collected the girls, May wrapping a squirmy Evelyn onto her back for the ride home and Julia settling into the saddle in front of Harry, and rode home after saying goodbye to Joseph and Willa. Adam took off, riding a few paces ahead of them, eyes scanning the darkening road and the stretches of land ahead, ever vigilant.

The trip home was uneventful, and Adam took the horses into the barn as their little family stepped up onto the porch, the evening sun casting long amber streaks over the land. Behind May, Harry lifted a sleepy Julia from the saddle, her curls loosened from the ribbon and tangled from the wind. Evelyn nestled contentedly against May's shoulder, her little fingers curled around a ribbon from May's blouse. The carnival had worn them all out.

From inside the house came the clatter of dishes and the soft sound of humming. A familiar voice, sweet and steady. May's chest ached with affection.

The door swung open before they could knock. "You're back just in time," Evangeline said with a warm smile. "The biscuits are nearly cooled, and the stew is still hot."

Harry smiled, lines softening at the corners of his eyes. "We didn't mean to keep you waiting."

"Bah. It's a joy to feed you all. And I knew you'd come back eventually, though I half expected you'd be toting another stray child by now," she said, giving May a wink as she held the door open wide.

The house smelled of thyme and onions, and something faintly sweet, apple peel and cinnamon, maybe. A kettle whistled on the stove. Evangeline took Evelyn from May's arms with practiced ease and carried her into the back room to begin the bedtime routine, her long gray braid trailing down her back like a silken rope.

May sat at the kitchen table, sighing as she pulled off her boots. She was pleasantly tired. The day had been long and full, and the memory of the carnival still buzzed behind her eyes: Julia shrieking with laughter on the pony cart, Harry winning her a carved wooden doll, Adam getting his face painted against his will by the town's schoolteacher.

Harry poured them each a cup of tea and sat beside her, his fingers brushing her knee. "Today was great."

May leaned her head against his shoulder. "I think so, too. Though I'm not sure Julia needed quite so many peppermints."

"She earned 'em. That beanbag toss was tricky."

They both laughed softly.

May leaned back in the parlor chair, her ankles tucked beneath her, a teacup warming her hands. She was still unwinding from the day's festivities, her body tired in the best way, sun-flushed, full of sweets, and softened by laughter. Harry stood and crossed the room, thumbed through the small stack of mail they'd brought in from town. He paused and held up one envelope.

"It's a letter from Tom Landry," he said. "I've been waiting on this one."

May straightened. "Is that…. It's about Edward and Mitchell?"

Harry gave a quiet nod and sat beside her, sliding a finger beneath the seal. His brows furrowed as he read, lips pressing into a line.

"They're in prison," he said simply. "Mitchell got twenty-five years. Edward got thirty. Hard labor."

May exhaled slowly, heart catching. "Thirty years…. My God."

Harry handed her the letter. She took it with careful hands, eyes scanning the page while the sounds of crickets and rustling summer trees drifted in through the open window.

"He says Edward didn't speak a word when they took him," she murmured. "And Mitchell…well, I doubt he's ever had to face the consequences of his actions before."

Harry didn't answer right away. His gaze drifted toward the girls' room down the hallway. "It should bring peace," he said. "And it does, in some ways. But it still happened. Beth still died. You were still tied to a chair in some godforsaken shack. That doesn't go away."

May looked over the top of the letter at him. "No. But you saved me. And now we can move forward. This is part of that."

Harry nodded, slow. "What about Evangeline?"

May folded the letter with gentle fingers and set it aside. "I was just thinking that."

"She deserves to know," Harry said. "But…I don't know. It's hard to guess what that kind of justice feels like, when it's your child they murdered."

May's throat tightened. "She hasn't spoken Beth's name much. Not since I've known her. But I see her look at Julia sometimes, and I can tell she's remembering."

Harry reached for his tea but didn't drink. "Maybe I'll tell her. I'll keep it to just the facts. Then, if she wants to talk about it, she can."

May nodded. "I think she'd appreciate that."

They sat in a stretch of companionable silence before May reached over, laid her hand atop Harry's, and offered a small smile. "You did good, Sheriff."

His eyes softened. "We both did."

Evangeline returned a little while later, wiping her hands on her apron. "Girls are down," she said, settling into the third chair at the table. "Not a peep from either of them. Though if Julia wakes up and asks for that candy apple again, I'll be blaming you two."

May grinned. "Thank you, Evangeline. Truly."

"Oh, hush," Evangeline said, patting her hand. "What else am I here for?"

The teasing tone made May laugh, but it faded into something warmer, softer as she glanced between the older woman and her husband. Her heart pulled unexpectedly at the thought that this was her family: a sheriff, a widow, a former matriarch, and two little girls sleeping in the next room.

Harry cleared his throat. "Evangeline, we got a letter today. From Sheriff Landry."

She looked up at once. Her face didn't change much, no sharp reaction, just a stilling of breath and a narrowing of eyes.

"They've been sentenced," Harry said gently. "Mitchell's to serve twenty-five years. Edward...thirty. Hard labor."

Evangeline was quiet. Then, "I suppose I ought to feel something."

"You don't have to," May said softly.

"I thought I would feel relief," Evangeline said after a moment. "Or anger. Instead, it just feels...done. Like a door's closed." She gave a tight nod. "That will be enough."

The three of them sat quietly together, the weight of the moment hanging gently but not heavily at their center.

The three of them sipped tea as the last of the light slipped through the windows in companionable silence. Outside, the cicadas chirred, and the breeze moved slowly through the grass. It reminded May of nights long ago, listening to her parents at the kitchen table long after bedtime, talking softly over tea, their hands sometimes brushing in the candlelight.

"You know," Evangeline said after a long pause, "I've been thinking it's almost time I head back home."

May frowned. "So soon?"

"It's been two months," Evangeline said. "You all don't need an old woman hanging about every day. I'll be fine. I still know how to use a rifle, and the hens need tending."

Harry chuckled. "You're as fierce as ever."

"That I am," she said proudly. "But I admit, I'm tired. And I worry sometimes, about being out there all on my own. Heard tell in town that there's been some trouble up by the railway, men looking to squat where they shouldn't. It's probably nothing, but I keep the doors barred at night just the same. I don't like leaving the place empty for long, however. It's time I get back."

Harry and May exchanged a quick glance, but Evangeline turned the conversation to lighter topics. The three of them sat together a little longer, watching the candles flicker lower and the shadows stretch across the floor. After a time, Evangeline sighed and eased to her feet.

"I'm off to bed. I expect you two will follow shortly, though maybe after some of that private time you keep pretending you don't make time for."

Harry grinned. "Good night."

"Good night, my darlings," she said, and left the room quietly.

They banked the fire and made their way to the bedroom. May washed up at the basin while Harry undressed, and they changed into their bedclothes, hers a soft cotton nightdress, his old undershirt and long johns.

May sat on the edge of the bed, brushing out her hair.

The glow of the lamp on the dresser spilled golden light across the room, casting soft shadows over the hand-stitched quilt and the clean-washed wooden floor. A breeze rustled the lace curtain by the window, bringing with it the scent of chamomile and summer hay.

Harry shifted slightly, tugging off his boots with a weary sigh. "I reckon I could sleep a week," he murmured.

May smiled as she tucked her legs beneath her on the bed. "If only the girls would allow it."

He chuckled. "No chance of that."

May paused, glancing toward the open door where the hallway now lay dark and quiet. "I've been thinking," she said. "About Evangeline. About asking her to stay."

Harry looked up from unbuttoning his shirt, surprise flickering in his tired eyes. "To live here? With us?"

May nodded, curling a bit closer to him. "She's been such a help. I know she complains about her hands aching when she kneads bread, and about how the roof creaks when it storms, but I think more than anything, she's lonely out there."

"She never says it outright," Harry said softly. "But I reckon you're right."

"And she loves the girls," May added. "She puts Evelyn to sleep faster than I ever can. That lullaby she hums, what was it again?"

Harry smiled. "'sailing, Sailing.' Beth used to sing it, too."

May returned the smile, but there was no tension in it, no sting of comparison. Once, she had been so afraid that the life she had built with Harry would never be enough. Now, she felt safe to honor his past together, and respect the woman who had created a beautiful little girl and been forced to leave too soon.

"There was a night," May continued, her voice gentler now, "when Evelyn wouldn't stop fussing. Nothing I did seemed to soothe her. I must've walked ten miles in that nursery. I felt like a failure."

Harry reached out, brushing her wrist with his thumb.

May went on. "Evangeline didn't say much. Just came in, wrapped Evelyn in a thick quilt she'd warmed by the hearth, and said, 'Babies don't just need rocking. They need reminding the world is warm.' She held her tight and sure, like she wasn't worried at all. Evelyn stopped crying within a minute. And I—" Her voice caught slightly. "I just sat there and cried instead."

Harry didn't speak, but he brought her hand to his lips and kissed it. She leaned into him.

"I never thought I would have to learn to be a mother without mine to guide me. I never got the chance to ask my mother questions, to hear from her what to do. But Evangeline...she answers them for me. In quiet ways."

Harry rested his forehead against hers, his voice low. "Let's ask her. First thing tomorrow. She belongs here."

May nodded, a soft, grateful smile on her lips. "I think she does."

They climbed under the quilt together, the scent of fresh lavender rising from the linens. Outside, the wind whispered through the cornfields, and somewhere down the hall, Evelyn gave a soft sigh in her sleep. The home was still, full.

Harry wrapped an arm around May, and she rested her head on his shoulder, letting the rhythm of his breathing lull her toward sleep.

"I love you," she murmured.

His voice, thick with contentment, followed a moment later. "I love you."

They drifted off, the house quiet and strong around them, the future stretching out ahead like a warm summer road.

THE END

Also by Ava Winters

Thank you for reading **"Their Nebraska Marriage Deal"**!

I hope you enjoyed it! If you did, here are some of my other books!

My latest Best-Selling Books

#1 An Uninvited Bride on his Doorstep

#2 Once upon an Unlikely Marriage of Convenience

#3 Their Unlikely Marriage of Convenience

#4 An Orphaned Bride to Love Him Unconditionally

#5 An Unexpected Bride for the Lonely Cowboy

Also, if you liked this book, you can also check out **my full Amazon Book Catalogue at:**
https://go.avawinters.com/bc-authorpage

Thank you for allowing me to keep doing what I love! ♥

Printed in Dunstable, United Kingdom